"Okay, princess. If I take my hand from your mouth, are you going to scream?"

She shook her head.

Cal didn't drop his hand. "Good. Maybe I won't have to kill anybody tonight." He looked almost disappointed. "If we're lucky, we can get out of here and no one will know we're gone until morning." He raked his critical eyes over her, taking in the diamonds, the low-cut gown, the high-heeled shoes. Slowly he dropped his hand.

"You're here to get me out?" Livvie asked.

"That's right, princess. I'm here to save your ass one more time."

Dear Reader,

The holidays are here, so why not give yourself the gift of time and books—especially this month's Intimate Moments? Top seller Linda Turner returns with the next of her TURNING POINTS miniseries. In *Beneath The Surface* she takes a boss/employee romance, adds a twist of suspense and comes up with another irresistible read.

Linda Winstead Jones introduces you to the first of her LAST CHANCE HEROES, in *Running Scared*. Trust me, you'll want to be kidnapped right alongside heroine Olivia Larkin when bodyguard Quinn Calhoun carries her off—for her own good, of course. Award-winning Maggie Price's LINE OF DUTY miniseries has quickly won a following, so jump on the bandwagon as danger forces an estranged couple to reunite and mend their *Shattered Vows*. Then start planning your trip Down Under, because in *Deadly Intent,* Valerie Parv introduces you to another couple who live—and love—according to the CODE OF THE OUTBACK. There are *Whispers in the Night* at heroine Kayla Thorne's house, whispers that have her seeking the arms of ex-cop—and ex-*con*—Paul Fitzgerald for safety. Finally, welcome multipublished author Barbara Colley to the Intimate Moments lineup. Pregnant heroine Leah Davis has some *Dangerous Memories,* and her only chance at safety—and romance—lies with her husband, a husband she'd been told was dead!

Enjoy every single one, and come back next month (next year!) for more of the best and most exciting romance reading around—only in Silhouette Intimate Moments.

Yours,

Leslie J. Wainger
Executive Editor

Please address questions and book requests to:
Silhouette Reader Service
U.S.: 3010 Walden Ave., P.O. Box 1325, Buffalo, NY 14269
Canadian: P.O. Box 609, Fort Erie, Ont. L2A 5X3

Running Scared

LINDA WINSTEAD JONES

Silhouette®

INTIMATE MOMENTS™

Published by Silhouette Books

America's Publisher of Contemporary Romance

SILHOUETTE BOOKS

ISBN 0-373-27404-1

RUNNING SCARED

LINDA WINSTEAD JONES

would rather write than do anything else. Since she cannot cook, gave up ironing many years ago and finds cleaning the house a complete waste of time, she has plenty of time to devote to her obsession for writing. Occasionally she's tried to expand her horizons by taking classes. In the past she's taken instruction on yoga, French (a dismal failure), Chinese cooking, cake decorating (food-related classes are always a good choice, even for someone who can't cook), belly-dancing (trust me, this was a long time ago) and, of course, creative writing.

She lives in Huntsville, Alabama, with her husband of more years than she's willing to admit and the youngest of their three sons.

She can be reached via www.eHarlequin.com or her own Web site www.lindawinsteadjones.com.

Prologue

Making a special trip to the grocery store to buy ice cream and cookies in the middle of the day was a definite indication that things were not as they should be. Wearing comfortable shorts and a T-shirt with Taylor Elementary School emblazoned across the front, her hair pulled up and back into a ponytail, Livvie looked like any other teacher enjoying summer vacation. It was the worst *vacation* of her life! She really should make an effort to do something fun, but a woman should be allowed a few weeks of self-indulgence after she discovered that her fiancé—make that *ex*-fiancé—was cheating on her. The rat.

Livvie studied the bag of chocolate-chip cookies that peeked out of the plastic bag as she placed a foot on the bottom step of the flight that led to her second-floor apartment. Twenty-five percent more chips. Good. She needed all the chocolate she could get.

An unexpected noise penetrated her dismal introspection, and she stopped with one foot on the stairway and the other on the floor. While she was tempted to dismiss the popping sound as something innocent, she couldn't. Uncle Max had once taken her to a firing range and she'd taken a few shots with a pistol that had a suppressor attached. Some newfangled toy he'd been trying out at the time, she remembered. The gun had made that exact sound. The popping, coughing noise had come from…she turned her head…*that* apartment. The door was open, just a crack.

The walls in this building were thin. If the hard-of-hearing woman in 1B had had her television on as usual, Livvie never would've heard the noise from 1A, open door or no. She listened for a moment more, and tried to dismiss what she'd heard.

She didn't know the woman who lived in 1A, but they said hello in the hallway on a regular basis. 1A was a very pretty, very quiet woman with dark hair and dark eyes. Hispanic, Livvie had guessed, since the name on the mailbox was Nina Garcia. There were two young girls in that apartment, girls who were as quiet and pretty as their mother. It was the thought of those girls that made it impossible for Livvie to ignore what she'd heard.

"Mrs. Garcia? Nina?" Livvie walked to the door, her grocery bag in one hand, the purse strap over her shoulder threatening to fall. "Hello? Is everything okay?" Nina Garcia would come to the door, tell her all was well, and Livvie could climb the stairs to eat her ice cream and cookies while she cursed Terry's name. The rat. And maybe she'd cry a little bit again, as she contemplated what she'd lost. Or rather, what she'd falsely imagined she'd found. Ice cream, cookies and tears. The ultimate pity party.

No one answered her call. Livvie slung the plastic handle of her grocery bag over her arm and took her cell phone out of her purse. She wasn't about to walk into that apartment. This was a job for the police, not a recently dumped elementary school teacher who had an overactive imagination and too much time on her hands.

"What's your emergency?" a dispassionate voice asked.

"I think I heard a gunshot," Livvie said. She gave the 911 operator her name and address.

"We'll have an officer on the scene shortly," the woman on the other end of the line said.

Livvie leaned against the wall and relaxed a little. "It's probably nothing," she said. "I just heard a…"

The door to the apartment opened slowly. For a moment Livvie thought she'd be proved wrong. Nina would walk into the hallway with a glass of champagne in her hand… explaining the popping sound…and Livvie would tell the 911 operator to call off the cops.

A gun, bulky suppressor attached, was the first thing she saw.

It wasn't Nina who stepped into the hall, but a man. Like the family in 1A, he was dark-skinned. Unlike the Garcias, he was *not* pretty. His nose had been broken at least once, there was a tattoo of a spiderweb on his neck, and most startling…a jagged scar marred his face from the corner of one eye to his jaw.

The man turned to her, startled to find her so close. In an instant he noted the cell phone, her groceries and her fear. His gun hand began to shift.

Livvie did the only thing she could think of. She swung the grocery bag up with all the force she could muster. The cookies didn't carry much weight, but a half-gallon of frozen ice cream could do a lot of damage, if used properly. She caught him off guard and knocked the gun out of his hand, then swung again and aimed for the scar.

And she screamed. Doors along the hallway began to open. Cautiously, yes, but she and the man with the scar were no longer alone. The distant wail of sirens grabbed his attention, and he ran. He scooped up the gun she'd knocked out of his hand as he made his escape.

The man with the scar glanced back, and his eye caught hers. She shuddered and turned away, pushing the door to 1A open wide.

"Mrs. Garcia?" The danger was gone. If the scarred man had had an accomplice, she'd know it by now because he'd be running, too. "Hello?"

The drapes in the living room had been drawn and most of the lights were off. The apartment was dim, and much too quiet. Livvie's instinct was to return to the hallway and wait for the cops, but what if someone was hurt? It wouldn't be right to leave them unattended, even for a few more minutes. Especially if those children were in here! The very thought gave Livvie a chill. She couldn't possibly stand in the hallway when those girls might be in the apartment, frightened out of their wits and maybe even wounded. Or worse.

The apartment was too quiet. Hysterical screaming would have been preferable to the ominous silence, but silence was what she got as she walked through the small rooms, touching nothing as she searched for the occupants of 1A. No one was in the living room, and the bedrooms seemed to be deserted. Livvie called out a friendly "hello" as she walked through the apartment, searching for signs of life.

Just when she'd decided that no one was at home, Livvie stepped into the kitchen and found Nina. She'd been expecting the worst, and still her heart leapt and she cried out in surprise. The woman's motionless body lay in a pool of her own blood. There was so much blood. The petite woman had been shot in the chest, and her once-white summer dress was soaked.

Pale fingers twitched, and Livvie jumped back, startled. A ragged, horrible sound echoed through the room as the woman on the floor tried to breathe. Nina wasn't dead…at least, not yet. Livvie pushed her fear and revulsion aside and knelt down beside Nina, trying to ignore all the blood on the floor and on the woman. Surely she should do something, but she didn't know exactly what. Livvie pressed her hand over the wound to quell the flow of blood, even though she was almost positive it was too late for such an effort. She had to try, at least. She couldn't possibly just sit here and do nothing at all.

"Help's on the way," Livvie said in a low, shaky voice.

Nina opened her eyes and fixed them on Livvie's face, surprising her. She'd thought the woman well beyond hearing and understanding. Livvie's wrist was grasped and held with surprising force.

"My daughters," Nina said frantically. "Don't let him hurt my Elsa and Ria."

Livvie glanced back toward the doorway. "He's gone," she said. "Where are the girls?" Oh, she prayed they had not been at home when Scarface had broken in. If they were here…

Nina struggled to take a breath. "They went to a birthday party," she whispered in a softly accented voice. "They will be home soon. Don't let him hurt them, please. Please…"

"He's gone," Livvie said with a sigh of relief. Children should not have to go up against men like Scarface. She shuddered at the very idea. "He's not going to hurt the girls, I promise."

"You give me your word?"

"Yes. I promise, they'll be fine."

Nina closed her eyes, and her grip relaxed. "Thank you," she whispered.

And then the quiet, pretty woman in 1A took her last breath. Livvie was still kneeling beside the body when the police arrived.

Chapter 1

Camaria, South America

A knot had formed in Livvie's throat long before she'd taken her seat at the general's dining room table, and it refused to go away. Her heart beat too fast, and she couldn't manage to take a deep, calming breath.

How on earth was she going to get out of here?

When a respectable attorney had approached her about escorting Elsa and Ria to be reunited with their father, General Menendez, it had seemed like a good enough idea. She'd even thought it might be somewhat of an adventure. The fact that she'd been offered a nice wage to stay on for a few weeks until the girls were settled was just icing on the cake. The small South American country of Camaria had been politically stable for years, making it a seemingly safe destination.

She had not realized that General Lazaro Menendez would be a wacko. How could she possibly have known? During their brief phone conversations, she hadn't had so much as a sliver of warning. The middle-aged man wasn't particularly handsome or ugly, just pleasant-looking in an ordinary way. He had a nice enough smile and an almost gentle voice, and was physically fit and clean-shaven. Most days he wore a crisp black uniform, but on many evenings he dressed in civilian clothing that was expensive and tasteful. His accent was almost non-existent; he'd explained that he'd attended school in Texas, of all places.

But after just a few days here, she'd begun to see a new and alarming side of the general. He was given to fits of temper that were almost childlike, and his initial fascination with his daughters waned quickly. He'd said Nina had run off with another man when the children were young and he'd been delighted to hear that Elsa had remembered her old home. But even a child would hardly forget this place.

Like every other corner in the general's palace, the dining room was elegantly furnished. Exotic flowers filled delicate vases, and if the Picasso on the far wall wasn't an original it was a very good copy. Tonight the long mahogany table had been set for two with the finest china, crystal and silver. The meal smelled delicious and looked… interesting…but Livvie couldn't take a single bite.

Her companion at the dinner table, the general himself, didn't seem to notice her lack of appetite. For a father who claimed to be devoted, he didn't care to talk much about his children. Throughout the meal he'd talked constantly, primarily about his sugarcane plantations and his diamond mines, and the way the people he employed loved him and would do anything for him. There was more than a touch of pride in his voice as he talked about how deeply he was adored by his people.

Livvie nervously caressed the necklace Menendez had placed around her throat shortly after she'd taken her seat. Extravagant and heavy, it was set with diamonds from his own mines. She'd protested the offer as he'd approached her with the necklace in hand, but he had insisted that she wear the jewels while they dined together. After all, the diamonds went so well with the gown he'd had delivered to her room this afternoon.

She had planned to leave the white satin gown hanging where she'd found it, upon retiring to her quarters after a long day with the children. But Dulcinea, the servant Menendez had assigned to Livvie upon her arrival, had insisted that she wear the elegant evening gown for this special night. Livvie had suggested her own outfit, a long skirt and a high-necked matching blouse, as an alternative, but that was apparently not at all acceptable. The general would be very upset, Dulcinea said, if his gift was refused, and it was not wise to upset the general.

The way Dulcinea had shaken her head and averted her eyes…Livvie hadn't wanted to get the older woman in trouble by refusing the general's gifts, so here she was.

The gaudy necklace was not a gift but a loan—he had made no bones about that. Livvie felt like the hideous thing was choking her. She'd never cared for anything heavy or restrictive around her neck, especially when it so obviously came with strings attached.

Well into his own meal, Menendez finally noticed that Livvie had not touched her food. His smile faded. He frowned and his normally expressionless eyes went hard. "The piranha is not to your liking?"

"I'm not hungry," she replied.

"Would you care for something else? The chef will make you anything you'd like."

Since coming to the palace she'd been taking her evening meals with fourteen-year-old Elsa and eleven-year-old Ria—who were better company than their father and who did not wait until this late hour to dine.

Livvie shook her head and refused the general's offer. She wanted this meal to be over, the sooner the better. She did not like the way he stared at her cleavage, such as it was. She'd never been busty, but her dinner companion didn't seem to mind that she was lacking in that department. Maybe he was staring at the diamonds that were draped across her flesh, and not at her. After all, he did seem quite fond of the jewels.

"You must have dessert," Menendez insisted. "Banana layer cake, the chef's specialty."

Before she could refuse, a liveried servant appeared with two huge pieces of cake and two cups of coffee. The knot in her throat loosened a bit. Banana cake and coffee? The cake would go straight to her hips, and the coffee would keep her up all night. Her stomach rumbled. A couple of extra pounds and another sleepless night; she had more serious matters to worry about, at the moment. Livvie ate a few bites of the cake and drank the strong coffee, and the general seemed pleased.

While she ate, he continued to speak. He droned on and on, as he had during the entire meal, always talking about himself, his plans, his accomplishments. Menendez told her that in a few weeks he'd be traveling to Santa Rosa, Camaria's capital city, for an extended stay. He wanted Livvie to join him. For the sake of his daughters, of course, he said as he once again fixed his eyes well beneath her neck.

It was not the first time he had asked that she stay on as the girls' private tutor long after the time of their original agreement ended. She adored Elsa and Ria, but a permanent job so far away from home? Working for *him?*

Livvie remained silent and noncommittal, and again she wondered how she might get out of here. Maybe she could concoct a family emergency to cut her planned one-month visit short. Or she could pretend to be horribly homesick. Oh, if only she could manufacture a believable contagious disease which would require immediate medical attention that was unavailable here! No matter what story she came up with to explain her quick departure, Menendez couldn't stop her from leaving.

Could he?

When Livvie's half-eaten cake and empty coffee cup were taken away, she reached up to unclasp and remove the heavy diamond necklace.

"No," Menendez said, his voice so sharp Livvie immediately dropped her hands. "The diamonds are so beautiful around your throat. Leave them." In spite of the bite in his voice, he smiled at her. She had never seen such a cold, lifeless smile. Not even from Uncle Max, who usually had the power to set her every nerve on edge. "I will remove the necklace myself. Later."

The knot in her throat reappeared. There was no mistaking his intentions. There could be no mistaking the strength of her response. "No," she said succinctly. "You won't."

Menendez was not affected by her refusal. In fact, he looked more amused than ever. That wasn't a good sign. She'd been here two weeks and three days. In the beginning days Menendez had flirted with her, but she'd dismissed his inappropriate comments and roving eye as meaningless—an unpleasant aspect of his character. In the past week or so he had been kept blessedly busy with more urgent matters, and she'd allowed herself to believe that since she'd refused his many invitations to dinner, invitations that came with suggestions that there would be more for dessert than banana cake, that he'd turned his attentions elsewhere and would leave her to do her job. Apparently she had been badly mistaken. Tonight's invitation hadn't been a request at all, but a command. Livvie had never been good with commands. Not from her father, not from her uncle…not from Terry, the rat. Then again, none of their commands had been delivered by uniformed men carrying automatic weapons.

Livvie reached up and again began to toy with the clasp. She was unfamiliar with the mechanism, and could only fumble without success. The trembling of her fingers didn't help matters at all. Wearing the necklace was like wearing a very pretty yolk, and she was desperate to get it off. What kind of clasp *was* this?

One of the general's soldiers walked into the room without greeting and leaned over to whisper in his leader's ear. Menendez stood crisply and laid cold eyes on Livvie. "One hour," he said simply, and then he stalked from the room.

"Great," Livvie mumbled as she stood and rushed from the dining room. "Just great." She continued to fumble with the clasp as she all but ran toward her room, her heels clicking on marble floors in the wide, elegant hallways. She'd lived in apartments that had less square footage than the hallway where the guest bedrooms were located! This palace was massive and extravagant, and she should be very happy here. Instead, all she could think about was how to escape.

The lock on her door had never struck her as being particularly sturdy. There were no weapons close at hand. Even if she were the kind of person who carried firearms or knives, someone here would have confiscated the weapons shortly after her arrival, of that she was certain. She had nothing with which to defend herself.

The palace staff was housed in another wing, and the girls' shared room was at the other end of a long hallway. Which meant Livvie could scream all she wanted and no one would hear. And all this time she'd accepted the general's explanation that he wanted her to have one of the finer rooms, that as his guest and a friend of his children she was a part of the family and deserved the best. In reality, he'd corralled her here.

Her quarters were very nice, much nicer than she'd anticipated when she'd agreed to come here for the month. She'd expected a room of her own in the palace, but she had not known that she'd have a series of rooms almost as large as her apartment. From the hallway she entered into a sitting room where she had her own desk, a comfortable chair and ottoman, a plush rug and a few lush potted plants. An alcove contained a small kitchen area, complete with microwave and refrigerator. The sitting room was decorated in varying shades of green, with infrequent gold accents. It was never without fresh flowers in bright, cheerful colors, thanks to Dulcinea's attentions.

Beyond another doorway was her bedroom, a huge chamber where she slept on a comfortable mattress in a four-poster walnut bed. There was a matching dresser, a private bath, a rocking chair and a reading lamp, and a walk-in closet. This extravagant room was also decorated in green.

Glancing through the doorway into that bedroom did nothing to still Livvie's fears. Someone, Dulcinea no doubt, had lit more than a dozen candles and turned back the sheets on her queen-sized bed. Flower petals, red and pink, had been scattered across the white sheets. The place smelled of perfume, as if someone had spritzed the general's sweet cologne all over the sheets.

"Gross," Livvie mumbled as she grabbed the chair at her desk and placed it at the door, wedging it beneath the doorknob. Maybe that would deter the general's visit. For a while, anyway.

That done, she entered the bedroom and crossed to the window to look out on the night. The bars that she had always thought were meant to keep people out now took on an all new significance. She was trapped.

Camaria had the potential to be paradise, especially here in the north. The weather was warm, but never unbearably hot, and a multitude of plants thrived. One rainy season had passed and another wouldn't begin for a few months. Perhaps if she'd arrived at a time when it rained almost constantly she'd think the place not so much like Eden, but for now…for now it was a lovely prison.

There were plenty of lights around the palace, but beyond the boundaries were jungle and darkness, and there was no telling what lurked in that black night. She glanced back at the bed. Could what was out there in the jungle be any worse than what awaited her here?

"If I get out of here, I will never again do anything impulsive. I'll even listen to Uncle Max, I'll even let him check out any potential boyfriends before I get in too deep," she whispered. "I'll be good, I swear." She glanced up at the ceiling. "Get me out of here, and I will never again be impetuous. I'll weigh the pros and cons of every decision. I'll come up with a plan for my life and I'll stick with it, no matter what." She sighed. "Rash decisions never work out for me. I should have learned that when I was fifteen." And agreeing to come here had been a rash decision, made as much for her own sake as for Elsa and Ria. Again, she turned her eyes to the darkness beyond the palace. "Just…get me out of here."

She glanced down. Candlelight sparkled on the diamonds that adorned her throat and chest. The V-shaped neckline of her white satin gown dipped much too low. First things first. She had to get the necklace and the gown off, and dress herself in something more practical.

There would have to be one more impetuous move, before she changed her ways and settled down into a life of predictable and rational decisions.

She was going to run.

He came with no warning. While she studied the frightening darkness beyond the window and fiddled with the maddening clasp at the back of her neck, a muscled arm circled her waist. Before she could scream a hand clamped over her mouth. Hard. Livvie kicked her feet as she was lifted off the ground, but the man who had grabbed her paid no mind to her struggle. He'd said an hour! And how had he gotten into her room?

Suddenly she realized that it wasn't the general who'd grabbed her. Whoever this man was, he hadn't drenched himself in sweet cologne, and he was taller and leaner than Menendez. He dragged her away from the window, away from the bed, and she kicked the whole way. She bit her captor's hand, but he didn't even flinch as he hurried to the closet. The clothes hanging in her walk-in had been shoved aside, and a door at the back of the closet opened onto a narrow, dimly lit hallway. Livvie's heart kicked all over again. The cleverly disguised door had been here all along. Locking her door at night had been a complete waste of time.

Livvie continued to kick as she was dragged into the secret hallway. She managed to land a couple of solid blows with her white heels, but most of her efforts were entirely in vain. Once they were in the small space, the man who had grabbed her placed her on her feet. Still, he kept her pinned against the wall as he closed the secret door.

This was another of the general's sick games, Livvie imagined as she glared at her captor's shaded face. His cheeks were smeared with some kind of dark green greasepaint, and the way his head was turned she couldn't see him well. But she was quite sure she hadn't seen this man in the palace since her arrival.

Still, he had to be one of the general's men. Since she'd had the gall to say *no* over dinner, he was going to have her delivered to him by one of his goons.

Low wattage lights had been placed sporadically in the hallway, and when the man who had grabbed her turned his face to hers she could finally see him well enough. That green paint had been smeared across his face, here and there, as if he'd swiped his fingers across the high spots so the light wouldn't catch the sheen of his skin. He had dark brown hair, slightly curly and a little too long, and a powerful build. He wasn't bulky, like some of the general's soldiers who apparently spent their days lifting weights. He was just big and lean and—she swallowed—mean. His eyes were hazel-green and piercing. The hand at her mouth and the knee that kept her pinned to the wall were hard and unrelenting.

"You!" she said in a voice muffled against his palm, as she remembered where she'd seen that memorable face before.

His voice, as he whispered, was harsh. "Okay, princess, here we are. If I take my hand from your mouth, are you going to scream?"

She shook her head.

He didn't drop his hand. "Good. Maybe I won't have to kill anybody tonight." Did he look disappointed? He raked critical eyes over her, taking in the diamonds, the low-cut gown, the high-heeled shoes. She saw the disapproval there, the disgust. Slowly, he dropped his hand.

"You're here to get me out?" she asked.

He nodded.

"That's right, princess. I'm here to save your ass one more time."

Max had sent him, she knew that. She'd been unable to reach her uncle by phone before coming to Camaria, but she had mailed him a letter telling him of her plans. For once, she thanked her lucky stars that her uncle was paranoid and bossy and always seemed to know more than anyone else. He'd obviously known that it hadn't been wise for her to come here.

She shook her head, and as Cal took her wrist in his hand and led the way down the narrow hallway, she glanced heavenward. It was a done deal. *Thank you!* No more impetuous behavior for Olivia Larkin. From here on out, her life would be deliciously dull.

"Can't I go back and change clothes?" The woman he all but dragged behind him took quick steps to keep up. Cal glanced back as they hurried down the first flight of stairs.

Olivia Larkin was prettier than she'd been four years ago. A little slimmer, a little more mature. Her dark blond hair was longer than it had been then, and her petite figure was warm and real in the white gown. The last time he'd been sent in to haul her ass out of trouble, she'd been wearing a baggy dress that hadn't done her justice. He preferred his women with a little more meat on their bones, especially up top. *Delicate* was definitely not his style.

An all-grown-up Livvie was definitely delicate. She was graceful, as if she had been made for white satin, as if she'd break if he squeezed her too hard. With those diamonds around her neck she sparkled like the princess she was. Menendez's princess.

It hadn't taken him long to discover which bedroom was hers. The room had been empty when he'd found it, but he'd known it wouldn't stay unoccupied for long. He had noticed the candles, the flower petals, and more than that, the way her bedroom had reeked of the general.

When he'd stepped into that room and smelled the cologne, he'd almost upchucked. God help him, he wanted out of this place. Now.

"I want to go back and change clothes!" she said again.

"No," he said, keeping his voice low.

"But…"

"I have proper clothes and boots stashed at the end of the tunnel." He had left his backpack there not knowing what he'd encounter when he found the package, not knowing how much Livvie would fight him. For all he knew she liked it here. Max hadn't filled him in on all the details, he'd just hired the Benning Agency to get his niece out ASAP. He hadn't specified *how*.

"But…"

"We're not going back." If all continued to go well they'd be long gone before anyone missed her. Still, he needed to know how much time they had. "When were you expecting him?"

"What?"

"Menendez," Cal said through clenched teeth. "How long before he discovers that you're gone?"

She hesitated before answering. "An hour, he said, but…"

"That's all I need to know."

"But…"

He stopped and turned to glare down at the package. That's what Olivia Larkin was, a package he'd been hired to pick up and deliver. "Honey, it really would be best if we didn't talk any more than we have to," he whispered. "These walls are not paper thin, but if we're speaking at the wrong place and the wrong time, someone might hear."

"Okay," she said, her voice lower than his. "But what about this?" She pointed to the necklace. "Help me take the thing off, and I'll leave it here. Someone will find it. Right?"

Cal grabbed her hand and started walking again. "Keep it," he whispered. He was sure she'd earned the diamonds around her pretty throat.

"But…"

"I will gag you, if I have to," Cal said. After that, Livvie stayed silent.

He merely glanced at the closed door, one in a series of solid doors, as they hurried past it. He didn't slow down, he didn't experience any panic.

But he did look very hard at that door, for a brief, heart-stopping moment. He knew too well what waited in that room. A memory that had been buried for a long time came back in a flash. He'd tried so hard to forget, but being here brought it all back. He could see and smell and hear as if he'd been in that room just yesterday.

To keep going, to get this job done, he had to push that memory away.

Benning had originally given Santana this assignment. No one had asked Cal to return to this place, not even Max Larkin. Cal had volunteered, knowing Santana wouldn't have a chance here. He didn't know the palace like Cal did, and there hadn't been time for a thorough briefing. Two weeks wouldn't have been long enough to prepare Santana for what would await him in Camaria. But two days? Impossible.

Besides, the package knew him, in a way. Even though it had been four years, he figured she'd recognize him and that would make explanations easier.

A second flight of narrow steps led into the escape tunnel. It was one of two routes, and the one with which Cal was most familiar. It was darker here than it had been in the hallway, though not completely black. Livvie tensed as they descended into the tunnel. He could feel it, as if her anxiety radiated through her wrist and into his hand. Much as he wanted to shake her off, he didn't. She was his responsibility for the next six hours. They would travel by foot to the rendezvous site, where they'd be picked up by helicopter. Benning had the rescue planned down to the last detail.

The tunnel narrowed and sloped slightly downward before leveling off for a short distance and then turning up, taking them unerringly toward the surface. All was quiet here, and Livvie didn't say a word. Cal saw no reason to say anything, either. Silence was best and besides…Olivia Larkin was everything he detested in the opposite sex. Spoiled little rich girl, getting her jollies by getting it on with a sadistic Third World general, living off her pretty face and whatever sorts of acrobatic tricks she could do in a man's bed. His job was to get her out of here and to safety, but that didn't mean he owed her anything. He would not treat her like a princess, he would not cater to her. She was just a job.

When they reached the ladder at the end of the tunnel he snagged his backpack from a dark corner. Inside the pack was everything they'd need: Clothes for Livvie, a satellite phone in case things went wrong and he needed backup, food, water, a first-aid kit.

Clothes were all he needed for now. He drew out the camouflage T-shirt and pants, a pair of sturdy hiking boots and thick socks.

Livvie turned her head and fixed wide blue eyes on him. "Where am I supposed to change clothes?"

"Here. Quickly."

"I can't change in front of you." She pursed her lips and screwed up her nose when he didn't offer a solution to her sudden attack of modesty. "At least turn your back. Be a gentleman."

"I'm not a gentleman and you don't have anything I haven't seen before so lose the damn dress before I lose it for you."

Like the spoiled girl she was, Livvie lifted her chin. "This is entirely unacceptable. When Uncle Max hears about this…"

In a fluid motion, Cal pulled his knife from the sheath at his belt, flipped it in his hand and drew it down the front of the white gown from low neckline to hem in one quick motion. The satin parted, and Livvie opened her mouth as if she were thinking of screaming.

Cal grabbed her and pressed a hand over her mouth. "We don't have time for this, and if you're thinking about screaming just remember that if we get caught here and now we will both end up dead. Now, get dressed or I will, by God, dress you myself."

There was murder in her eyes, but she got the message. He dropped his hand, took a step back and tossed her the traveling clothes. As she caught them, the ruined gown parted like an unbelted robe.

"You're a jerk," she whispered as she shrugged off the gown and very quickly pulled on the long-sleeved T-shirt. She wasn't so quick that Cal didn't get a nice, if all too brief, view.

"So I've been told."

"If I wasn't desperate to get out of here I'd...I'd..."

"You'd what?" he asked as she stepped into the pants. Nice legs, too, for a short woman. He should've remembered that.

"Scream," she said. "I don't suppose you could've come to the front door and told the general you were here to escort me home."

"I don't suppose," he said softly.

"Isn't this a little overly dramatic?"

"Max doesn't think so."

She sat on the floor to pull on her socks. "So I'm just supposed to waltz into the jungle with *you?*"

"Pretty much." She'd said she was desperate to get out of here. It didn't take much of an imagination to figure out why. "Did he hurt you?" Cal asked in a lowered voice.

"What?" She glanced up as she tied the laces of one boot.

"Menendez," Cal said. "Did he hurt you?"

She shook her head and gave her attention to the final

chore of tying one last shoe string. "No. But what a creep! When I came here I had no idea what he was like." She stood and brushed off the back of her pants, as if she might've picked up some dust on her butt.

Livvie hadn't been here very long, he knew that. Maybe she didn't know exactly how creepy her lover could be, when the mood struck him.

"Stand still," he ordered. He squirted a generous dollop of insect repellent onto the palm of his hand and smeared it over her neck. She sputtered when he quickly swiped his hands over her face, and tried to yank her hands away when he smeared the insect repellent there. The process took less than thirty seconds.

"Let's go." He grabbed her discarded shoes and gown and stuffed them, along with the repellent, into the backpack. He didn't want anyone stumbling across the evidence that she'd left by this route.

"Up there?" she whispered, glancing up the long metal ladder that would lead them to the surface.

"It's the only place to go from here, princess."

She stepped onto the bottom rung and he gave her a little shove to hurry her along. He had an hour or less to put some distance between them and the palace before the general discovered that his woman was missing.

Cal climbed, staying close to Livvie. He hadn't thought he'd ever be in Menendez's palace again, and in spite of the instinct that told him to get out of this place as quickly as possible, he was tempted to spend a little time. He could drop in and leave his mark, and make sure the general knew who'd been here. By the time Menendez figured out what had happened, Cal would be at home, sitting in his favorite recliner sipping on a cold beer.

If he ventured into the palace again, maybe he'd even stumble across the general himself. He had a score to settle, and this was his chance. The only chance he would ever have.

But his job was to get Olivia Larkin out as quickly and quietly as possible, and that's exactly what he was going to do. No more, no less.

She climbed as quickly as she could, moving a little more quietly without the high heels and the rustling gown. At the top of the ladder he reached past her to grab the handle on the trapdoor, throwing it open on a dark night.

They emerged into the jungle that surrounded the general's compound. Back on solid ground Cal closed the trapdoor and made sure it was well concealed, as it had been when he found it. He took Livvie's wrist in an iron grip once again. Walking quickly, they left the palace behind. They'd encountered no trouble in the tunnels, and he didn't expect trouble here. Even if someone had already discovered that Livvie was missing, the odds were no one would be searching this particular spot.

Menendez didn't trust easily. It was the only reason he'd survived so long. Only a handful of his most trusted soldiers knew about the maze of secret hallways and the escape tunnels.

Cal had once been one of those soldiers.

Chapter 2

Livvie gratefully took a long, deep breath of air. The tunnels had had a stale odor about them, a stench she was grateful to escape. Out of the palace, away from the general, she felt suddenly free. She wouldn't feel entirely safe until she was home again, but still…her heart almost soared, and the muggy air seemed to carry the scent of freedom.

Cal turned and walked away from the tunnel after making sure the exit was well-disguised by the plants that grew around it. Did he hope that no one would realize how they'd escaped? With the chair blocking her doorway, she imagined they would figure it out, sooner or later. Probably sooner, since Menendez had planned on visiting her tonight.

"We should hurry," Livvie said as she followed close behind Cal, suppressing a deep shudder. The T-shirt and cargo pants he had provided fit her perfectly, the boots were her size. Of course they were perfect. Uncle Max sometimes bought her clothes and shoes for Christmas. The things he bought were usually more conservative than anything she would've chosen for herself, and she didn't exactly have wild tastes.

Cal was a little older, but he hadn't changed much in the past four years. Livvie tried very hard not to think about the first and only time they'd met, but unfortunately it hadn't been a forgettable time.

She'd been straight out of college and living in Texas at the time. Oh, she'd thought she was so grown-up, so independent. Ha. Uncle Max had known she was in trouble before she had, and just when things had been about to get ugly Cal had shown up to whisk her away. She certainly hadn't expected it to become a habit. Neither had he, she imagined.

Tonight he had dressed appropriately in a black T-shirt, dark jacket, jeans and sturdy boots. That smear of green across his face was almost frightening. It made him look a little vicious, as if he were capable of doing anything. And he probably was. Otherwise, he wouldn't be here.

Four years ago they'd spent twenty-four hours together, most of that time in a car going well over the speed limit. Those first few moments had been frightening, and she'd been so angry and scared and indignant. Once she'd accepted that he was telling the truth, she'd actually been grateful that Cal had shown up when he did. For a few minutes of those twenty-four hours, she'd almost found herself pleasantly intrigued with the too-macho and not-altogether-bad-looking guy.

Almost. For the other twenty-three hours and fifty minutes or so, he'd just been exasperating. He was definitely not Prince Charming material.

Livvie wondered for a moment if there were weapons under Cal's jacket, maybe something other than the knife he'd used to cut her dress off. She answered herself with a silent, "Of course there are." He wasn't the kind of man who would enter the palace unprepared. Still, from her vantage point she saw nothing to alarm her.

She almost laughed. Alarm her? These had been the most alarming two weeks of her life!

Cal didn't seem interested in holding a conversation, and she couldn't blame him. This was no place for chit-chat, and he hadn't been exactly chummy last time. Still… "How have you been?" she finally asked.

His response, a short bark of laughter, was terribly rude.

She pouted, and didn't feel too bad about it since he couldn't see. After a few silent minutes, he said, "Fine. I've been fine."

Livvie hurried to catch up with him. "That's good." She waited for him to ask how she had been, but of course, he didn't. "Your hair's longer. I like it. And I'm glad you shaved the goatee. I'm not a big fan of facial hair."

He glanced down at her, but he didn't actually tell her to shut up.

"Sorry," she said. "I ramble when I'm nervous. I'll get it out of my system pretty quick, I promise." She took two more steps. When she wasn't talking the jungle was too noisy. Even when she was talking she couldn't ignore the sounds of small critters and a multitude of insects. She and Cal might be the only human beings in the vicinity, but they were *not* alone. The jungle was alive, and they were the intruders.

Oh, she could not bear to think about what was out there, just beyond her reach. "What does Cal stand for?"

she asked, trying desperately to take her mind in a new and less alarming direction.

"What difference does it make, princess?" he answered. As they stepped farther into the darkness, he came up with a flashlight. It wasn't very bright, but the beam did illuminate their path. "Six hours from now you'll be on your way home and with any luck you'll never see me again."

"Six hours? We're not going to walk for the entire six hours, are we?"

"Yep," he said softly.

She had no one to blame but herself. Since she'd been prepared to walk on her own, she should just be grateful that she wasn't alone and that Cal apparently knew where he was going and how long it would take to get there.

He was definitely the kind of man who would know how to get where he was going, even in a place like this. Back in the States he probably had an isolated cabin and a big dog, and he could live off the land for weeks at a time. He'd be a meat and potatoes man, she imagined, who spent a lot of time in seedy bars getting into knife fights over big-breasted bleached-blond women named Bambi or Heather. And winning.

"Calvin," she mused. "Caleb. Calbert."

Cal stopped and turned to meet her face-to-face. "Calbert?"

"That's it."

"No." He turned his back on her and continued walking, shaking his head.

"How did you know about the tunnels and the doorway into my room?" she asked. Her heart leapt, and she felt a decidedly sick churning in her stomach. She'd thought the chair at her door might stop the general. If she hadn't gotten out in time he would have laughed at her efforts and entered through that hidden door.

Cal didn't answer her question, but barreled forward, pushing past thick foliage that grew over this poor excuse for a path as if he knew his way around this jungle well.

Too well. Livvie had a sudden and terrifying thought. Just because Uncle Max had sent Cal after her the last time she'd gotten herself in hot water, that didn't necessarily mean he'd sent him in *this* time. She came to an abrupt halt. The man before her took only a single step before he turned to face her, as if he had known she was going to stop before she did. With the flashlight shining down and to the side she couldn't see his face, only a vague outline of his tall, muscular body.

"Listen, princess…"

"And don't call me princess," she interrupted. "You know very well that my name is Olivia Larkin. My friends call me Livvie. You can call me Miss Larkin. That's only fair since you won't even tell me your name."

He grinned, teeth bright in the night. "Fine, Miss Larkin. My name is Quinn Calhoun. My friends call me Cal. You can call me Mr. Calhoun. Now that we've been properly introduced can we *go?*"

She pursed her lips and withheld the childish urge to stick out her tongue. "Did my uncle send you?"

"Yes."

"How did he know I needed rescuing?"

"Apparently it's a semi-permanent state for you," Cal said impatiently.

She was in no position to argue with him—she knew that. She was out of the palace, away from Menendez…stuck in the middle of a dangerous jungle with Quinn Calhoun.

"I just want to be sure," she said more calmly.

Cal leaned down so he was close to her. "We don't have time for this. I was hired to get you out of General Menendez's palace. Are you complaining? Would you like me to take you back?"

"No," she answered quickly, suppressing a chill. "You arrived at a very opportune moment, and I'm grateful, I really am, but…"

"Save your breath," he said sharply. "We have a long walk ahead of us."

Fine. She didn't care what he thought, anyway. "How did Max know…"

"Ask him when you get home. Who knows, maybe he'll even tell you."

Home. Oh, she should argue. She should plant her feet and insist that Cal tell her all the details of this rescue. But the very mention of the word *home* made her rush to keep up with his long stride.

They hadn't been walking more than ten minutes before a sharp noise broke the night. Palace alarms. "An hour my ass," Cal said as he quickened his step. "Apparently you've been missed."

"Maybe something else happened," Livvie said too brightly, a trace of hope in her voice. "Maybe someone was trying to break in."

"Princess, no one breaks into the general's palace. Trust me." Could have been some poor son of a bitch trying to break out, though.

No, the alarm was for her. He'd be foolish to consider any other possibility, even though they were well short of the hour she'd said they had.

"We're going to have to pick up the pace." He attached the dim flashlight to a hook on his belt and drew a short machete from the sheath inside his jacket. If they had to leave the path, he'd need it. "Can you handle this or am I going to have to carry you?"

"You are not going to carry me," she said indignantly.

He grabbed her hand and started jogging at an easy gait, for the moment following the trail that would lead them away from the general's palace. The glow from the flashlight was no longer steady, but bounced a bit and sent faint rays of light into the growth around them. It was possible that they would have to leave the path, and he was prepared for that possibility. But if they did have to alter the planned route, it would cost them precious time.

The guards would spread out. Menendez would send his men toward the hidden exits of his escape routes, and some, the most trusted, would even come through the tunnels. Others would take to the road…some headed toward the little town where many of the soldiers passed their time when they weren't on duty, others toward a rural village where some of the general's plantation workers lived. Maybe when they didn't find what they were looking for they'd spread out, but with any luck they wouldn't bother until morning.

All of them would be traveling without a complaining, mouthy woman slowing them down.

He had been here in the past, on this very route. He had run from the palace before.

"The general probably won't look for me very long," Livvie said breathlessly. "Once he realizes I'm gone he'll…"

"Menendez doesn't like to lose," Cal said sharply. "He'll

look for you until he knows you're out of the country. And even once you get home, you might want to see about keeping a low profile for a while. A *very* low profile."

For once she didn't argue with him. There was no quick, breathless "But…" in answer to his suggestion. Cal glanced over his shoulder. The princess was white as a sheet.

Livvie ran to keep up with Cal. He didn't run, but there was no hesitation in his step. For Livvie, it was a matter of pride not to slow him down any more than she had to, but it wasn't long before she was breathing heavily and struggling to match his stride.

Had they been out here for hours? Or had time simply stopped for this excursion? It was as if they were lost in the middle of nowhere. Literally. As if no one else existed, as if they would be running away from the general forever. Always afraid he was right behind them, always waiting to be found. She was caught in a nightmare.

From a distance the jungle had always been beautiful. Exotic. Up close it was scary and suffocating. And dark. The canopy high overhead didn't let in so much as a ray of moonlight or starlight. If not for Cal's flashlight the darkness would be complete. It wasn't as hot as she'd thought it might be, but the humidity was high. She'd begun to sweat as soon as they'd picked up the pace.

It was such a noisy place. The deeper into the jungle they traveled the noisier it became. The night whirred, chirped, clicked and occasionally screamed. Even though the animal screams were far away, they always made her heart skip a beat. Cal wasn't affected at all…as if he *had* a heart to skip a beat!

They stopped once for water, and Cal asked her if she

were hungry. She said no, not wanting to slow down their journey, even though dinner had been cake and coffee and she'd eaten a light lunch.

Other than his offer and her refusal of food, they didn't speak. Cal made surprisingly little noise for a man who was barging through the jungle in the middle of the night. Even though they were on a path of sorts, the jungle refused to recognize the boundaries. Plants grew over and across the trail, blocking their way on occasion. Livvie made noise; she knew it, but couldn't help the fact. Her step seemed louder than his, and she had a tendency to run face first into the large leaves Cal managed to avoid. She sputtered when that happened, but did not complain or cry out. She found it incredibly annoying that he wasn't even breathing hard.

They had left the lights of the palace behind long ago, but that did little to ease her fears. The flashlight that hung from Cal's belt, with its faint ray of light, was the only thing between her and total darkness. Livvie wouldn't admit as much, but she was scared. As scared as she had ever been. With every step she became more terrified. And rightly so.

Even though she had met him once before, Livvie knew very little about Quinn Calhoun. He worked for her uncle on occasion, but was not an employee of the company for which Max Larkin now worked in a consulting capacity. And she doubted very much this rough-looking man and her *GQ* uncle were friends.

Which meant Cal was available for hire to just about anyone. Anyone who knew where she'd gone might've hired him to kidnap her. Was this a kidnapping or a rescue? She couldn't be sure.

The alternative, returning to the palace and General

Menendez, was unthinkable. But had she simply jumped out of the frying pan and into the fire? The man had cut her dress in half in order to hurry her along. What would he do to her if she slowed him down now?

They had been making steady progress through the jungle, but suddenly Cal stopped. He switched off the flashlight and squeezed her wrist tight.

"What…" Livvie began.

Cal dragged her off the path, swung her around, clapped his hand over her mouth, and pressed her back to the trunk of the tree. All before she had a chance to protest with anything more than a sharp intake of breath. She couldn't move, she couldn't make a sound. Her worst fears were coming true, here in the middle of nowhere in the middle of the night, in a place where no one would ever find her. Cal hadn't set her free, he had kidnapped her. Who had hired him? Someone who wanted something from Max, of course. Money or information.

All this—the rescue, the quick walk through the jungle, the sense of urgency—it was all a farce. She tried to push against Cal with her hands and her body, but he was too strong. He'd pinned her to the tree, and the hand over her mouth was like a rock. The body he pressed to her was like stone, too. Warm stone, but hard as rock and just as immovable.

In his free hand, he held a very sharp machete.

She was about to bite him anyway when she heard voices. Two men spoke in rapid, low Spanish. Those voices, and footsteps, came closer and closer.

It was dark here. Unbelievably dark. Cal was right in front of her, his face no more than two inches from hers, and still…she couldn't see him. She could feel him, though, warm and solid. She trembled as the men on the path came nearer. He didn't.

He hadn't hurt her, though he had frightened her more than once. And if he wanted a ransom, then why hadn't he taken the diamond necklace she continued to wear? The thing was worth a small fortune. And this was Cal, after all. She knew him. They had a past, in an odd sort of way. They had nothing in common, they would never be friends, they would never even carry on a decent conversation. But she did trust him. Heaven help her, what choice did she have?

She began to relax, her body and mind unwinding slowly. Cal had grabbed her because he'd heard the guards approaching long before she had. He had only been trying to keep her still and quiet so she couldn't give away their location.

Her hands relaxed and rested on his shoulders. She nodded once, and Cal slowly dropped his hand from her mouth and lowered it to her waist where it rested solid and warm. They stayed there, perfectly still, bodies pressed together, and didn't make a sound. She couldn't even hear him breathing, and she did her best to make her own breaths as easy and quiet as his.

Out of the corner of her eye a small portion of the jungle was illuminated by the flashlight the soldiers carried. The light didn't reach them, thank goodness, but if Cal hadn't heard…

Livvie realized, as they waited for the men on the path a few feet away to pass, that she had truly never known anyone like Cal. Her earlier imaginings about what his life might be like were mere fantasy, a way to pass the time and at least pretend that she knew this man, but in truth he was unique. Her male acquaintances were teachers, restaurant owners and local politicians. They were very nice, perfectly ordinary men who would have no idea how to make their way through the jungle. No one she'd ever known would have dared to cut a woman's dress off, and the way he had handled the knife, as if it were an extension of his arm, well…that certainly wasn't the norm.

But he was like other men in one very telling way. With their bodies pressed so close together, she couldn't help but feel his response. The length of his arousal pressed against her. Any other man would have shifted away and drawn back, embarrassed. But Cal didn't move. Maybe he thought the men who were searching for them would hear even that.

Maybe they would. The soldiers were close, and they had stopped on the path to discuss their plans. One of the men decided that Miss Larkin had not taken this path. If so, they would have seen signs of her by now.

Livvie listened, but her mind was elsewhere. Her mind was on the man who pressed his body against hers. *Oh, my.*

After a moment's discussion, the guards continued along the path, even though they were certain that the American woman could not have traveled so far.

Livvie's mind was not on the soldiers who were searching for her. She became suddenly and assuredly convinced that Cal didn't remain motionless and pressed against her because he was afraid someone would hear. He didn't care. To know that she felt his response…he simply did not care.

Only after the searchers had passed and she could hear no more steps on the path, no more frantic voices, did Cal step back. He switched on his flashlight and turned his back to her. "Let's go." He headed away from the path, making his own way in the dark wilderness. He made good use of the machete in his hand this time.

Livvie followed, staying close. She didn't want to make too much of his telling reaction as he'd restrained her. If he didn't care, why should she? It was just a normal guy thing, she reasoned as they continued on silently. An unwanted and unprovoked physical response. If she'd thought Cal was the kind of man to be embarrassed, she'd say something funny to lighten the mood. But knowing him as she did, briefly but much too well, she imagined he had already dismissed the incident as insignificant. She walked quickly to keep up with him, grateful for the boots he'd provided.

He really needed to get laid if hanging onto the princess for a couple of minutes got him hard. Cal forged onward, not looking back and not holding on to Livvie's wrist. She was keeping up well enough as he created a crude path. She stayed close, and for this leg of the journey he didn't need to lead her along.

He'd been without a woman too long, that's all it was. Olivia Larkin wasn't his type and never would be. Not that she wouldn't do in a pinch…

"Can we stop?" she asked, her voice low.

"Why?" he snapped, turning to face her. All he wanted to do was get her on the helicopter and out of his hands. Once they were in Guyana she'd be someone else's problem.

She glared up at him. "I have to pee."

"Now?"

"Yes."

"It can't wait?"

She answered with one of those soft girlie grunts that spoke volumes about her frustration. Finally she said, "If you're going to insist that I drink water, then you're going to have to let me stop and pee."

Grumbling, he swung the backpack down and off, opening it with one hand. The guards were either headed in another direction or on their way back to the palace, and he didn't expect any more trouble. If anyone was out looking for them they'd be in the small towns nearest the palace. Not here, not now. A small roll of toilet paper was stashed in the backpack, next to one of her white shoes. He pulled the roll out of the backpack and tossed it to the princess.

"Thank you," she said sarcastically.

"You're welcome."

She offered her empty hand. "Can I borrow the flashlight?"

He handed it over and she illuminated a not-too-overgrown path that took her away from him.

"Not too far!" he ordered when she'd taken a few steps. "And take a good look around before you drop your drawers."

"I'm just going behind this tree." She shined the flashlight on the trunk of a tree not four feet in front of her. "But thank you for that thoughtful and oh, so gentlemanly advice."

"Smart-ass," he muttered.

She turned off the flashlight, after doing as he'd instructed and examining the immediate area, leaving them in total darkness. He heard the rustle of her clothing, and then silence.

"Maybe you should sing," she said.

"I don't sing."

"Never?"

"Never. If you're all that shy, you sing."

After a moment's hesitation she did. She began to sing "I Will Survive" in a soft, horribly off-key voice that was surprisingly husky.

Cal stood on the path and waited impatiently. He tapped his foot, rotated his head and snapped a crick out of his neck. Standing still while a good number of soldiers who had better weapons than he did hunted him down wasn't his way of doing things. Baby-sitting wasn't his thing, either.

"One time I beat the crap out of a guy for singing that song," he said.

Maybe Livvie was done. The singing stopped, and once again he heard the rustle of clothing. "Well, that was very rude of you," she said as she switched the flashlight on and came toward him again.

"I hate that frickin' song," he said softly.

"I'll sing something else next time," she said as she handed him the flashlight and the roll of toilet paper.

Cal didn't respond. With any luck, there wouldn't be a next time.

"So," she said, sounding much too casual, "you actually beat a guy up just for singing?"

"I was drunk," Cal explained, "and he couldn't carry a tune."

"Did this episode take place in a seedy bar?"

"Is there any other kind?"

"Of course there is." Now that she'd had her breather, she sounded downright chipper. "But I assumed you'd fight over women named Trixie or Kiki, not old disco tunes."

"I never fight over women," Cal said.

"Why not?"

"They're not worth it."

By the time she saw the murky lights of a small town before them, Livvie was breathless. Finally! A bathroom.

A place to sit. Maybe a telephone. Now that she was safely away from the palace she didn't have to stay with Cal if she didn't want to. She could find a phone and call…someone. Uncle Max? He'd just tell her to stay with Cal until he delivered her home, and she'd end up agreeing even though that wasn't what she wanted to do. Mary Ann? She was a great friend, the best. But she'd have no idea how to go about getting someone out of a foreign country. Terry, the rat? No way in hell.

Which left her in Cal's hands, for the moment.

Far from the edge of the jungle, Cal dropped to his haunches and went very still. Livvie did the same, lowering herself to hunker down beside him.

"What are we doing here?" she whispered.

"The pickup spot is on the other side of town." He pointed. "We can stay in the jungle and walk around the town, or we can go straight through and hope no one is there looking for us just yet."

"Don't you have a plan?" She didn't intend to sound snippy, but it had been a very long night. And it wasn't over.

Cal looked at her. Dark as it was, she could feel the heat and the anger radiating from him. "I had planned to stay on the path and then go around town, staying under cover in the jungle for as long as possible. But that was before I knew your boyfriend would miss you so soon. The detour we took after we heard the soldiers on the path cost us some time."

"I don't have a boyfriend," she snapped.

"Sorry," he said. "Lover? Beau? *Amante?*" His accent when he spoke the single word was flawless, as if he were a native.

She knew what he was thinking, and she knew why. The

dress, the diamonds. The way Dulcinea had prepared her room for the evening... "You're wrong," she whispered.

"None of my business, princess."

"I'm not a princess!" she snapped, losing her patience with the man.

She didn't like Cal, not at all, so she really shouldn't care what he thought about her. He was a hired hand, a man who obviously led a rough and uncertain life. And while he was...interesting, she supposed, he certainly wasn't pretty. In any other place, at any other time, they wouldn't even have reason to exchange names. No wonder he'd laughed at her when she'd very politely asked him how he'd been. Polite was not even a part of his vocabulary.

So why did she care what he thought of her?

"The fact is we're behind schedule," he said calmly, "and in order to reach the helicopter on time we're going to have to walk straight through town."

"Won't it wait for us?"

He shook his head. "This is a hired ride, and the pilot knows if he gets caught he's in a heap of trouble. So, if we're not there on schedule he'll leave without us. There is a backup plan, but it'll definitely be best if we can get you out of here before sunup."

Livvie nodded.

"No talking."

Again she nodded, grateful for the chance *not* to speak to Quinn Calhoun. He didn't hang on to her wrist, which was just as well.

Sporadic streetlamps lit the narrow paved streets, and while they were few and far between, her vision, and his, was much better than it had been in the jungle. Where there was no artificial light, moonlight lit their way, since they were no longer under the canopy of the jungle. The town slept, quiet and still.

All of the houses were small, simple homes made of cedar, with tiny windows set high in the walls. Most of the houses did not have electricity, but a few did. The occasional yellowish light of a low-wattage lightbulb broke through a small window, even at this hour.

Cal's head snapped up, seconds before Livvie heard the noise. He took her hand again and yanked her out of the light and into a narrow alley. As she took a breath to ask him what the hell he was doing, she heard the roar of an engine. A car, moving fast, was headed their way.

She hadn't seen the gun until now, but Cal reached into his jacket and came out with his hand cradling a small, deadly looking pistol.

"We can hide until they go away," she whispered as softly as possible.

Cal glanced up and down the alleyway, and then he led her away from the street. There was a cross alley, a passageway between the houses so narrow a large man wouldn't be able to fit. He gently pushed her into the darkness and said, "Stay here. If I don't get back…"

"Don't say that," she whispered.

"If I'm not back in three minutes, you head north. There's a clearing, and a helicopter will be there in…" He checked his watch. "Fourteen minutes. Princess, you have to be there."

"So do you!"

He didn't answer, but left her standing there in the dark. Alone. Her back against a cedar wall and her heart beating so hard she could feel it pounding against her chest.

North. Which way was north? She thought she knew, but

couldn't be sure. He'd pointed from the shelter of the jungle. That way? Or that? The trip through the jungle and through the little town had been a winding one, and she had been turned about and around until she was hopelessly lost.

Besides, annoying as he was, she didn't want to proceed without Cal. She didn't like him, not at all, but he had gotten her out of the palace in the nick of time. She had prayed to be rescued, and he'd appeared. She couldn't leave without him.

Cal had two objectives as he crept toward the road and the noises that broke the stillness of night. Olivia Larkin was going to make it out of here, and he was not going to let himself be captured. Not again. Never again.

The engine stopped. Two car doors slammed in quick succession, then another. He heard footsteps. Low voices. There were three of them. Decent odds. He'd faced worse.

The men were talking in low voices, but they weren't close enough for Cal to hear their words. Not that it mattered. His job was cut and dried. Get the package out. Kill anyone who tried to stop him.

He glanced back, but only once. Three minutes had come and gone. Livvie had to get herself to the helicopter. She could do it, if she'd just get moving. All he had to do was lead the general's men away from this alley and give her a clear shot.

Behind him—far behind—he heard a frantic whisper. "Cal!" Why hadn't she headed north yet? Surely her survival instincts would kick in once the gunfire started.

The three men from the car exchanged a few more words and then split up. That was a stroke of luck. They probably thought they were searching for a lone runaway woman, and that meant they'd be sloppy. Good. Only one was headed this way. Very good. Cal holstered the Colt and drew his knife. It fit comfortably in his hand. He felt more in control with a knife than a pistol. Besides, wielded properly, a blade was quick and silent.

Footsteps along the street headed his way. Cal flattened his back against the wall and waited. For a moment he forgot about the princess, the people who slept in the houses around him, the helicopter that would soon land. The general's soldier came around the corner and Cal made his move. Hand over mouth, head jerked back, one smooth swipe. Before the man knew what was happening he was face-down on the street, throat cut fast and clean.

Cal dragged the body into the dark alley and glanced back. The princess should be well on her way to the pickup point, but she wasn't. She stood not ten feet behind him, her eyes on the soldier's body, and then on the knife, and then on his face.

She was close to panic, actually looked like she could pass out at any moment. God, he didn't have time to deal with this. Not now.

He took her hand and turned her away from the body, leading her through the alleyway and toward the edge of town. "I thought you'd be halfway to the drop point by now."

"I wasn't sure which way was north," she said in a small voice. "And besides…I didn't want to leave you behind."

Ridiculous. He could take care of himself and she couldn't, it was that simple. Didn't she have any self-preservation instincts at all? They ran from the alley in a burst of new speed. Cal heard the distant whir of the helicopter; the two soldiers who remained in town would hear, too, he knew that. He and Livvie had a head start, but not much of one. Not enough. He ran faster, and forced Livvie to do the same.

They ran into the clearing just as the helicopter began its descent. The side doors were open—missing, in fact. This would be a rough ride, but once it was over Olivia Larkin would be back where she belonged and Cal...

Cal had a strong urge to put her on the helicopter and go back. Back to the palace, back to General Menendez. The place scared him more than he liked to admit, but he had unfinished business here, and it had been preying on his mind.

No, it was his job to get the package to Guyana, but once that was done maybe he'd come back. Prepared, next time.

When they reached the helicopter he swung the woman up and in, then jumped in himself. He slipped off the backpack and tossed it beneath his seat as he gave the pilot the signal to go.

But before the pilot could obey the command two soldiers ran into the clearing. Reiner and Alejandro, of course. Who else? They were two of Menendez's best men—the wiry, pale German and the six and a half foot tall native. Reiner silently commanded the pilot to shut down his engines, and the automatic weapon Alejandro had trained on the helicopter's cockpit compelled him to do just that.

Cal swung down and out of the helo.

"Hand over the gun," Reiner commanded.

Since Alejandro now had his M-16 trained on Livvie, Cal complied.

"Well, this is a surprise." Reiner grinned widely once Cal was unarmed. He stuffed the confiscated Colt into his waistband. "I thought you were dead. Lazaro will be so very glad to see you."

"Wow," Cal said without emotion. "You're on a first name basis with the general these days. Good for you."

Reiner crooked a finger at Livvie, but she stayed put.

"I tell you what," Cal said, placing himself between the mercenary and the woman he had been sent here to collect. "How about you do me a favor, for old times' sake, and just let her go."

"I suppose you think I should let you go, too, after you cost me a night's sleep."

Cal knew he wasn't that lucky. "I'll stay. You let her go." He didn't even turn to look at Livvie's face. None of this was her fault. He should've been faster. He should've found another way.

But he hadn't.

"She comes with us," Reiner said, his German accent as heavy as it had been six years ago. He motioned with his pistol for Livvie to leave the helicopter, and she did. She immediately moved close to Cal, almost hiding behind him.

Reiner grinned widely as he leaned into the helicopter and spoke to the pilot. "It is your lucky day, my friend. If you're out of here in two minutes you get to live."

The pilot didn't think twice. As Cal, Reiner and Livvie walked away from the helicopter, the engines came to life again. Seconds later it lifted off the ground. Cal fingered the knife at his belt. With the knife alone, he could take both men and shield Livvie with his body, but not until Alejandro was closer. And the big guy was headed his way. Not quickly, but an inch at a time. Cal calculated distances and wrapped his arm through Livvie's so he could push her behind him before the fighting began.

When the helicopter was perhaps fifty feet off the ground, Alejandro lifted his M-16 and started firing. The report of the automatic weapon was deafeningly loud; Livvie dipped her head and covered her ears. Cal automatically rested his hand over the knife at his side, but before he could react a bullet found its mark and the helicopter exploded in mid-air. A ball of fire lit the sky as if sunrise had come with a bang.

"You said you'd let him go!" Cal shouted as Livvie turned her face into his chest and screamed.

"I lied," Reiner said as he watched the pieces of the aircraft fall to the ground in flames.

Chapter 3

Livvie stopped screaming, but she couldn't bear to look at the flames and the wreckage that continued to fall and burn. She pressed her face to Cal's chest and clutched at his jacket, eyes closed tight while the two men shouted at one another. This couldn't be happening…the nightmare couldn't be getting *worse*.

Suddenly the shouting stopped and Cal pushed her away. Surprised, she practically flew backward to land on her rear end and then roll awkwardly down a small embankment. Shots were fired, a few quick bursts, and again Livvie screamed as she fought her way up into a sitting position.

She wished she had Cal in front of her so she could hide from this sight. Eyes wide open, she couldn't help but see the flames and the carnage on the field. Flames, and charred debris, and men fighting. The big man who had shot down the helicopter swung his weapon toward Cal and took careful aim, but a shouted order from the other man kept him from firing. In frustration he tossed the weapon aside, drew a knife of his own, and went after Cal. The three men fought, with knives and fists and feet. Two to one should be unfair odds, but Cal held his own.

The sky was no longer completely dark. The sun would soon rise, and a touch of morning light lit the sky and the scene before her. Villagers arrived, a few at first and then a larger group, to see what had caused that awful noise.

Cal moved quickly and with a deadly grace, as he had when he'd killed the man in the alley. No movement was wasted; there was no doubt in his actions, he never faltered. Livvie held her breath, but she watched. Hiding wouldn't make things any better.

Until she'd found Nina in her kitchen, Livvie had never seen anyone die. In the span of a few minutes she'd witnessed two more deaths. The general's soldier in the alleyway; the pilot who had come here to rescue her. And they wouldn't be the only ones to die today. The fair-haired man Cal called Reiner fell back, and Cal took that opportunity to finish off the soldier who had shot down the helicopter. With one unhesitating swipe, Cal cut the big man's throat. The soldier dropped to the ground as if he'd gone boneless.

Reiner got up quickly and resumed a fighting stance. Livvie trembled. Was he *smiling* or was it a devilish trick of the light that made it seem so?

Cal didn't take his eyes off Reiner, but he spoke to her. "Run, princess," he shouted. "I'll be right behind you."

"Stay where you are, Miss Larkin," Reiner responded. "This won't take long and I will be quite annoyed if I have to chase you."

Livvie rose to her feet and sidled toward the townspeople who had gathered a few feet away, at the edge of the clearing. Cal advised her to run, but where on earth was she supposed to run to? The helicopter—her transportation out of Camaria—had been destroyed. The pilot was dead. She couldn't go back to the palace.

Max. If she could just get in touch with him, he'd know what to do. A phone, that's all she needed. Surely someone in that town they'd just passed through had a telephone!

Cal and Reiner struggled, fighting hand to hand and with a ferocity that made Livvie hold her breath as she watched. She stood beside a tall older man and watched, praying that Cal would win, knowing that her very life depended upon who survived this fight.

Both men fell to the ground and the struggle continued. It didn't matter what had happened to this point; she didn't want to see Cal hurt. She certainly didn't want to see him killed. He had come here to save her, and if he died…

If the worst happened, his death would be hers to bear. Cal was crude, he was arrogant, he was overbearing…but she didn't want to watch him die.

Cal swept out his leg and flipped Reiner onto his back. In an instant, Cal was in charge and the fair-haired mercenary was at a disadvantage. With a twist and a grunt, and a quick slash of the knife Cal wielded, the fight was over. Reiner was dead.

For one blessed instant, Livvie was certain that somehow everything would be all right. Her knees went weak in relief. And then Cal stood and took a single step. He swayed, dropped to his knees, and fell forward to lie prone and motionless on the ground.

Livvie broke from the crowd and ran toward him.

"Cal?" she cried as she dropped to her knees beside him. "What's wrong?"

He was breathing, thank goodness, but in the light of the rising sun she saw blood. Blood and long slashes in his jeans and jacket. There was blood on his neck, even in his hair. She looked to the crowd that remained motionless. "Someone help me. He's hurt!" Very gently, she rolled him onto his back. The view from this angle was even worse.

Cal reached up and gripped Livvie's arm. "My pistol."

"I don't know where…"

"Reiner has it. Livvie, get my pistol."

Because it seemed he wouldn't rest until she did as he asked, Livvie ran to the fair-haired soldier's body. The pistol had been stuck in the waistband of Reiner's pants, and it had remained there throughout the fight. Why hadn't he fired? Why hadn't he drawn the weapon and shot Cal with his own gun? When Reiner had called the other man off, she'd thought he wanted to kill Cal himself, for some reason. But why hadn't he used the gun?

She shouldn't look a gift horse in the mouth. Cal was alive; Menendez's soldiers were not. She very gingerly retrieved the weapon Cal asked for. Even though the safety was on, she was much too cautious to stick it in *her* pants. She ran back to Cal with the barrel pointed to the ground.

"I have it, see?" She offered him the weapon and he took it, holding on and closing his eyes.

"No," Livvie said frantically. "Don't close your eyes, Cal. Please, don't close your eyes!" She turned toward the group of disinterested villagers again. "Help him!"

A young woman who was braver than the rest stepped away from the crowd, even though others cautioned her to stay back. "We cannot be involved," she called. "We must leave them as they are, where they have fallen. If we assist a man who kills the general's soldiers, Menendez will burn the village to the ground and murder a dozen innocent people to express his displeasure."

A few of the villagers were already backing away from the scene. They were going to walk away. They were going to ignore everything they'd seen because they were too afraid to get involved. "You can't just leave us here! We need help. A phone!" Livvie said crisply. "I need to borrow a phone."

The woman shook her head. "There is only one telephone in our village, and General Menendez's soldiers monitor all calls in and out."

More of the locals were leaving, turning their backs on Cal and the wreckage of the helicopter and the general's dead soldiers. "Wake up, Cal," Livvie said softly. "Tell me what to do next. I don't know what to do."

Unconscious, he didn't respond.

"Dammit, Quinn Calhoun," Livvie said in a louder voice. "Wake up!"

The woman who had been speaking to Livvie stepped forward at last. "Quinn Calhoun?" She wasn't alone. A few of those who had lagged behind came forward, too. Cautiously. Suspiciously. More than one of them whispered his name. "This man is Quinn Calhoun?" the woman asked.

"Yes," Livvie answered. "Do you know him?"

The woman shook her head and dropped to her knees. It was all Livvie could do to keep from crying. Cal had been stabbed at least twice, scratched deeply a number of times, and if she wasn't mistaken he'd been shot in the thigh before Reiner had made the other soldier put his rifle away. That nasty tear in the denim stretched over Cal's thigh didn't look like a knife slash to her. It was ugly and raw and damp with blood.

"He's going to bleed to death," Livvie whispered.

The woman who had come to her aid looked Livvie in the eye and said, in a stern voice, "No, he is not."

Cal opened his eyes slowly. Half a dozen men and women leaned over him, their unfamiliar faces concerned, their voices low and comforting.

He should be in pain, he knew that…but there was no pain. He was numb. It felt good to have no feeling in his limbs, no more sting there at his side where Reiner's knife had gone deep.

Just as he was about to drift to oblivion again, he saw one more face. Hers. Heaven above, she was beautiful, wasn't she? Her hair was dark gold, her lips full and dark pink. The diamonds at her throat caught the light from lanterns and the rising sun and sparkled at her neck. Diamonds on camo fabric. Diamonds and camo and a pale, soft neck. It was a nice enough sight to die to.

But she shouldn't be here. "I told you to run, princess," he said gruffly. "Why didn't you run?"

"I couldn't just leave you here," she said softly, her voice drifting to him from a far-off place.

Cal tried to tell her that she was supposed to leave him here. She had to get out, she had to get away from this place before Menendez sent more men to see what had happened to Reiner and the others. But he couldn't speak. The world faded until there was just her face, and then even that was gone and there was only darkness.

* * *

Right before he'd passed out, it had been quite clear that Cal was annoyed with her for not following his instructions. Like she would have known where to go without him!

She'd been willing to make her way out of here on her own, before Cal had dragged her out of her room at the palace, but now that he was here…she didn't want to go on alone. And no matter what he said, she was not leaving him here. Not like this.

Once the worst of his wounds had been hastily bandaged to slow the flow of blood, Cal was moved into the nearest house and carried into the single bedroom where he was placed upon a narrow bed. The men who carried Cal and the women who cared for him handled him gently, almost reverently. She heard his name whispered several times in awed, hushed tones. She knew some Spanish, enough to get by in the palace, at least, but their words were so low and quick she was unable to make out every one.

Apparently, he was *the* Quinn Calhoun. A hero. A saint. Their savior. Livvie was sure there had to be more than one Quinn Calhoun in the world. Maybe they were confused. The man she knew was no saint.

Of course, he *had* saved her. Twice.

Three older women—one thin, two broad—expertly moved everyone else, including Livvie, away from the bed. Then they began to work with nimble hands. Livvie closed her eyes when they removed Cal's jacket and the makeshift bandage, and cut open his shirt to expose the ugliest of his wounds.

Livvie bit her lip and stifled a cry. She would not faint. She would not weep. The last thing these people needed was a hysterical woman to take care of. At the moment, all their attention was needed for Cal.

The woman who had been first to help sidled up close to Livvie, her eyes on the motionless man on the bed.

"Won't more soldiers come now?" Livvie asked the question in halting Spanish, but the woman answered in English.

"Yes, but we will all swear that we saw nothing."

"Will they believe you?"

"We can only pray that they do."

One of the three older women who were intently caring for their patient began to clean the wound in his side. Another took a pair of scissors to his jeans and began to cut them to expose what was indeed a gunshot wound on his thigh. They were openly relieved to find that injury less serious than the stab wound just above his waistline. A bullet had grazed his thigh, leaving a long, ugly abrasion but no bullet to be extracted. The third woman rushed from the room muttering beneath her breath.

Livvie kept her eyes on Cal's too-pale face and too-still body. "It seems that everyone knows him," she said. "Why is that?"

"Quinn Calhoun is a champion," the woman said proudly. "A very brave man."

"Yes," Livvie said impatiently. "I understand that much. But what did he *do?*"

"Silence." The smaller of the caretakers lifted her head for a moment and glared at Livvie. "She works for General Menendez. Tell her nothing."

"I don't…" Livvie began.

"Nothing," she repeated sternly.

Livvie watched for a moment while the women tended

to Cal. They seemed to know what they were doing, much more so than she would have. She turned to the woman beside her. "My name is Olivia Larkin," she said. "My friends call me Livvie."

The woman nodded her head. "I am Solana."

"Thank you so much for your help, Solana. I don't know what I would have done without you."

Solana's dark eyes hardened. "The help is not intended for you, but for him."

Before Livvie could explain her situation, Cal came awake with a start. He sat up quickly, and there was nothing the women who were attending to him could do to stop him. Immediately, his eyes went to Livvie and stayed there. "You're not supposed to be here," he said weakly. "Dammit, woman, don't you know how to take orders?"

The smallest of the caretakers tried to tell him to lie down, but he ignored her. "There's a second pickup point and time, in case of a screw-up."

Livvie would definitely call what had happened in the past few hours a screw-up. "When?"

"Tomorrow."

Tomorrow! Oh, she couldn't wait that long! A moment later Livvie calmed herself. Of course she could wait. She was out of the palace, Cal was alive…a single day's delay was nothing.

The woman who had left the room returned with a steaming coffee cup. "Drink this," she ordered.

"I don't…" Cal began.

"Now!" she insisted, her demeanor that of a demanding grandmother.

"Take it," Livvie said. "We can talk about getting out of here later, after they've patched you up."

Cal allowed the woman to place the cup to his lips, and he drank deep. When he tried to stop, the woman urged him to drink more. He did. When she was satisfied, she removed the cup and placed it on the floor by the bed.

Cal turned his eyes to Livvie again. "Even if I can't get out of here tomorrow, you're going to be on that helo. Got it?"

She wanted nothing more than to get out of this place. "Got it. Just tell me where and when."

Cal swayed, a puzzled expression passed over his face, and then his eyes rolled back and up and he fell to the bed to lie flat and still once again.

First there were dreams, and then there were nightmares, and then there was nothing. Darkness and peace enveloped Cal in a warm cocoon. He felt no pain. He had no worries. There was no past.

He liked it.

Someone moved him, an annoying interruption to his peace, but he didn't have the strength or the will to fight. He was simply aware of the commotion, and then he drifted toward peace again. He had never known peace, not like this. There had been good moments in his life, but he had never known contentment.

Voices interrupted the peace. Heated, angry words. *Her* voice. Why was she still here? A job. A princess. The package. Max Larkin's niece and General Lazaro Menendez's woman. He didn't want to believe it could be true, but her room had stunk of Menendez, had reeked of that sweet cologne that still invaded his nightmares on occasion, and he couldn't deny what he saw with his own eyes. What he smelled.

But she had been eager enough to leave his palace, hadn't she? Had she become bored so quickly? Or in her weeks at the palace had she seen glimpses of Lazaro Menendez's true nature?

When he'd first heard who he was to extract from the palace, he'd noted dispassionately that Livvie was the general's type. Petite, blond and blue-eyed, almost innocent looking. Almost. She had this fire in her eyes that kept her from being entirely innocent. Was the face she presented a mask for the world? For Max and for him and for everyone else but her lover? In the past there had been women like that in Menendez's palace. Women who would play meek in public, who would provide Menendez with the chase he loved and then give in when he was tired of the game.

Maybe Livvie was like that; maybe not. She did have a tendency to attach herself to the worst kind of man. No wonder she drove her uncle crazy.

He wanted to believe that she wasn't one of those women. On the inside, maybe Livvie wasn't the general's type at all. She looked the part, but underneath it all she possessed a genuine decency. A goodness. A soul. Tonight she had seen a man die, and she hadn't liked it. She'd been repulsed and saddened and shocked, as a truly good person should be.

But in her room he had breathed in that sweet stench....

She was a puzzle, his princess. His princess. For the moment she truly was his. He had rescued her, he had killed for her, and until he delivered her home she was *his*.

Olivia Larkin. Livvie. The nickname suited her much more than the more formal Olivia. Livvie was a fitting name for a real girl, a woman who sang "I Will Survive" so he couldn't hear her pee, a woman who walked mile after mile without a word of complaint.

Well, maybe a word…

The voices faded, one by one. Hers was last to go. He drifted away to the sound of her voice…and once again Cal found that rare and comforting peace.

Cal waited in the hallway that led to the restrooms. In twenty minutes this place was going to be raided, and Derrick Arnold and everyone around him was going to jail.

Everyone but her.

This wasn't exactly the toughest job he'd ever had, standing in the shadows of a Texas bar with a beer in one hand and his eyes pinned to a woman who wasn't all that hard to look at. She was a little prissy for his tastes, and she sure as hell had lousy tastes in boyfriends.

If she didn't head this way soon, he was going to have to go in there and collect her from the table, and that could get ugly.

Finally, she leaned in and kissed Arnold on the cheek, collected her purse, and headed Cal's way. Her longish, yellow dress floated around her legs without shape or form. She wasn't in any hurry as she headed for the ladies' room. Cal set his half-empty beer bottle on the floor and stepped deeper into the shadows to wait.

Olivia Larkin was small and unprepared. Cal slapped his hand over her mouth, picked her up, and carried her out the back door to the alley and his car. He dumped her in the back seat and as soon as she opened her mouth to scream he said the magic words.

"Max sent me."

She obviously wasn't sure if she should believe him or not. Cal tossed her his cell phone. "He said you should call."

Cal didn't know what Max said to calm his niece down, but all of a sudden she went still and quiet. No more hysterics, no more righteous anger. She disconnected the call and handed Cal his phone.

By the time she realized that the rear doors didn't open from the inside, they were on their way, taking a bump as the car pulled into the street.

She leaned over the seat. "I can find my own way home."

"Not this time you can't," Cal said.

"I'll have you know I'm twenty-two years old and perfectly capable of taking care of myself, no matter what Uncle Max says."

Cal didn't answer. Explanations weren't part of the job.

"We're a good thirty minutes from my apartment," she grumbled. "Can you stop at the next gas station? I need to use the restroom."

"I'm not taking you to your apartment," Cal said as he took a corner too fast.

"What?"

"I delivering you to your uncle, as ordered."

"Uncle Max is in Washington D.C.!"

Cal stepped on the gas. "I know."

They refused to slow down to accommodate her. Livvie was sure the men who carried Cal through the jungle on a narrow stretcher would be perfectly happy to leave her behind if she couldn't keep up. It would probably suit them just fine if she was lost in the jungle. The very idea of actually being alone here made her rush to keep up.

Ever since the old woman had informed everyone that Livvie worked for Menendez, no one but Solana had spoken to her. Even then, it was very clear that Solana didn't trust her. They were simply stuck in a bad situation together. Since the heroic Quinn Calhoun had been protecting her they couldn't leave her entirely alone.

No, she was not a favorite of the locals. Fortunately for her, none of the men in the small Camarian town had the heart to shoot her. They were not soldiers, they were simple farmers and merchants who lived in the shadow of the general's palace.

But they were smart enough to know that eventually the general's men would search the town for her and for Cal, and their hero wasn't safe there.

Their hero. What on earth had he done?

Livvie carried Cal's pistol in a huge pocket of her cargo pants, after double-checking and then checking again to make sure the safety was on. She didn't think the weapon had anything to do with the men's hesitation to approach her. Anyone who saw her handling the weapon would surely realize she had no idea how to use it.

Daytime noises in the jungle were different from nighttime noises. Not as scary, but that was probably because she could see to a much greater distance. The plants were varied and lush, and amazing flowers grew everywhere. Most of them were red, but there were other colors here and there, bright and startlingly beautiful.

The men who carried Cal spoke quickly and in low voices, perhaps hoping that she would not understand. But she understood their language better than they knew and was able to pick up some of what was said. They were taking the saint Quinn Calhoun to a safe place.

Her they would have handed over to Menendez without a second thought, given the chance.

Livvie trekked along the path in her jungle camouflage

and diamond necklace and combat boots. If you could call this tiny, overgrown trail a path. There were several times when she was sure she and the men who carried Cal's litter were blindly walking in a huge circle. The scenery didn't change much, and after a while even the red flowers ceased to draw her attention. Her legs ached and she was so tired she could barely take a deep breath, but she would not allow herself to fall behind.

If she'd run as Cal had instructed her to, the men who grudgingly allowed her to follow along might have found the courage to kill her. Solana had made it clear that the punishment for the offense of helping Cal would be dire, and no matter what she said they refused to believe that she was completely on their side. Cal was a treasure to them…Livvie was basically a willing prisoner. And she would stick close to Cal, because she was still depending on him to get her out of this mess.

But not today, she imagined. Whatever the ladies in town had given him last night had knocked him out completely. He wouldn't be telling her where the pickup point was. She glanced at the afternoon sky. It was probably already too late.

She ran to catch up with the stretcher and glanced down at Cal. He really did look bad. What he needed was a hospital and the best doctors money could buy. What he was going to get was a small village in the jungle, an uneducated healer and her.

Could she keep him alive?

Cal opened his eyes to darkness and pain. Where was he?

For a moment, he was sure his worst fears had come true. The general had found him. He was locked in *that room,* and the general was coming. In the recesses of his mind, he could hear the footsteps in the hallway. He could feel the bonds that entrapped him—steel at his wrists, rope around his ankles. He could smell his own blood and sweat. Footsteps continued, growing louder, crisper. They were getting closer. Closer. *Here.*

"You're awake," a soft voice whispered.

A match was struck, the flame flickered, and a lantern was lit to cast pale light around an unfamiliar room. Cedar walls, unpainted. No adornment, no amenities. He was lying on a narrow cot and Livvie Larkin sat on a stool at his side. A mosquito net hung around his bed, making her image misty.

"Why are you here?" he asked, his voice raspy. "You'll miss the pickup."

She smiled. "We missed it three days ago."

"Crap." He tried to sit up, but she reached through an opening in the netting and laid a hand on his chest to very gently push him back to the cot. "There's a satellite phone in my pack."

"Your pack was on the helicopter when it…when it exploded," she said. "Don't you remember?"

Suddenly, he did remember. "Reiner."

Livvie nodded.

"Where are we?"

"Some little village where no one will find us."

Benning and a handful of his boys would be here soon, if they weren't already. They might give Cal a few days to fight his way out of whatever had delayed him. Then again, they might already be in Camaria, searching for him and the package. Larkin would be pissed.

"We have to get out of here."

"You're not well enough to travel."

He could hire a couple of locals to get Livvie to safety

and a telephone, but there was no one here he trusted. He was in a strange place, surrounded by strange people, and besides…Cal only trusted a small handful of people, and they were all thousands of miles away. He wasn't about to let Livvie out of his sight.

"Sleep, Cal," she said in a soothing voice. "When you're better, we'll make our way out of here together."

The man who was treating Cal seemed to know what he was doing, but Livvie could not be sure. For one thing, he didn't look to be much more than twenty-five years old. When Solana had assured her that there was a talented healer in this village, she'd envisioned an old, wizened man with white hair and wrinkled skin. Raul was younger than she, and he was not at all wizened. In fact, he came just short of qualifying as a stud muffin.

So, she counted his age against him. And if he was so talented, why was he here? This place they had chosen to secrete Cal…it wasn't even big enough to be called a village! There were a few proper buildings, all made of cedar with thatched roofs. She and Cal were staying in the back room of one of those buildings. Much of their food was gathered from the land around them. Fruit and wild pig was a large part of the diet, along with some bland, boiled root they ate with almost every meal.

Then there were the chickens. There were chickens everywhere, which meant they had eggs and the occasional spicy chicken stew.

Most of those who lived here in the small village worked on the general's sugarcane plantation; even the children. The day after she and Cal arrived here, two soldiers in a jeep came by to question the workers about a missing

American woman who was probably traveling in the company of a man. The general wanted very badly to speak to these people, and would pay a handsome reward to anyone who was able to assist him in his quest. Everyone who was questioned lied well. They swore they had seen no one who did not belong here. The soldiers believed them.

These were the people Menendez said loved him. Apparently they loved Cal more.

Livvie had finally been able to work the clasp of the damned necklace Menendez had put around her neck, but not before the people who lived here had had a good look at it. They knew what it meant; that she was somehow connected to the general. That she worked for him, as they did…and yet not as they did. While she'd been enjoying fine meals and every possible comfort in the palace, these people who had helped to make the general's fortune had been living in close quarters, with food they gathered themselves and not even the dream of a four-poster bed with a soft·mattress.

Considering the circumstances, they treated her well. Livvie wasn't exactly greeted with smiles when the local women brought in food and water. But they did feed her, and she never felt threatened. She was tolerated.

Raul's English was excellent, not nearly as awkward as Solana's. She wondered if he'd been educated elsewhere and then returned here to live. She didn't know Raul's reasons, but she wasn't about to second-guess the luck that kept him here. For Cal's sake, she was grateful.

Like the others here and in the other small towns, Raul was a native Camarian, a product of the indigenous Indians and the Spanish settlers. They were a beautiful people, like Nina. Like Elsa and Ria.

After a few days, Livvie finally had to admit that Raul did seem to know what he was doing. At least, he didn't kill Cal with his potions and salves. Cal slept almost around the clock, and after a couple of days he started eating again. Livvie actually began to hope they'd be out of here soon.

Raul had examined the worst of Cal's wounds by the light of an old oil lamp. He had no nurse to assist him, no pharmacist to fill prescriptions, no expensive machinery to monitor his patients' vitals. By day he worked in the sugarcane fields, like everyone else. By night he took care of these people, because the general would not.

Cal was not a good patient. He grumbled as Raul examined him, insisting that he was fine and needed nothing more than a good night's sleep. The medicine Raul administered made Cal sleep a lot. The healer said that was a good thing, but it scared Livvie to see Cal this way. He should be grumbling and cursing and dragging her through the jungle toward safety. Instead, he slept.

When Raul moved away from the bed, Cal dropped back into oblivion.

"When will he be able to travel?" Livvie whispered.

Raul glanced at his sleeping patient. "I don't know. Most of the wounds are healing well. Some were minor to begin with and didn't need more than a bandage to keep them clean. But the one here," he laid his hand over his own side, "it's not looking good. It's getting infected. I'm afraid if the infection progresses it will kill him." Raul didn't pull any punches.

"Isn't there anything you can do?" Livvie asked. The idea of losing Cal now, after everything they'd been through…she couldn't bear it.

"There is a medicine I can try." Raul studied the patient. "I don't like to use it if there's any other choice, because it has dramatic side effects."

"Such as?" Livvie prodded in a too-sharp voice.

"Chills, increased heart rate and in some cases hallucinations."

"I thought you didn't have any medicines except the herbal teas and salves you make yourself?"

"This is herbal, and I did make it myself." He gave her a half smile. "Plants are the foundation for most medicines, Miss Larkin."

"Yes, but wouldn't it be better if you had some real medicine?"

"Trust me, this is very real."

Livvie sighed. She wanted antibiotics, dammit! And some plain old painkiller. The locals had provided chicken soup, when she asked, so at least they had that covered. "I just want him to get better."

"I can see that."

"And you're the only one who can save him." It was scary to know that Cal's life rested in this young man's hands. A young man who needed a haircut and was dressed in worn cotton pants and a shirt that had seen better days. He would surely get carded if he tried to buy beer at any convenience store in the States.

"I will," Raul assured her. "We can wait until tomorrow to try the medicine. If Mr. Calhoun is better in the morning, perhaps we can proceed without using it. Is that plan satisfactory, Miss Larkin?"

"Yes it is, and you really should call me Livvie." She had instructed him to do so at least half a dozen times. She'd even asked for his last name, once, and he had told her in an almost-too-friendly voice that his name was of no importance. "After everything you've done for us…"

"I really shouldn't," he said.

"Why not?"

Something on his face hardened, and suddenly he didn't look quite so young. "We're not friends, Miss Larkin," Raul said. "You are here because Mr. Calhoun is here. You are safe because he is here."

She decided to ask Raul, since no one else would tell her…. "What did he do to make you all care for him so much?"

Raul hesitated. "Let us simply say that Mr. Calhoun is not precisely what he appears to be."

That was *no* help at all.

"I'll check back in the morning." Raul turned to walk away, but Livvie stopped him.

"Wait!" She reached beneath the cot where the patient slept and snagged the necklace, which she'd wrapped in what was left of Cal's torn, laundered shirt. She unwrapped it slowly, revealing the incongruous sight of diamonds resting on ripped black cotton. "I think you can use this more than I can." She wasn't going to attempt to return the jewelry to the palace. She wouldn't even mail it to the general after she got home. These people deserved it much more than Menendez did.

Raul shook his head. "I cannot accept this."

"I know the diamonds will be difficult to sell, but it can be done, and just think of what you can buy with the proceeds." Medicine, food, clothing.

The healer finally extended his hand, and Livvie gave him the necklace. "Do something good with it," she said in a soft voice. "These people certainly deserve to have something from the general."

"That is true," Raul said as he closed his fingers over the jewels. "I will see you tomorrow morning," he said as he left the room.

Livvie sat on the cot beside Cal's bed and watched him sleep. Having that necklace out of her possession was a weight off her chest. She felt as relieved as she had when she'd finally worked the clasp and taken the damned thing from around her throat.

She was surprised when Cal opened his eyes, not as a man who was just waking would, but as a man who had been playing possum might. "You gave away your necklace," he said, not bothering to pretend that he hadn't heard her conversation with Raul.

"It was never mine."

He sat up slowly, moving with caution but also with more strength than he'd shown yesterday. He ran fingers through his longish hair, and then raked one palm across his cheek as if to check the status of his beard, which was now several days old. "I thought diamonds were a girl's best friend," he said as he leaned against the wall.

Cal had been bathed and dressed in a well worn pair of cotton drawstring pants. He wore no shirt. There was nothing covering his chest and arms but a few white bandages and a number of scars.

She wanted, so badly, to ask him about some of those scars.

"Depends on where they come from, I guess." Livvie moved the netting aside and sat on the edge of the cot so she could reach out and touch his face. She didn't care about the state of his beard—at the moment, she wanted to know if he still had a fever. He was a little warm, darn it.

"Where should a woman get her diamonds from?" he asked as her fingers left his face.

Simple, but not as simple as she'd always believed it would be. "From an honest man, if there are any left. There are moments when I have my doubts about that."

"Honest."

She nodded. "I used to think that wasn't so much to ask. Now I'm not so sure."

Cal studied her with hooded eyes. He was pale, he was sick, he needed a shave and a haircut and a week in a really good hospital. So why was there still an undeniable strength about him? A strength that made her shiver. Why was he still dangerous?

No man had ever looked at her this way, as if he could see through her. She had the feeling she could never fool him; that if she tried to lie or trick or cheat him, he'd know.

"You could have used that necklace to buy your way out of here," he said in a gruff voice.

She shrugged. "And leave you behind to fend for yourself?"

"I can."

"I know." If anyone could…

"I've been fending for myself for a very long time."

"That may be true, but we're in this together," she said.

He snagged her wrist, and though his hand was overly warm and he had been sleeping more than not lately, that grip was strong. Surprisingly so. He tugged a little, and she listed closer to him. Her heart started to pound. The way he looked at her, the way he held on…was he going to kiss her?

What would it be like to kiss a man like Quinn Calhoun? She didn't think he would be shy about such things. No, Cal wasn't *shy* about anything! He was raw. Darker and harsher than any of the men she had kissed in the past. Cal was more…male. There would be no tentative pecks if he kissed her. No trepidation. He would probably devour her…and that might not be such a bad idea. She needed to be devoured. Just this once. Her heart leapt. Her mouth went dry.

But Cal did not kiss her.

"You're not what I expected," he said in a low voice.

"What did you expect?"

He didn't answer that question, and maybe that was just as well. "And Raul is wrong, princess. I am exactly what I appear to be."

Chapter 4

Cal hadn't had an opportunity to speak privately with his so-called doctor, but this morning he insisted that Livvie leave the room as he was examined. He used modesty as an excuse, which anyone who knew him well would realize was a crock. Even Livvie saw through the charade.

But she did leave the room.

"How much time do we have?" Cal asked as the healer examined the worst of his wounds.

"What do you mean?" Raul probed the injury with easy hands, and kept his eyes on his work.

"Cut the crap. I don't have time for it." He should have regained his strength by now, but he hadn't. His temperature was high this morning, and the fever left him feeling light-headed and out of control. Cal dearly hated not being in complete control.

"I don't care about your revolution," he said tightly. "In

fact, I wish you the very best of luck. But my job is to get Miss Larkin out of the country before the situation gets ugly, and if I don't do that before you and your friends stir things up it's going to make my job much more difficult."

Raul hesitated a moment before answering. "Four days."

Cal laughed harshly. "Four days. That's just great." It wasn't enough time, not unless everything fell into place perfectly. In his experience, that never happened.

"How did you know?" Raul asked softly.

"You bought weapons from someone who talked. That's all the information I have." Raul looked understandably concerned about the slip in security. "Menendez doesn't know, if that's what you're worried about."

With competent hands, Raul rebandaged both the wound on Cal's side and the one on his thigh. Cal was as cooperative as he knew how to be, until Raul reached into his bag of tricks and pulled out a dark bottle of medicine.

"No more. That stuff knocks me out, and we're going to have to get out of here today."

"You're not ready."

"I'll be fine." Cal pointed to the innocent-looking bottle in Raul's hands. "I'm not taking any more of that jungle concoction. I can't afford to sleep until the general finds us."

The younger man did not put his bottle away. "This is not what I've been giving you since you were brought here. It's something new, for the fever and the infection."

Cal shook his head.

"Without it you'll be dead long before you can get Miss Larkin to safety." Raul wasn't one to dance around the truth. His bedside manner was a combination of real concern and the naked truth. "There's no need to worry about the general finding you here, at least, not in the immediate future. He's expanded the search well beyond this area. When he finds no trace of Miss Larkin in Santa Rosa or at her home in the States, he will come back. But we have time before that happens. Time for you to heal."

Not nearly enough time, Cal suspected. "If I kick the bucket, the girl's all yours."

"I have problems of my own, as you well know," Raul argued. "If you don't get well and escort Miss Larkin out of here yourself, Menendez will eventually find her."

Cal glared at the kid, but Raul wasn't intimidated.

"If all goes well, you'll be ready to travel by morning."

"What do you mean *if all goes well?*" Cal asked as Raul poured a generous dose of the potion into a tin cup. Dark green, thick and grainy, it did not look at all appetizing.

Raul handed the cup to Cal. "I have used this many times, and with some degree of success."

"You're not instilling me with great hope, doc," Cal muttered.

"Some call it Raul's magic potion."

That *some* did not get past Cal. "And what do the others call it?"

The healer smiled. "Raul's loco juice. It sometimes causes hallucinations."

Cal stared down at the unappetizing brew. It was not only thick and grainy, it stunk. A repulsive bubble rose to one side of the lumpy surface, threatening to pop. What choice did he have? If the fever worsened and he dropped in the jungle, Livvie wouldn't leave him where he fell. She'd insist on staying with him, on getting help…and in the process she'd alert the general to her whereabouts and all this would be for nothing.

He had no choice at all. "If something happens to me, I want you to get the girl to Guyana."

Raul shook his head. "I cannot leave until after we have taken the palace."

"After, then," Cal said sharply. He didn't even want to contemplate what might happen if Raul and his rebels failed in their attempts. "With any luck, you'll run into some of the men I work with. I'm sure they're in the country by now, searching for us."

"That is unlikely." Raul reached into his bag and drew out a sloppily folded piece of newspaper. It had been crumpled and torn, but Cal could read the article well enough.

According to the Santa Rosa newspaper, Olivia Larkin and two unknown males who had been attempting to kidnap her had been killed when a helicopter crashed and exploded in the jungle. There was a photograph of helicopter wreckage. One of the white shoes Livvie had been wearing when he'd grabbed her—which was no longer white but had been scorched and damaged—was positioned front and center. Cal read the article twice. Menendez had managed to put his own spin on the story.

If everyone thought Livvie and whoever had helped her escape were dead, no one would come to Camaria looking for them. Thanks to the dead bodies of his soldiers, Menendez had to know Livvie hadn't been alone as she'd attempted to make her escape. Anyone who'd spent five minutes in her company knew she wasn't capable of slitting a man's throat.

But Menendez couldn't possibly suspect that Quinn Calhoun had returned, unless the villagers were talking. He didn't think they would. After all, they seemed to think they owed him. They didn't, but talking would get them all in trouble with the general, and they knew it too well.

If Benning thought Cal and the package were both dead, no one was out there looking for them. There was no rescue right around the corner, no team to fall back on. Not this time.

"And this crap will cure me?" Cal said suspiciously as he took an unpleasant sniff.

"I hope so. If it does not, I will do as you ask and escort Miss Larkin to Guyana. After I have done what I must do."

A task that could take years, if the kid survived the first few days. "I'll be able to leave here tonight."

Raul nodded. "Tonight, or perhaps tomorrow morning."

"Tonight." Cal drank the medicine, quickly gulping the bitter brew. After he had drained the cup, he returned it to the healer who had surely saved his life. "Do me a favor," he said as he fell back onto the cot.

"Anything," Raul answered almost reverently.

"Don't tell her you're going to use the diamonds to buy weapons." His head began to swim.

"What makes you think I would use her gift in such a way?"

"Aren't you?"

Raul hesitated. "Yes."

"It's fitting," Cal said. The medicine had gone to his head quickly. He could practically feel it rushing through his blood. His eyes drifted shut; he could no longer keep them open. The lids were just too heavy. Once his eyes were closed, lights danced behind the lids. Bright, colorful, intense lights. "I like the idea of the general's diamonds being used to buy weapons for the rebels. But still…don't tell her."

"She would not approve."

"No, she would not." The light that danced beneath his

lids took form, and images danced behind his eyes. Good and bad, from the past and the present, they were so real he thought perhaps he was already dreaming.

Livvie had never before fully appreciated the simple pleasures and convenience of a shopping mall. They'd been in this village for five days, and she was beginning to see the light. Drug stores, grocery stores, restaurants...department stores with clothes and shoes!

Her lack of amenities was a small annoyance, compared with Cal's dilemma. Fortunately the medicine Raul had given Cal this morning seemed to be working. He slept, as he had so much in the past couple of days, but when she touched him his skin seemed to be a bit cooler. His temperature was almost normal.

Knowing that Cal was finally getting better was a real relief. Not only was he her ticket out of Camaria, he had risked his life to save her. She owed him. She even liked him, a little.

Four years ago, Cal had kidnapped her from a bar—a very nice club, not one of those seedy places he probably patronized—where she'd been sitting with her new boyfriend Derrick, a handsome and well-dressed man who had told her he was in sporting goods. Cal had literally whisked her out of the bar moments before a police raid.

For a few minutes she'd been afraid of him, and then she'd been angry...and then, when Max had explained to her that Derrick's "sporting goods" were drugs and women, she'd been grudgingly grateful. Over the next twenty-four hours, while Cal drove her to Uncle Max's apartment, she'd very often hated his guts for being such a macho jerk. There had been a couple of fleeting moments when she'd thought she might like him in other circumstances, but that feeling had never lasted very long. She'd been twenty-two years old, naive, and alone in the world. A dangerous combination.

For a few weeks after the rescue she'd actually wondered if he might call her, even though he had shown no interest during their long trip. Even though he was so clearly *not* her type. Cal hadn't called, of course, and she'd written her momentary inappropriate fascination off to gratitude that she wasn't sitting in jail combined with the fact that he was very good-looking in a crude sort of way that appealed to *some* women.

Cal didn't look so great at the moment. He needed a haircut and a shave, and his face was much too pale. He wasn't a broad man, but was tall and tough and lean. Maybe a little bit too lean. She would really like to feed him, if she ever got the chance.

He'd tossed the blanket off so often she'd finally quit trying to tuck him in. The lightweight woven cover came to his waist now, leaving his chest and shoulders bare. Beneath that blanket he wore a pair of linen drawstring pants someone had donated on that first night, when they'd cut his bloody clothes away.

Cal looked pretty rough today, but his color was a little better than it had been yesterday and his wounds were healing. He needed a shave in the worst way. A dark, bristly beard covered his cheeks. Softer dark hair was dusted across his chest, and he had a few small scars there. One on his side, near a rib. Two close to the center of his chest. The newest knife wound at his side was going to leave yet another scar, a nasty one, as was the place on his thigh where a bullet had grazed his flesh.

The first time she'd seen his back, she'd almost cried. It appeared that someone had beaten Cal with a whip, leaving long, ugly scars that crisscrossed a muscled back that would be absolutely beautiful, if not for the marks. There weren't just one or two, but so many she couldn't count them all. This was the twenty-first century! People didn't get *whipped!* There had to be another explanation for the scars, but she hadn't dared to ask, and he hadn't volunteered any information about himself.

Even though Max had sent him in to do this job, Quinn Calhoun was a man to be frightened of. Hardhearted, scarred…he had led a violent life and wore the evidence of that fact on his skin. There was nothing soft or gentle about him. Nothing. Not an amiable smile or the occasional softening of his hazel-green eyes. No tenderness in the way he held her hand as he led her through the jungle. If he worked for Uncle Max she didn't want to know what kind of life he led, she didn't want to know why he was so hard.

All that aside, Cal had rescued her, and the people here loved him…for some reason.

Cal rolled over, and Livvie had a clear view of his scarred back. The mosquito netting that hung around his bed did little to soften the sight. A lantern lit the small room well enough for her to see the details of each scar. Some were worse than others—wider, longer, more prominent—while others were so thin and faded they were almost invisible. She reached out, parting the netting to touch one and then another, running her fingers gently along the length of one mark and then beginning again with another. There were so many…

Moving gingerly, he rolled over again so that he faced her. Her hand snapped back.

"I'm sorry," she said softly. "I didn't mean to wake you."

He cast her a crooked grin on a roughly bearded face. The unexpected smile was oddly enchanting, overtly sexy. She had never seen Cal smile before, and it was downright uplifting. Her heart did strange things.

"Don't ever apologize for touching me," he whispered.

Livvie's heart skipped a beat. Her stomach climbed into her throat. A chill rippled through her body. She did her very best to ignore the reaction. "You need your sleep."

"You're so beautiful," he said, his voice low, his eyes hooded.

Again, that thing with her heart and her stomach.

"Stop it, Cal. You need to rest. You need to get better."

"I need you." He offered his hand.

Livvie was tempted, but she didn't take that hand. From the beginning, Cal had made it clear she was an annoyance, a job. A princess. There had been that incident when he'd pressed up against her in the jungle, but she hadn't thought that to be anything but strictly physical.

"You're mad at me," he said.

"No, I'm just…confused."

"Don't be confused about me, baby. The first time I saw you, I was a goner. And now, after everything that's happened…I don't want to waste another minute."

She understood too well. When she'd thought he would die, she'd been so scared. It didn't make sense to waste precious time when she didn't know how much time she had left. All the hours she'd spent watching Cal, tending to him, studying him…yes, there was definitely something going on here. She had dismissed her feelings as misplaced gratitude, but if he felt the same way…

He scooted toward the wall, moving cautiously. "Come on. Keep me warm," he said. "I'm cold."

Livvie knew that if she crawled into that narrow bed, she'd very likely end up doing more than keeping Cal warm. Much more. Her implant meant she didn't need to worry about pregnancy, which was a concern since she had no idea if her feelings for Cal, or his for her, would survive once they returned home.

But at the moment those feelings were intense. Maybe Cal was so hard because he'd never known gentleness. She could be the one to offer that new sensation to him. Tenderness. Love.

She had sworn not to make any more impulsive decisions, but when it came to love surely one shouldn't make a detailed list of pros and cons.

Love? Who was she kidding? Maybe all she and Cal had was a purely sexual chemistry, or maybe they each just needed someone to hold on to in this terrible situation. Someone familiar. Someone close.

Moving carefully, so as not to jostle his wounds, she parted the mosquito net and climbed onto the bed with Cal. There wasn't much room on the thin mattress, so it seemed very natural that she fit up against him just so—that the arm he draped around her was warm and snug, not at all cold. An unexpected flutter danced in her chest. And lower, too, in the pit of her stomach.

Cal's mouth immediately dipped to find her neck. "You taste good," he whispered as he raked his lips across her throat. He pushed her T-shirt up just far enough to expose her belly, his fingers gentle on her skin. A quiver worked through Livvie's body—a deep, telling shudder. It was so easy to forget all the reasons she shouldn't be here and get lost in the reasons this was right. It felt right. With her body, even with her heart…it felt right.

Cal cupped her rear end and pulled her tightly against him so she could feel his erection pressing against her. His entire body was hard…everything but his lips. He used those lips well, tasting her. Kissing her throat until she felt like she was flying.

She was so glad to be here. To be alive, to be safe. To be holding Quinn Calhoun.

The scent of him was heady, erotic, and his flesh touching hers was deliciously sensual. When Livvie put everything but what she wanted out of her mind, she craved him to distraction. She adored him. She knew that together they would be dynamite. Fireworks. Beauty.

"I want you," Cal said softly. "I wanted you the first time I laid my eyes on you, but I didn't think it could ever happen."

The first time he'd seen her…he'd been dragging her to his car for that long trip to D.C. Had he wanted her even then? Apparently so. She never would have guessed. Knowing that he had wanted her even then made her silly musings about a possible phone call after the fact seem not so silly after all. "At first I thought you didn't like me much," she whispered.

"How could I not be crazy about you?"

She took his face in her hands, tilted her head to one side, and kissed him deeply. With all her heart she kissed him, and he responded. His entire body reacted, and so did hers. She spiraled out of control, and so did he. Quinn Calhoun, out of control. She hadn't thought it was possible. But his breathing changed, as hers had. He looked at her as if there was no other woman in the world, as if he were starving for her. Just for her.

"I don't want you to hurt yourself." She barely touched the bandage at his side.

"I won't."

"Are you…sure?"

He smiled at her, and oh, if she had ever doubted that she wanted this, those doubts disappeared. "Absolutely."

"I want you, too."

"It's been such a long time," he whispered.

"For me, too," Livvie answered just as softly.

It had been so long she'd forgotten how a kiss and a caress had the power to sweep her away. She closed her eyes and got lost in sensation, as Cal touched her. How could hands so large and rough be so gentle? How could a man who was hard and unyielding love so tenderly? Had she thought he didn't know tenderness? She was wrong.

He touched her, and she boldly laid her hands on him. Not just his scars, this time, but all of him. His shoulders, his hard belly, the curve of his hip. She traced a small scar on his chest with one finger, and then lowered her head to kiss that scar before rising up to once again lay her mouth on his.

When they kissed she felt the world spin. Cal's tongue speared into her mouth and he moaned, long and low. Livvie's body throbbed in time to her heartbeat, and she couldn't get close enough. She draped one leg over his hip, cupped his head in her hand, and answered his demanding kiss with one of her own. Deeper and deeper she fell.

His hands were no longer completely gentle, as he learned the curves of her body. He reached beneath her camouflage T-shirt and cupped her breasts, fluttering his fingers over the taut nipples. She was almost certain she felt those fingers tremble. Was Cal just as affected by this as she was? Did he spiral out of control? With more than a touch of impatience, he whisked her shirt off and tossed it onto the floor. And then he kissed her breasts, one and then the other, taking her higher…closer…

While he took a nipple into his mouth and drew it deep, Cal unfastened the single button at her waist and lowered the zipper. He shifted the pants down a couple of inches, and then slipped his hand inside.

His intimate caress wasn't delicate, but then Livvie herself was far from needing to be treated delicately. Cal stroked and kissed and held her tight, and she felt as if he were drawing her inside him, somehow. As if he absorbed her. Every touch sent her closer to the edge, and she answered Cal's telling moan with one of her own.

She was overcome in every way. Cal was hers. Physically, they were drawn together. Emotionally, there was something going on that she could not explain. He was hers. She was his. Her body wanted to open for Cal, to take him in and cradle him. To show him what love was like, what true sharing could be. A shudder worked its way through her body in anticipation. Together they worked the cargo pants down and off, and she impatiently kicked them aside.

He rolled atop her, and she yanked at the drawstring and pushed his trousers over his hips, freeing him. He guided himself to her and pushed. Gently at first, and then harder, until he was cradled inside her.

They moved together, fast and breathless and deep. So deep. Sweating and trembling. No one had ever loved her this way before…in a way so primal she felt as if she were not herself and never would be again. She was no longer alone, but was joined with Quinn Calhoun forever. He needed her, she needed him, and the way their bodies came together…surely this was meant to be.

Ribbons of pleasure shot through her body, making her moan, making her gasp. Cal draped his arm around her leg and lifted it higher, pushing himself even deeper.

"I wanted this so much," he whispered.

"Me, too," she said breathlessly.

"You drive me crazy, but I can't live without you. I tried but I can't." He filled her with a swift, hard lunge. "I can't."

She speared her fingers through his hair and pulled his mouth to hers, kissing him deeply, tasting him and drawing his breath into her mouth while she lifted her hips to take him. He touched her in places she'd never been touched before, relentless and without restraint.

Cal moved faster, and Livvie cried out as she shattered. Her release came on intense waves, unlike anything she had ever known before. And Cal joined her. Moaning, shuddering, giving over to pleasure and release.

He dropped down over her, using his arms to keep his weight from her body. His head rested beside hers, and he breathed deep and slow.

She had never known making love could be like this. Intense and beautiful, breathtaking and magnificent and raw. Who would have thought, when Cal grabbed her from behind and dragged her into the hidden tunnel, that they would end up here. She raked her fingers through his hair and muttered an almost breathless "wow."

Her legs were wrapped around his, her arms wound around his neck. Oh, she wanted to hold on to him forever. She wanted to stay right here, where she was warm and safe and entwined with Cal.

Her clothes were scattered across the room, where

they'd been thrown, and he was almost as naked as she was. She held him tight, her skin and his pressed together. She didn't want to let him go, not ever.

Her heart pounded so hard she thought it might come through her chest. Surely Cal felt it. His heart pounded, too. Fast and hard, it pounded. The world came creeping back. She wasn't ready for that to happen…she liked being so lost there was no one and nothing but the two of them in the world. Sensation so powerful couldn't last, she knew that. But, oh, she wanted to lose herself in Cal again.

He kissed her shoulder and skated one warm, possessive hand down her side. Yeah, they were in this together. They had…something.

"I love you, Claudia," he whispered hoarsely. "I love you, so much."

Cal opened his eyes, and for a moment he had no idea where he was. His heart thudded hard once, and then it all came back to him. The princess; Reiner; the fight. Raul; a fever; the medicine. *Dreams.*

Oddly enough, he felt good. In spite of being shot and stabbed and taking bitter medicine and dreaming of things best forgotten, he felt very good.

"You're awake."

He sat up slowly. Livvie sat on a stool on the opposite side of the room, just a few feet away, and she was not happy.

"What time is it?"

"Almost ten," she said crisply.

"Did you get any sleep today?"

"No."

"You should have. Didn't Raul tell you that we'd be traveling tonight?"

Her face paled. "You can't possibly be ready to travel."

Cal swung his legs over the bed, pushed the mosquito net aside, and stood slowly. "I don't have any choice." Surprised by a stinging in his side, he pressed a hand to the wound. Damn thing had opened up a little and was bleeding again. But not badly. He'd survive.

"Well, when you get where you're going you can send someone else back for me," Livvie snapped.

The last thing he needed was a hissy fit from Livvie at this point in the fiasco. "What's your problem? Did you get ants in your drawers? That can be dangerous in this part of the world, princess."

She stood slowly. A few days ago he had been able to intimidate her with a look, but not now. Maybe it was because he was wounded and she thought that would slow him down. Then again, maybe she was just royally pissed because she was here with him instead of at home. "Let's get a few things straight, Mr. Calhoun. You're not to call me princess, not ever again." She walked toward the cot where Cal had slept the day away, as he had slept for days before.

Days. Dammit. He couldn't believe he was so far behind schedule. "Yes, ma'am," he said dryly.

"You're not to touch me in any way," she said softly. "If you draw your knife and even look at me like you're going to remove so much as a button with the blade, you will regret it." She stopped a couple of feet from the cot. "And if you ever again insinuate that I was involved with General Menendez as anything other than a caretaker for his daughters, I will see that you never get a dime of whatever money you're owed for kidnapping me."

"So I don't suppose I should point out that the general's

children live with their mother, a woman who wisely left the son of a bitch years ago."

She sighed. "They did, until a few weeks ago when she was killed in a robbery attempt."

Kids in the palace. How many? He couldn't remember. By the time Cal had moved into the general's palace, Nina Menendez had already made her escape. Apparently the general had finally caught up with her. It was very unlikely that her violent death had been random.

Livvie seemed very serious and even indignant, but if her employment was so innocent, how did you explain away the diamonds, the roses on the bed, the stench of the general in her bedroom? Not that he cared. "Sweetheart, your arrangement with Menendez is your own business."

"I agreed to stay with the girls for a few weeks until they were accustomed to their new surroundings, Mr. Calhoun. General Menendez offered me a salary that was more than fair, and since school is out for the summer I agreed. After I arrived here I realized that was a mistake, and if you hadn't shown up when you did…" She went silent—she even blushed. "I am grateful that you got me out of there, but that doesn't mean you can treat me like a…like a…"

"Hooker?" he offered.

She slapped him. Swung out and gave him a good one across the cheek. And he let her.

Her lower lip trembled, ruining her tough act. And it was all an act. Maybe she was telling the truth about the general. She did look more like a teacher than a mistress, with her face scrubbed clean and her camo T-shirt hanging loose, though he had the sudden thought that she could be hot, if she wanted to. Very hot.

But she did have lousy tastes in men. Some women

were like that. No matter what choices they had in the romance department, they always took the path that would lead to heartbreak or disaster. Or both.

The jungle wasn't agreeing with her, he noticed. He'd thought her kinda tough, to this point, but her tough act was falling apart. She looked like she was on the verge of tears, and when she turned her head just so it seemed she had a pink rash of some kind on one cheek.

"I just want to go home," she whispered. "Now."

"I'll get you there, I promise."

His simple words got her hackles up all over again. "Why should I put any stock in a promise from a man like you?"

"Maybe because I don't make very many of them," he said truthfully.

Livvie had changed while he slept. She wasn't the woman he remembered. Then again, maybe the concerned face he'd thought he'd seen watching over him had been a hallucination. She was definitely not concerned at the moment. Not about him, at least.

"I think you're not a very nice man," she said softly.

"No, I'm not. Being nice isn't a job requirement for my current occupation."

"Which is?" she prompted.

"Getting pretty girls out of troublesome situations."

For a minute he thought she was going to try to slap him again. He wouldn't let her get away with it this time. Fortunately for both of them she decided not to hit him. "Not very good at it, are you?" With that she turned on her boot heel and stalked out of the room, and Cal had a vivid and unexpected vision of Olivia Larkin naked. Beneath him. Moaning.

He shook his head. Raul had warned him the medicine

might cause hallucinations, but he hadn't expected erotic dreams about the princess.

Weird dreams or not, the doc should bottle that stuff. Cal felt a hundred percent better than he had that morning. Not only was the fever gone, he felt…good. Wounds, princess and all, he felt damn good.

Chapter 5

Livvie was determined to stand by her new no touching rule, by God, which meant she followed Cal without that iron grip on her wrist, this time. She didn't have any difficulty keeping up with his pace, since he moved a little slower than he had on the night he'd led her out of the palace.

But he did move briskly and steadily, ignoring the wound she knew wasn't completely healed.

He'd insisted that she get a few hours sleep, while he'd packed two rugged backpacks Raul had provided for what Cal said would be a two-day walk. Two days! Well, it could be worse. She could be back there in that tiny room, watching Cal sleep and remembering with horror and embarrassment that she had fallen for what had to be his best lines.

He didn't even remember what had happened yesterday afternoon. Either that, or he was pretending not to remember so he wouldn't have to face what he'd done. What *they'd* done. She didn't think that was the case. Cal didn't seem like the kind of guy who would be embarrassed by anything, let alone what he'd surely see as a little recreational sex. Release, pleasure, a little fun on the side. Nothing more notable than that, unless you counted his blunder in calling her by the wrong woman's name before passing out.

So, who was Claudia?

They'd left the small village long before sunrise, each of them wearing one of the heavy backpacks, Cal carrying a small flashlight to light their way. His pack was significantly heavier than hers, which she'd protested more than once. He was, after all, still healing. But Raul's medicine had worked very well. In the morning light Cal looked just fine. Too fine, even with a new beard, an untended hairstyle, and someone else's clothes.

"Why do these people think you're such a hotshot?" she asked.

Cal glanced back at her, surprised that she'd spoken. "We have a long way to go today," he said. "You should conserve your energy."

"I don't see any reason why we can't walk and talk at the same time," she said sharply.

Wounded or not, he walked through the jungle almost gracefully. His step never faltered, especially now that they had daylight to show them the way. There was no confusion or trepidation in his movements, no uncertainty. Raul had provided clothing more appropriate for travel than the worn drawstring pants that had been left behind. Cal now wore heavy, dark green trousers and a matching T-shirt. The boots and socks were his. They were the only pieces of his original wardrobe that hadn't been ruined, either by

Reiner's knife or a pair of scissors wielded by a caretaker. She shuddered, remembering that night.

"Why do you care what happened?"

"I'm just curious," she answered. The way Raul had talked about Cal, the way the villagers had rallied around him, they way they literally risked their lives to keep him safe… What had he done that made him so special? She wanted to know.

Besides, maybe if he talked about something else she would stop remembering how easily and wholeheartedly she'd given herself to him. Maybe she'd stop remembering how good he had felt.

"It's not all that important and it happened a long time ago," he said, quickening his pace.

Why did she think it *was* important, even now?

She wanted to be furious with him, but no matter how she tried she couldn't quite pull it off. Yes, he had slept with her and called her by another woman's name, but it wasn't as if he'd forced himself on her. She had been swept away by the moment, and even now she wasn't actually sorry. She had never known passion so unyielding that it could carry her away, she'd never known she was capable of anything so primitively beautiful. Terry the rat had told her, on that last, terrible day, that she was too staid and boring, and that's why he'd turned to other women. Staid! Maybe she was cautious, but she was much too young to be called staid.

What had happened back there had been a mistake, she knew that. It had been wrong, she knew that, too. But it had *not* been boring or staid.

She had to quicken her own pace to keep up with Cal. Traveling through the jungle during the daylight hours was much easier than trekking around in the dark. Even though the canopy above shaded them, there was light. There were rough sorts of paths here and there, as though the natives traveled these routes often. Still, the growth threatened to block the paths.

The jungle was every bit as beautiful as she had known it could be. Wild and lush, green and steamy. And there were surprising flowers everywhere, again more red than any other color. Today she saw butterflies, too, large and colorful. Every now and then she heard the screech of a monkey, but they'd stayed far, far away from the two travelers.

The terrain and the wildlife were fascinating, and they almost took her mind off of Cal.

This was the adventure that she'd come here looking for. Not life at the palace, not fending off the general for more than two weeks and being trapped each night in lovely rooms. There were dangers here. Insects, animals, snakes, rough terrain, physical challenge. But those dangers were offset by an incredible beauty and an unexpected power. This wilderness was the world that she knew existed outside her own small domain. It made her problems seem small, for a while. It made her heartbreak seem less significant.

"Are you married?" she asked, running to catch up with Cal.

"No." He sounded horrified as he wagged a bare ring finger at her.

She was relieved to know that much, at least. She did not want to be the other woman. Not even for a day, not even unknowingly. "Not every married man wears a ring, you know," she said.

His answer was a grunt, of sorts.

Cal was definitely not interested in carrying on a conversation to pass the time. But she was. "It must be very interesting, to be a… What is your job description, anyway? Mercenary? Bodyguard? Jack-of-all-trades?" And master of at least one, though she would certainly not tell him so. "I'll bet you've seen lots of fascinating places." She glanced through thick foliage when something beyond the path moved and made leaves shake. Yes, she knew very well there were dangers in the jungle as well as beauty, but those dangers were staying well clear of the travelers who did not belong here.

Cal didn't do his part and give her a proper job designation or name one or two of the fascinating places he'd been, but continued on as if she hadn't spoken. So she persisted:

"Of all the places you've traveled to, what was your favorite?"

"I hire out to do odd, dangerous jobs no one else wants," he snapped. "I'm not a damn travel agent."

"There's no reason to be testy."

"Yes, there is." He stopped, turned, and glared down at her. "With any luck, in a couple of days you'll be in a real hotel room with room service and a real bed and a real bathroom. And you won't have to see me again, so it doesn't matter if I'm married or not, or why some of the people around here have a mistaken idea about me, or what damn country I like best." He leaned down a little bit, trying to intimidate her.

"Well, someone got up on the wrong side of the bed this morning."

Cal closed his eyes, took a deep breath, and then turned his back on her. "I am not getting paid enough for this frickin' job," he muttered as he walked away.

A capable man could live in the jungle forever and not have to worry about going hungry or thirsty. As long as he knew what to eat and what not to eat, could differentiate good water from bad, and had a knife in case of emergency, he'd be fine.

Then again, Cal though sourly, what man would want to live in the jungle forever with a woman who simply would not shut up? The clearer he made it that he didn't want to talk, the more Livvie chattered.

But that wasn't what had him in such a bad mood. As the day wore on, he began to put the pieces of one very bizarre puzzle together. That rash on her face was already fading, but he'd finally accepted it for what it was. A man's beard had irritated her delicate skin. Even worse, he was beginning to suspect it had been *his* beard.

Raul's loco juice really had made him loco. He'd dreamed of Claudia and it had seemed so real. So good. He hadn't dreamed of her for years, and when he had she'd appeared in a nightmare, not an erotic dream. Then as the day continued and he listened to Livvie's voice, fragments of a memory came back to him. This memory teased all his senses, until he could see her beneath him, feel her skin, taste her mouth, hear her moan. And he could smell her, too, a pleasant, uncomplicated scent of woman.

He had gotten it on with Livvie Larkin, and while he'd seen and heard and felt Claudia at the time, he was gradually remembering what had really happened. Everything was so fuzzy. Fuzzy and indistinct and much more real than any dream could ever be. Exactly how powerful was Raul's homemade medicine?

Not so powerful that Cal could entirely block out what had happened. He put the pieces of the puzzle together, unable to deny the truth.

When he'd awakened, Livvie had been sitting, tense

and obviously upset, on the other side of the room. She'd ordered him not to touch her ever again. She'd even tried to stay behind, but he couldn't allow that and she hadn't argued with him when he'd insisted. Not much, anyway. Everything in his fragmented memory indicated that when she'd joined him on that cot she'd been more than willing.

More than willing.

Max was going to kill him.

"Where are you from?" she asked, once again quickening her step to keep up with him.

Cal turned his head to look at her, but he didn't slow down. "What?" Her face was a little flushed, more from the quick walk than the beard burn. A sheen of sweat made her face glow.

She sighed, obviously growing exasperated with him. "When you're at home, where are you? Where does your family live? Where do you go for Christmas and Thanksgiving?"

"I move around a lot, I don't have any family, and I don't do Christmas or Thanksgiving."

She faltered a little, but Cal didn't slow down. "What do you mean, you don't *do* Christmas or Thanksgiving? Everyone does something."

"I don't."

For a couple of minutes she was silent. Cal enjoyed the silence for a few moments, and then for some reason he wished she'd start chattering again.

"Sorry," she finally said. "I'm such an idiot. I was raised by Ozzie and Harriet, and sometimes I'm so naive it's embarrassing."

"You were raised by Ozzy Osbourne and someone named Harriet?" he teased.

She laughed lightly and it sounded quite natural, as if

she laughed often. "You know what I mean, don't you? That old television show. A mother and a father, a white picket fence, home cooked meals, someone to tuck me in at night. My parents protected and loved me so much. They gave me the ideal childhood. I didn't know there was anything or anyone bad in the world until I was—" she hesitated for a moment, and then she finished in a lowered voice "—fifteen."

She went quiet again, and Cal knew he should be glad. Hadn't he been wishing for silence for the past two hours? The jungle was never completely quiet. It was too alive, too vibrant.

"What happened when you were fifteen?" he asked after a few minutes. Heaven help him, he had to know.

"They died in a car crash," she said, the liveliness gone from her voice.

"Sorry," he said softly.

"Yeah, me, too. It was one of those stupid, senseless things. Nobody's fault, really, just…" she hesitated, took a deep breath, and then continued. "Anyway, all of a sudden my whole life was turned upside down. I have never, not before or since, felt as alone as I did at that moment when the police came to the door to tell me what had happened."

"You don't have any brothers or sisters?"

"No, it was just me." She sighed. "And Uncle Max, who I barely knew at all back then. My parents died and Max was there, and I had to move to another city and he was much stricter than my parents had been, and…I really hated him, for a long time.

"I ran away," Livvie added after she'd taken a few more cautious steps. "A couple of months after I moved into Uncle Max's place, I packed a bag and ran."

Cal couldn't help it. His heart hitched, more than a little. "How'd that work for you?"

She laughed again. "Not well. Max was with the CIA at the time, and he sent a team of agents after me. They were annoyed at being given that kind of duty, but they found me in less than two days. I had to pretend to be upset, but in truth I was so relieved. Kinda like when you showed up. This time," she clarified. "Once I'd recognized you, of course. It took me a few minutes to decide you really weren't the enemy on our last encounter."

Funny, he had never realized that she felt anything but annoyed. Annoyed he could handle. Grateful came with too many obligations. Obligations he didn't need or want.

"Poor Max," Livvie said softly. "He's always so in control, so calm and cool. I don't think he's ever made a mistake, not in his whole life. He must hate this, sending people in to rescue his screwed-up niece."

"You're not screwed up." Cal insisted.

She snorted, in an entirely feminine way. "I have a tendency to always be in the wrong place at the wrong time," she argued. "And I unerringly pick the wrong man. Derrick. Terry. When I first spoke to the general on the phone, I had no clue that he was…evil. And he is, I think. Really, truly evil. I didn't see what was wrong with any of them, I didn't even have a clue. How do I manage that?" She laughed again. "And how does Max always know?"

Max Larkin had retired from the CIA a few years earlier. Cal had no idea exactly what his current *consultant* job entailed, and he didn't want to know. He had a feeling the less he knew about Max Larkin the better off he'd be. Max had gotten him the job with Benning, a couple of years back, and he threw a good bit of work their way. Jobs Larkin and his company couldn't or shouldn't handle.

And who the hell was Terry?

"We need to go a little farther before we set up camp for the night," Cal said.

He expected a response from Livvie, but all was silent. And then he heard it. She whispered his name in absolute terror.

He turned and drew his knife in one move, but relaxed and lowered his hand when he saw why Livvie was terrified.

She stood nose to nose with an iguana who was perched on a low-lying tree limb. He hadn't paid the four-foot-long lizard any mind at all when he'd passed by, but the reptile definitely had Livvie's attention.

"It won't hurt you," he said as he retraced his steps.

"Are you sure?" she whispered. "What if I turn my back and it attacks me?"

He couldn't help but smile. "Not likely."

She wrinkled her nose. "This is the ugliest creature I have ever seen."

Cal lifted the knife in his hand. "Tastes like chicken."

The thought of eating the lizard was apparently more repugnant to Livvie than the possibility of being attacked. "Ewww! I'll stick to protein bars and the occasional banana, thank you very much." She backed away, her eyes on the lizard. "You're sure it won't jump on me?"

"Positive."

She scurried toward him, stepping sideways and backward so the reptile wouldn't have a chance to jump on her back. He had a feeling she'd stick a little closer for the next few miles.

"You never said where you were from," she said as

they quickly moved away from the iguana. She did glance back. Once.

"I move around…"

"I know that. But where do you live right now?" Livvie was obviously frustrated, and Cal finally got it. She was trying very hard to get her mind off of her troubles with this casual conversation. She was reaching for a touch, just a touch, of normalcy in her very *un*normal life.

"Alabama," he said. "The agency I work for is located there. I travel a lot, though, so I'm not home very much."

"Oh. I've lived in Indiana for the past three and a half years. Uncle Max lives in D.C., as I'm sure you know, and even though we fight all the time we do manage to get together for the holidays. One, at least. Sometimes we can manage to get together for Thanksgiving and Christmas, but some years he just can't manage both. And last year…" She stopped speaking with an abruptness that caught Cal's attention.

He glanced at Livvie to make sure she hadn't seen a snake or a wild boar or something else more startling than an iguana. No, she was frowning, lost in thought, but she wasn't afraid. "What about last year?"

"Max met my fiancé for the first time, and…"

"Your *what?*" Cal stopped on the path and so did Livvie. She'd been shacking up with the general, she had come to him willingly enough—if his memory was at all correct—and she was *engaged?* Was this the same woman who'd asked him to turn away while she changed clothes, who sang so he wouldn't hear her piss, who managed to look downright haughty on occasion?

"My fiancé," she said. "Well, ex-fiancé now, but back then we were still engaged. Terry," she said. "These days better known as Terry the rat."

Cal breathed a little easier. "What happened?"

She puckered her mouth, just slightly. "He was fooling around, and I was the last to know. We're teachers in the same elementary school, and everyone there knew what was going on before I did. It would have been humiliating enough even if no one else had known, but once the news came out I couldn't walk down the hallway without knowing that everyone there felt sorry for me. 'Poor Livvie, she wasn't good enough for Terry and we knew it all along, but what a terrible way to find out.'"

He had a feeling Livvie was much too good for Terry the rat, but he didn't tell her so. This conversation was already getting out of hand. He didn't do personal, not like this. "We need to keep moving," he said, turning his back on her. "Another half hour or so and we'll set up camp for the night."

"Fine with me," she said breathlessly. "My feet are killing me."

Cal was one of those nature-loving guys who could set up a camp in no time, wounded or not. And he had all the right equipment, thanks to Raul. There was a tent that folded up into almost nothing and fit into his backpack, but opened into a decent sized tent for two, thin blankets, bottled water and nasty tasting protein bars.

Livvie was a bit surprised that Raul had access to such things, but she wasn't about to complain. The alternative would be sleeping in the wild and eating unrecognizable fruit and iguana—and she wasn't that much of an adventurer.

She had a feeling that would suit Cal just fine, though, if he didn't walk straight through without any rest or sleep or food. The guy just wasn't human.

No, she conceded as he sat down a few feet away from her, using the raised, gnarled root of a tree as his chair. Cal was as human as the next man. He had flaws and hopes and dreams like any other person, he just chose not to share them.

It wasn't yet dark, but darkness was coming. Soon. And here darkness fell so quickly it took her breath away.

While he'd been setting up camp, Cal hadn't so much as glanced at her. All day he'd led the way without hesitation, without so much as a hint that he might not know what he was doing or where he was going…though to be honest the terrain all looked the same to her. He took his responsibilities toward her very seriously, and she had no doubt that he could get her to safety. But she could count on one hand the number of times he'd really looked at her today.

Now, as he sat on his jungle chair at the end of a very long day, he stared into her eyes the same way he did everything else. Bold. Fearless. With an intensity she felt as if it were tangible. Maybe he wasn't human, after all.

"Could you be pregnant?" he asked without warning.

Livvie blinked twice, and her breath caught in her throat.

"The Pill," he prompted when she didn't immediately respond. "The patch, a condom. Anything."

"Hormone implants," she said in a small voice.

There wasn't much light left, but it was enough for her to see his obvious relief. "Smart girl."

"I didn't think you remembered," she said.

"I didn't, for a while. It was that loco juice of Raul's."

She should probably just let it go. Laugh it off, dismiss what had happened as unimportant.

But she couldn't do that. "You thought I was someone else."

He didn't answer, and while they sat there it happened. Darkness enveloped Livvie, and for a while she didn't mind. If she couldn't see Cal, he couldn't see her. Thank goodness. There was no way he could see the single, stupid tear that slipped down her cheek.

"Who is she?" Livvie asked, glad that at least she didn't sound like a brokenhearted girl. It was easier this way, in the dark. Cal had a battery operated lantern, but he hadn't turned it on. Darkness was best for this conversation. "Claudia. Is she your girlfriend back home?"

"No."

"An old girlfriend, then."

"It doesn't matter who or when…"

"You love her," Livvie said. Saying that shouldn't hurt, but it did. She had no claim on Cal. No claim on his heart, at least. Men and women had casual sex all the time, right? She never had, but there had to be a first time for everything, she supposed.

For a long moment, all was quiet. What if she'd gone too far and Cal had just walked away? He could do it. He could walk out of here without making a sound, if he wanted to. What if she was all alone in the dark, and he just left her here? What if…what if…

"I don't," he finally responded.

Livvie sighed in relief. No, he wouldn't leave her here. He wasn't the kind of man who would walk away from his responsibilities. "You said…you said you loved her."

"A man will say anything to get into a woman's pants, you should know that by now." His voice was unnecessarily harsh.

"When you said those three magical little words my pants were already on the other side of the room," she said briskly. They had definitely been past the point where he'd needed to charm her out of anything.

He'd been inside her, still, his heart and hers beating too fast, her impossible imagination running away with her...

Finally she heard him move. A shuffle in the dark, a boot on the ground. A click, and a soft light bathed their campsite.

"You should get some sleep." Cal had his back to her, but she could tell he was wound so tight he was about to pop. What happened when a man like this lost his temper? She didn't want to know.

"So should you."

There was the one small tent, but it had room for both of them in it. Barely. Cal was still healing, after all. He had to rest.

"We'll sleep in shifts," he said. "You sleep as long as you can, and when you wake up I'll get an hour or two before we head out."

"Do you think the general's soldiers might find us here?" Livvie asked as she moved toward the tent.

"No. We're a good distance from the road, and Raul said the general's search has moved outward. The odds of anyone finding us tonight are extremely slim."

"But not impossible."

"Nothing is impossible."

Livvie crawled into the tent and sat down on the blanket Cal had laid out there. She removed her boots and wiggled her toes, but left the thick socks and everything else on. Tent or no tent, the insects were brutal at night, and she wasn't going to take any chances. Cal watched her through the narrow opening. Once she was settled, he'd likely zip the tent closed and turn off the lantern. Oh, she hoped she could sleep. She was so tired.

"Where is Claudia now?" Livvie asked as she folded the blanket over her legs and laid back. And why weren't they together? No matter what he claimed, she couldn't see Quinn Calhoun saying *I love you* lightly, and he'd surely never had to lie to get a woman into his bed.

"Dead," Cal said simply.

Suddenly she was sorry she'd asked. He'd loved this Claudia woman and she'd died. It was a tragedy, worse even than finding out that Terry the rat was a philanderer. Was that why Cal was so tough and seemingly unfeeling? Because he'd lost the woman he loved?

"That's awful," she said. "I'm so sorry. What happened?"

Cal stared at her hard, his eyes catching and holding hers, a muscle in his jaw twitching. His lips thinned and went hard. Just when she'd decided he was not going to answer, he said, "I killed her."

Chapter 6

Cal sat outside the tent where Livvie slept, the lantern and flashlight turned off, the night almost completely black. He had good night vision, and had been sitting in the dark long enough for his eyes to adjust. There was nothing out there. Well, no *one*. The jungle rustled and hummed with night-life, but the critters stayed well clear of the intruders.

Even if he had been willing to sleep without a proper guard, he wouldn't get any sleep tonight. Too much crap was running through his usually ordered mind. Claudia, yeah, but more than that he found himself looking back at other things best left forgotten.

Olivia Larkin really was a princess. She'd grown up in her perfect little world, living the kind of life he'd always believed to be nothing but fantasy. She'd been safe, she'd been happy. She'd been surrounded by people who cared about her and protected her.

He didn't mind for himself that he hadn't had a sitcom childhood. His life had made him who he was, and he had no regrets. But his little sister…Kelly should've had better. And dammit, he should have been there to go after her when she'd run away from home, seven years ago.

If she really had run away. What if she was dead? What if that bastard of a stepfather had killed her, disposed of the body, and then reported her as a runaway? Kelly had been seventeen at the time and she'd run away from home once before, so the police hadn't looked very hard. They'd filed their reports and forgotten.

Cal hadn't forgotten. Kelly was the reason he worked for the Benning Agency. Benning had the resources and the manpower to keep the search going, even though Cal had never found so much as a trace of his sister.

She was out there, somewhere. He had to believe that, or else he had nothing left. The stepfather who had either killed her or forced her from home was dead. Cal would have killed the SOB if he'd had the chance, but the bastard had died of a heart attack before Cal could get his hands on the man. He could have made the old man tell the truth, if only he'd lived a few months longer.

There had been no CIA agents to search for Kelly Calhoun when she went missing. Since her mother had recently passed and her no-good brother was in Camaria at the time, there hadn't even been anyone around to miss her when she ran.

If she truly had run. Neighbors had reported hearing an argument the night Kelly disappeared. What if their stepfather, a violent and unstable man who was given to getting really nasty when he drank, had murdered her that night? Cal knew his mother would have protected Kelly with her own life, but once she was gone…no one had been there for her.

He should have been there, but instead he'd been in Camaria, working for the general and screwing Claudia and doing what he did best. Quinn Calhoun was a soldier, through and through. The Army at eighteen, a year of being lost after his tour was done, Camaria and General Menendez at twenty-four. When he'd come here he'd put his past behind him, and he hadn't even known what had happened to his sister until he went home, two years later. By that time Kelly had been missing almost a year.

The people here thought he was a hero, but that was a lie. There had been times when he'd done what he had to do, but there was nothing heroic about the man he had become.

In the dark alley behind the gas station Cal stood in shadow, his back against the wall. If he was wrong and Max's niece left by way of the ladies' room door, he'd hear her. If he was right…

The small window not ten feet away opened slowly. It creaked a little, a whispered curse from the ladies' room reached his ear, and then for a moment all was quiet.

Her purse was first, flying out of the window and landing in the alley with a shush and a rattle. He heard a soft grunt, a rustle, and then another grunt. One bare leg made it through the window. A very fine leg, he noted. Her shoe fell off and landed beside the purse, and Olivia Larkin whispered a mild curse again.

This assignment wasn't much better than baby-sitting, but Max was paying him well. These two days of work would give him enough cash in hand to search for Kelly for a month. Longer, if he was frugal. Still, hauling a spoiled princess away from trouble and delivering her to her uncle was less than exciting work.

At least she was making it interesting.

Her other leg made it out, and the shoe on that foot stayed put. She twisted around slowly, hanging tightly onto the window frame as she maneuvered, and then she lowered herself a couple of feet. Her loose dress was caught on the window, so she came out with wiggling bare legs and then panties showing.

She made so much noise as she worked her way out of that window and down...did she think he was deaf? Or stupid?

With a grunt, a squeak of the old window and another curse, Olivia Larkin managed the feat of easing herself through the window and let herself fall to the ground. Instead of landing solidly on her feet she fell backward and ended up on her ass.

Cal put his hands together. Applause was definitely called for.

Her head snapped up. If looks could kill he'd drop dead on the spot. Lucky for him, Olivia Larkin's glare wasn't fatal.

She scrambled to her feet and grabbed her purse and shoe from the ground. "How long have you been standing there?"

"Since you went into the little girls' room."

She smacked him with her shoe as she walked past. "You could have said something!"

"And miss the show?" He followed her from the alley and into the soft glow cast by the gas station's lighted sign. She stopped and slipped on her shoe.

"This is ridiculous," she said softly. "I'm not a child, I'm a grown woman! All I want to do is go home."

"It's three o'clock in the morning and you're a long way from home."

"I can catch a bus, I can hire a cab, I can hitchhike!"

"Sorry, sweetheart."

She glared at him again. If she wasn't such a spoiled brat, he might find her pretty. Messing around with Max Larkin's niece would surely be suicide.

"Can't you find a real job?" she asked as she turned away and headed for the car. "As if anyone would have you. Not a big market for hoodlums, is there?"

Yeah. Definitely suicide.

A car accident, maybe, Livvie thought as she followed Cal along the narrow trail he made for them with a machete, and he'd been driving. Or something had happened to Claudia when he wasn't around and he blamed himself. Or they'd been doing something adventurous, like skydiving or mountain climbing, and there had been a tragic mishap. Why else would Cal say he'd killed Claudia?

She remembered the way he'd slit a man's throat in the alley, the way he'd killed the two soldiers without so much as flinching, and she couldn't help but wonder if it hadn't been something so simple as an accident after all.

No matter how curious she was, she couldn't make herself ask.

Cal had slept for an hour and a half after she'd gotten up just before dawn. That couldn't be enough, could it? He was still recuperating, or should be. Besides, she always needed at least seven hours of sleep a night, and eight was better. That requirement had gone out the window, lately, but how could anyone function on less than two?

Since she couldn't probe deeply into Cal's past, and idle chatter did not appeal to her today, she remained silent as they walked along the path. Cal said it was unlikely they'd reach Guyana by tonight, but tomorrow morning was almost certain…as long as they didn't run into any trouble.

Every now and then he glanced back as if to make sure she was still there. What would he do if she wasn't? What if she just stopped and refused to go forward? Her legs ached, her feet hurt, her shoulders were strained by the backpack and she needed a shower in the worst way.

But she wasn't going to stop, and if she did Cal would most definitely come back for her. Max wouldn't send a man who was willing to fail after his niece.

She took a few quick steps to catch up with Cal. "So, I guess you know my Uncle Max pretty well."

"Not really. I've worked for him a few times, that's all."

"He trusts you. If he didn't, he'd be here himself."

"I'm more qualified than he is for this particular job."

"Why?"

"Because I've been here before."

"In Camaria?"

He glanced down at her. "In the palace, princess."

She'd told him…*ordered* him…not to call her princess. But since he didn't say the word as if it were an accusation, she let the infraction pass without comment. "Why were you in the palace, and how did you know about the secret hallways and the escape hatch?"

He took a few steps before answering. "I used to work for Menendez."

Something very cold rushed through her veins. Somehow she doubted he'd been the chef or the groundskeeper. "Doing what?"

"Whatever he told me to."

That was how Reiner knew him; they'd once worked together. She had hated Cal, on more than one occasion. She had cursed his name and thought him the lowest of the low. But she had also liked him, envied him, been thrilled by him. Yes, in spite of everything she expected better of him. "How could you work for a man like that?"

He didn't slow his pace at all. "At least I didn't sleep with him."

Suddenly she'd had enough. How many times had she tried to tell Cal that she had worked for the general as a companion for his daughters and nothing more? He simply refused to listen. She stopped on the path and dropped her backpack. Cal kept walking.

"You're a son of a bitch," she said.

He was a good fifteen feet away before he stopped and turned to face her. "Yeah. So?"

"Why do you refuse to believe that I was not involved with the general?"

"Why do you care if I believe you or not?"

She shouldn't care. Cal was her uncle's employee, and that's all. He had been hired to get her out of here, and so far things had not gone well. They were not friends, they were not colleagues, and once she got home she'd never see him again, because her days of getting into trouble were over. Besides, she knew darn well that Quinn Calhoun had done things much worse than anything he could accuse her of doing.

He had also given her the most magical, exciting, passionate…and humiliating night of her life.

"I'm not moving until you admit that my only reason for being in the palace was to take care of Elsa and Ria."

He moved forward slowly, and when he reached her he bent down to snag the backpack she'd tossed to the ground. Then he tossed her over his shoulder, moving so quickly she didn't know what he was planning until it was too late.

"Put me down."

"No." He walked a little more slowly than before, but still managed to move unerringly forward.

"You're going to hurt yourself."

"No, I'm not."

She had seen the wounds, and she knew darn well he wasn't physically able to do this. "I just want you to admit that…"

"Your bedroom reeked of him," Cal said darkly. "The dress, the diamonds, the flowers and candles, maybe you can explain all that away. But you can't explain to me why you and the room stunk of his cologne." He took a deep breath, as if he were calming himself down, as if he were pulling himself together. "God, that stench…" For a moment he held his breath, as if he could still smell the cologne, and it was choking him. "He was due in an hour, you told me that yourself, princess. And if you're down here looking after two little girls, why do you need hormone implants to keep yourself from getting pregnant?"

"Put me down before you hurt yourself," she said calmly.

After taking a few more steps he did as she commanded, placing her on her feet almost gently.

"Now, give me that backpack."

He handed it over.

"If you must know…"

"I don't need to know anything. It's none of my business. Just don't lie to me."

Livvie planted herself before Cal, there on the path. She shouldn't care what he thought of her, and she certainly didn't owe him anything. But she wanted him to know the truth. She needed him to accept that she had never been involved with the general. Why? He knew about Derrick, he knew about Terry. Why should one more bad choice in the romance department matter?

"I've never lied to you," she said succinctly. "Menendez said he was coming to my room that night, but he had not been invited and I'd made it more than clear that he would not be welcomed. While I was trying to choke down dinner, someone else prepared the room. If you'd stepped into the sitting room you would have seen that I had a chair wedged under the doorknob. Not that it would have done any good, with those secret hallways, but I didn't know about them." Cal's expression didn't change. "I have hormone implants because Terry the rat decided he didn't want children for at least a couple of years, and it seemed like a good idea at the time. When I found out he was cheating on me, I didn't run to the doctor to have them removed. I ran here instead."

There was a faint, almost imperceptible softening of Cal's eyes. "Princess…"

"Call me Livvie," she snapped. "After all, we have slept together."

He glared at her without apology, without embarrassment. Yes, they had slept together, and it hadn't been entirely Cal's doing. She'd wanted him. Heaven help her, she still wanted him.

"You saved me," she said in a softer voice. "I don't know what I would have done if you hadn't shown up when you did, and I will be forever grateful. But that doesn't mean you have the right to insult me. I made a mistake in coming here, I understand that. I doubt Uncle Max will ever allow me to forget it."

Sleeping with Cal had been another of her colossal mistakes…hadn't it? Oddly enough, she didn't think so. Those moments had been too special, too passionate, too beautiful to be thought of as a mistake. And even though she should count Cal as another of her romantic blunders, she was glad she'd taken his hand when he offered it. She was glad that for a short while she'd believed he thought she was special and exciting. She couldn't be sorry. He probably was, though, if he gave their time together any thought at all.

"I just don't want you to think I'm…"

"Why do you care what I think?" he interrupted.

"I'm not sure why, but I do."

Cal shook his head. "I'm not sorry I'm wrong, not this time. It was the smell that did it," he said in a low voice. "That cologne he bathes himself in." He needed a shave, he was hard as nails and without any hint of gentleness, and still…his nostrils flared as if he could smell that cologne even now. "A woman like you shouldn't come within a hundred miles of a man like Menendez."

"What does that mean, exactly—*A woman like me?*" Livvie asked. Was it an insult or a compliment? She couldn't tell.

"Let's move, prin…Livvie. We have a long way to go today." She moved aside and he stepped past her.

Cal wanted to go back, sneak into the palace, find Menendez, and cut the man's heart out. It was unlike him to get so proprietary about a job, a woman, a package. But the look on Livvie's face when she'd told him he'd arrived just in time…

He almost smiled as he dipped down to avoid a low-lying branch. He didn't need to go back. The rebels would take good care of Menendez. And if Raul and the other rebels didn't get the job done…maybe he'd come back to Camaria once Livvie was safe, and if he had to he'd do the job himself.

"Can we take a break?" she asked breathlessly.

The woman had a bladder the size of a pea. And an off-key repertoire of old disco tunes and twangy country songs. "Sure." They'd be near the Guyana border by nightfall. One more night of sleeping on the ground. Tomorrow night Livvie would be in a hotel room awaiting pickup by either her uncle or Major Benning, and Cal would be sleeping in his own room…or heading back into Camaria.

What he really wanted to do was share a room with her. His memories of their one time together weren't quite clear enough. They maintained a dreamlike quality he could not shake, but he suspected she had been extraordinary. He wanted her again, and this time he'd be clearheaded.

Not likely. As a matter of fact, it was damned unlikely.

Livvie sat on a fallen tree trunk and took a deep breath. Maybe this was a pit stop of another kind. She just needed to rest a minute. Cal swung his backpack off and down. They were making decent time, and he could use a breather himself.

"What are you going to do when you get home?" she asked, as if they were on a cruise ship or a golf course.

Get laid was probably not the answer she was looking for. "I'll grab a burger and a beer and then sleep for a few days."

"Sounds good," she said with a smile. "I want a bubble bath first, and then a cheeseburger and beer."

"You don't look like the burger-and-beer type."

"What type do I look like?"

He looked her up and down, from the top of her head

to the tips of her combat boots. It didn't matter how dirty or tired or ragged she was, the woman had dignity and grace. Definitely not his type. "Wine and smelly cheese."

She grinned. It was a great smile, without artifice. He hadn't known it was possible for a woman to be without artifice. Some of them were so damned good at it, deception became their reality.

"Wine goes straight to my head," Livvie said, "and I prefer my cheese melted over a hamburger."

"Looks can be deceiving."

"Thank goodness. Uncle Max likes wine-and-smelly-cheese women."

"He does?"

Livvie lifted her hair off her neck and took a deep breath. "I actually met the last one, and she was…well, she had this huge stick up her butt. She had no sense of humor at all. They dated for almost two years, and I never did figure out what Uncle Max saw in her."

"Maybe she was good in the sack."

"You're such a romantic," Livvie said dryly, not as offended as Cal had thought she might be.

"Well, he's going to be glad to see you." He hadn't told her yet about the newspaper article, but before she called her uncle she needed to be warned. Her phone call was going to be quite a shock to Larkin. "There's something you should see before we get moving."

"I don't think I can move again," she said, rotating her head as if to work some kinks out of her neck.

"Want me to carry you a while?" Cal asked as he retrieved the scrap of newsprint Raul had given him.

"No," she said sternly. "You're in no shape to do that."

"I'm fine."

She didn't argue, but she didn't look like she agreed, either. When he handed her the article their fingers brushed, just a little. That innocent touch shouldn't have been erotic—but it was. It was a cell memory of that time together, he imagined. A time he couldn't remember nearly well enough.

All the more reason to have her once more.

"Oh, my God," she said as she read the article. "At least we don't have to worry about Menendez looking for us. He thinks we're dead. But poor Uncle Max…"

"Menendez knows damn well we're not dead," Cal said sharply. "There was one body on that helicopter, not three. But if he reports that we're dead, then if he does catch us, nothing's going to stop him from doing whatever the hell he wants."

She went pale. "I will be so glad to get home. I'm going to kiss the ground and never leave the country again. I won't be impulsive, I won't crave anything exciting in my life. Dull Miss Larkin, schoolteacher, from here on out. That's it for me." She stood. "I need a few cats, I guess," she added in a slightly dismal voice. "And I should start collecting something. Potato chips that look like famous people, or antique door knobs or ceramic turtles."

She would never be dull, but how could he tell her that? "We should get moving."

With a sigh, she lifted her backpack. "You know, someone needs to stop General Menendez. He's…he's a bad person," she added as she slipped on the pack and adjusted the straps so it fit snugly. "He's the kind of man my parents and Max always tried to protect me from."

"Don't worry about the general," Cal said as he lifted his own pack. "I don't think anyone will have to worry about him much longer." He turned around and started walking, but he instinctively knew that he was alone. When he turned he saw that Livvie hadn't moved.

The woman who had once taken the time to brush a little bit of dust off her rear end now wore more than her share of dirt, and her hair tangled wildly around her face. Her cheeks were flushed, her eyes were tired. So why did she look so damn good? Prettier than he remembered. Sexier than any woman wearing baggy camouflage had a right to be.

She would be even more beautiful if she'd smile, but she definitely wasn't smiling at the moment. In fact, she looked downright stunned.

"It all makes sense, now," she said softly. "The way Uncle Max sent you in. The way you're getting me out, when you should be in bed recuperating." She closed her eyes in a long, frustrated blink. "What's going to happen? When?"

He could lie to her, but why? She'd probably be relieved to know that the general's own people were going to take care of him themselves. "Rebel uprising. A couple of days. We don't want to be anywhere near Menendez's palace when it happens."

She took a step backward. "What's going to happen to the girls?"

"How old are they?"

"Elsa is fourteen, Ria is eleven."

He wished he could assure her that the girls wouldn't be hurt, but he couldn't do that. "I'm sure the general will get them to safety. They're his kids, after all."

"But what if he doesn't? The rebels won't hurt them, will they?"

He didn't answer. If Livvie knew what the general had done to the children of some of those rebels, she might understand. No, he didn't think she would ever understand that kind of thinking. His silence was enough to alarm her.

"They're innocent," she whispered. "They have done nothing wrong."

"If you're looking for someone to tell you that life is fair, you're looking in the wrong place," Cal said harshly.

She knew who he was, what he was, what he'd done. And this was the first time she'd looked at him as if she truly understood. "How can you leave them there?"

"How can I leave them there?" he repeated as he stepped toward her. "They're not my problem. *You're* my problem."

"Not anymore." She took a single step back. "You're fired."

"You can't fire me!"

"Yes, I can. You did your job. You got me out of the palace and away from Menendez. When you get home, tell my uncle you did your part. Tell him going back for the girls was my idea. He won't hold you responsible."

"I can't let you do that."

"You don't have any choice."

Cal raked a hand through his hair. He could tie her up, if he had to, and carry her the rest of the way to Guyana. It wouldn't be easy, but it would definitely be better than allowing her to go back to Menendez's palace.

"I know what you're thinking," she said softly. "And I imagine you're right. You're stronger than I am, even in your current condition. But you'd be wasting your time, because the minute we got where we were going and you turned your back I'd be on the first ride to Camaria I could find. I will *not* leave those girls unprotected. They are my responsibility and I will do whatever I have to, in order to make sure they are safe."

Cal shook his head. The confidence and surety in her voice reminded him of Max. There was no way she'd turn back now. "If you do that you'll get to the palace about the same time the rebels do. Bad plan."

"Then maybe you'd better just let me go now." With that she turned and started walking, retracing their steps.

"Holy crap," he muttered as he followed her. "Plan B. I take you to Guyana, drop you at a safe place, and then I come back for the kids."

"No."

"Why not?"

"I don't trust you."

It was the first smart thing she'd said all day.

She shouldn't have told Cal she didn't trust him. He hadn't said a word since, and how on earth could she be sure that he was leading her back to the palace? The jungle paths all looked the same to her, though he didn't seem to falter at all.

Besides, it had been a lie. She did trust Cal, as much as she could trust any man who'd made wildly passionate love to her and then called her by another woman's name. But the delay of getting her to safety before going after the girls might make all the difference, and besides, Elsa and Ria didn't know Cal. They'd be frightened if he just swept in and grabbed them up.

The jungle was a noisy place, but she was getting accustomed to the screeches and buzzing. After they'd been walking a while, a new and gentler sound joined the chorus. It sounded like…water. Cal cut off the path they'd been following and began to make his own trail once again. After a few minutes of hacking through thick growth, he cut his way into a clearing. The sight that was revealed took Livvie's breath away. A small lake, clear and blue, spread before them. To the right, a small waterfall fell gently into the water. Straight ahead, on the opposite side of the lake, a cliff rose straight and tall.

Water lilies floated atop the water here and there, and the bank was lush and green. The view was like something from a postcard.

Cal dropped his backpack. "We're going to rest here a while."

"Do we have time to stop?"

He stared at her. "If we were going to Guyana, no. But since there's been a change of plans we have the time." He stripped off his shirt, exposing a hard, scarred chest and one large bandage. Was he thinner than he'd been a week ago? She thought so. A little. He needed bed rest and good food and a good woman to make sure he took better care of himself.

Cal unfastened his pants.

"What are you doing?" she asked frantically.

He checked the ground around him before untying and kicking off his boots. "I'm going for a swim. I'm hot and I didn't get enough sleep last night. It'll help."

Livvie steered clear of him as she walked to the water's edge and peered down. The lake was clear, but this was the jungle after all. "Is it safe?"

"Safe enough. Definitely safer than what we're planning to do. Just stay away from brightly colored frogs and all snakes."

"Snakes?"

"Most of them aren't poisonous."

"Well, *that* makes me feel better," she mumbled.

She very purposely didn't look at him while he finished undressing. Not that she hadn't seen him before, but still…the man had no shame. Not that he had anything to be ashamed of.

Livvie didn't so much as glance Cal's way until he dove under the water and came up with a splash, tossing his head back so his hair was slicked away from his face.

It wasn't fair. He was so cool and relaxed, and the water looked so good. It had been days since she'd had even a halfway decent bath, and the very idea of plunging her entire body into that cool water was enough to make her tremble in anticipation. She was sticky with sweat and, dammit, she was hot.

Livvie dropped her backpack. "Swim over there," she said, pointing to the left. "And look the other way."

"Livvie…"

"I know. You've seen it before. I occasionally suffer the delusion that you're a gentleman. Humor me anyway."

He swam away, oddly obedient, and she quickly stripped. She was even more cautious than Cal had been, checking the ground around her and the water as she stepped into the lake. No frogs, no snakes. The water on her feet and legs felt heavenly. Cool and refreshing and…she closed her eyes as she swam out toward the middle. This could so easily be paradise. The secluded lake was beautiful in an awe-inspiring way, and it was a miracle and a gift that she found herself here, even if only for a few minutes.

As she dipped her head beneath the water, Livvie tried to convince herself that Cal's presence had nothing to do with that idea. It didn't work. He belonged here in a way she never could. He was a part of the beauty that overwhelmed her and touched her heart.

It wouldn't be paradise without him.

Cal kept his distance as they swam in the cool water, but he was never too far away. If she saw anything to alarm her, if he decided this was no longer a safe place to be, he could be with her in a matter of seconds. But he didn't come so close that she could reach out and touch him, or he could reach out and touch her.

Livvie didn't kid herself, as she plunged beneath the water and came up out of the lake with her face presented to the sun. They didn't have all day, this was not an exotic vacation. It was a few moments of pleasantness in an entirely unpleasant situation. Nothing more. She glanced toward Cal to see if he was watching her. He wasn't.

She was an idiot. He didn't care about her. No matter how she tried to convince herself otherwise, no matter how she tried to turn a quick roll in the hay into something romantic…she knew what had happened between them had been a mistake, one of the worst of her mistake-filled life.

So why didn't it feel like a mistake?

Since she'd never again be in a place like this one, and she suspected Cal did not plan to stay here for very long, Livvie swam to the waterfall. The lake danced gently near the base of the cascading water. She walked into the churning pool and reached out her hand so that the waterfall splashed onto her palm, then she closed her eyes and lifted her face. Water pummeled her body, caressed it…and it felt so good. For a moment she allowed herself to forget everything, and she simply enjoyed the feel of water on her skin. Her muscles ached from all the walking, and she'd been dirty for days. No shower had ever felt this decadent and sensuous and simply *good*.

When she opened her eyes she found Cal closer than he

had been when she'd first come to the waterfall. With his hair wet and pushed so severely away from his face, there were no strands to soften the harsh lines. Maybe his nose was a little bit too severe, and the stubble on his cheeks was definitely rough. He was tough inside and out, all muscle and sinew and scars. With his hair slicked away from his face she discovered another scar. A small one near the hairline. She wanted to touch that scar, the way she'd touched the others. She wanted to know how he'd been injured, who had done it, whether or not it had hurt…things she had no right to ask.

Cal continued to stare at her, and Livvie didn't try to hide beneath the water. She didn't squeal and dip down and tell him to turn away. Why should she? He'd cut her gown off and watched her dress, he'd taken off her clothes and made love to her. She had nothing to hide.

He had lifted his hand and invited her in, once. If she lifted her hand right now, if she invited him to come to her…would he? Before she could work up the courage to do such a brave thing, the moment was gone.

"Time to go," Cal said gruffly, and then he turned and swam away from her.

The village they came upon a couple of hours after leaving the lake was a surprise to Livvie, and it seemed to pop up out of nowhere. There was a rough dirt road, a clearing where the growth was slightly more well managed than the jungle, and a collection of buildings.

She actually smiled. Civilization, even such rough civilization, looked very, very good.

She rushed forward and grabbed Cal's arm. "Oh, they'll have a phone here, right? We can call…"

He shook his head. "No phone."

Her heart fell.

"This isn't a tourist town," he explained. "There are no phones, no bus stop, no television, no Internet connection, no…"

"I get the point," she snapped. "Why is this town here? I mean, is there anything else around?"

Cal looked at her, his eyes deeper than usual. "There's a bar, a restaurant, and a cathouse. This is where the general's soldiers come for R&R."

Livvie glanced at the town with different eyes. It no longer seemed like a comforting stop on their journey. Cal really had circled around to bring them close to Menendez; she'd had no idea they were once again close to the palace.

"We don't need to stop here," she said softly. "I don't mind the protein bars and the bottled water, and real bathrooms are overrated. Let's just move on, straight to the palace."

"You're staying here," Cal said. "I'll go in and get the kids and then come back here for you."

Livvie shook her head. "No way. The girls don't know you. You'll frighten them if you just go in and…"

"Do I need to remind you that this was your idea?" Cal snapped. "I can't take you back into the palace. If we both don't end up dead, Max will kill me when we get home. My job was to get you out of there, not play white knight and nursemaid to the general's daughters, so if you don't want to stay here and wait for me then we'll continue on to Guyana right now." He grabbed her wrist and turned away from the small collection of buildings.

"Wait!" Livvie said as he dragged her a few steps deeper

into the jungle. "I'm sorry. I didn't mean to push. We'll do it your way."

Ah, she found the magic words. He stopped and dropped her hand, then turned to look down at her. "Honey, if we were doing this my way we'd be a long way from this place."

"I'll wait here while you go collect the girls," she said calmly. "It's the least I can do."

He started walking toward the village. "There's one woman here I can trust. You'll stay with her while I'm gone, and you won't talk to anyone else, you hear me? No one."

Not a problem.

He was cautious, moving into town not down the main street but through a narrow alley filled with garbage. Livvie wrinkled her nose and wondered who he would be leaving her with. Someone in the cathouse, she imagined. A hooker he knew from his stint in Camaria. A woman who was probably still in love with him. Cal wasn't pretty, and he certainly wasn't suave. But he was all male in a way that made *some* women drool and sigh. The Quinn Calhoun she knew had surely left women all over the world weeping over his departure. Her imagination worked overtime as they skulked down the alleyway.

Apparently she did trust him, since she was about to let him drop her off in some godforsaken place and leave her. No phones, he'd said. Not much else from the looks of things. Just food, booze and women for the general's soldiers.

Maybe she was wrong and he'd take her to the restaurant to leave her in the hands of a grandmotherly type who would feed them stew and bread and hide Livvie from the soldiers.

Cal entered the largest building in town—a two story

wooden building—by way of a door off the alley, and took a narrow flight of stairs to the second floor. He held Livvie's hand. Not for comfort, she supposed, but to make sure she stayed where she was supposed to—close behind him.

A door down the long hallway opened, and Cal did a quick turnabout. The backpack came off in a smooth, quick motion, and he dropped it to the floor as he pressed Livvie up against the wall and kissed her, shielding her completely from view and presenting whoever had opened that door a view of nothing but his backside.

Her mouth latched onto his as if she were hungry, as if she needed this kiss to calm her heart and feed her soul. Why did she continue to think there was nothing soft about Cal when he kissed this way? The way he held her, the way his mouth moved over hers…he stirred butterflies in her stomach and dreams in her heart. After a long, very nice moment, she remembered where she was and why Cal had kissed her.

Livvie moved her mouth from Cal's and shifted her head so she could peek around his shoulder. A smiling half-dressed woman stood in the doorway to the room, saying goodbye to a…Livvie wrinkled her nose…a customer. The man glanced toward Livvie and Cal and almost immediately dismissed them as unimportant.

Livvie clutched at Cal's shirt, she shifted her head again so it was buried against his chest and there would be no chance for the man down the hall to get so much as a glance of her face or her hair.

The grinning man leaving the room of a prostitute was the scarred robber Livvie had seen leaving 1A. It was Scarface, the man who'd murdered General Menendez's ex-wife.

Chapter 7

Livvie sat in the only chair in the room, silent and watchful, while Adriana hugged Cal and told him how good it was to see him alive and well. Cal couldn't give his old friend his undivided attention. Something was wrong with Livvie, and he had no idea what had set her off. She'd gone pale and her knees were actually shaking. Was she offended that he'd brought her here? What had she expected? A suite at the Waldorf?

"Quinnie." Adriana stepped back and patted his cheeks softly. "You haven't changed at all. I believe you are even more handsome than you were the last time I saw you."

"That's not saying much," he answered softly.

Her wide smile faded. "I can't believe you've come back here. How foolish."

"I can't believe you're still here. You should be out by now."

Adriana cast a suspicious glance to Livvie. "Things have not changed," she said in a lowered voice.

Livvie stood. "I really need to talk to you," she said sharply. Her gaze was pinned to his in an almost frantic way, the blue bluer than before, the fear more palpable.

"About what?"

"I need to talk to you now, and alone," Livvie insisted, cutting her eyes momentarily to Adriana.

"Anything you have to say to me you can say in front of Adriana."

"It's all right," Adriana said sweetly. She went up on her toes to kiss Cal's cheek. "You two talk. I'll bring up some hot food in a few minutes." She smiled at Livvie before she left the room.

"I have to get out of here," Livvie said as soon as the door closed behind Adriana. "I can't stay here alone, Cal, you can't…"

"We can trust her," he said, trying to calm an almost frantic Livvie. "She helped me before when I needed her."

Livvie snorted. "I'm sure she did."

Cal took her arm and held on tight. He didn't owe her any explanations, but he wouldn't have her making accusations. There were two people in the world to whom he felt a lifelong obligation. Adriana was one of those people, and he didn't need attitude from the princess.

"We are putting her life in danger just by being here," he explained. "I know that, and so does she. I promise you, she'll take good care of you while I'm gone."

Now it was Livvie who grabbed him. Her grip on his arm was much stronger and more desperate than his. Her face had gone paper white, and the sheen of unshed tears made her blue eyes shine. "You can't leave me here," she whispered. "The man in the hall, the man who was leaving this room, he's the one who killed Menendez's ex-wife!"

"Are you sure?"

She jiggled the arm she gripped as if she thought she could shake some sense into him. "Yes, I'm sure! That's not the kind of face you forget. I saw him up close, Cal. The scar, the tattoo on his neck... It's Scarface." She shivered, and her frightened expression changed to one of pure horror. "Oh, God. He must work for Menendez. When Nina asked me to keep the girls away from him, she wasn't talking about the scarred man, she was talking about her husband. She'd changed her last name and run as far away from Camaria as she could, all to protect herself and the girls, and what did I do? I delivered them to the man she asked me to protect them from."

"You couldn't have known," Cal said, trying to comfort Livvie because she seemed to be taking this new revelation so hard.

"No." She shook her head. "I should've known that something was wrong. Uncle Max would've known. You would've known. But not me. I have the worst luck with men! I don't even see what's right in front of my eyes. You know that better than anyone. You saved me once before, when I had no idea what Derrick was like. None. He put on a show for me and I took him at face value. And Terry, I don't even want to go there. Two and a half years of my life, wasted, and you know what? I still don't see it. Knowing what I know now, I can look back and I still don't see the deception. What I've done this time is just as bad. No, it's worse. The girls told me who their father was and I contacted the embassy. When the general called asking to make arrangements for his children, it never even occurred to me that his ex-wife hadn't remarried some guy named Garcia and divorced or been widowed. The girls had been away so long they didn't remember much about their father, and they certainly didn't seem scared. I just packed my bags and dropped Uncle Max a note and trotted on down here without a care or a concern to deliver those little girls into the hands of a…a monster. And you…" She took a deep breath, then closed her eyes. "I am so incredibly…"

He kissed her. In part to shut her up, but also in part because he wanted to. With her cheeks flushed and her hand grasping his sleeve, she was too tempting, too close. The brief kiss in the hallway had been intended only as a way to disguise themselves from the man in Adriana's doorway, but the feel of her lips on his had been enough to jar his memory of how she tasted, enough to make him want more. Livvie didn't fight the kiss, but parted her lips and let him devour her. She devoured him back, after a moment had passed.

He wrapped his arms around Livvie and kept on kissing her, long after he should've stopped. Dammit, he could almost remember making love to her. Almost. The memory teased him, as if he were trying desperately to remember a dream that threatened to fade into nothing. He wanted to make love to Livvie again, with a clear head this time. And why not? Max was already going to kill him when they got home…if they got home…

Livvie took her mouth from his, slowly. The kiss had excited and calmed her, it had chased the fears away and reminded her of a moment she'd obviously prefer to forget. Her cheeks were flushed, her lips slightly swollen and damp. "Don't leave me here," she whispered.

"It's best…"

"It's not! Elsa and Ria don't know you, but they know me. It'll be easier if I'm with you. Not only that, I know where their rooms are, and what the daily schedule is. I can help."

"You can tell me everything I need to know before I leave here."

Once again, her fingers tightened around his sleeve, and she held on tight. "No. It's my fault they're in that damn palace, and I want to be a part of getting them out."

"It's too dangerous," he insisted, hoping to talk some sense into her. If he had to tie her up and leave her here, he would. But it would be so much easier if she'd just admit that she had no business tagging along.

But Livvie didn't back down easily. Did she ever? She looked him in the eye, determined and frightened and as stubborn as any woman he'd ever known. She looked at him as if he were someone he would never be.

"Cal, when Nina asked me to protect her girls from *him,* I thought she was talking about Scarface. But she was talking about Menendez, I can see that now. I promised her…"

"I'll take care of it."

"No," she said softly. "This is mine. My burden, my charge. If I thought I could go in alone and get the girls out without your help, I would. They're my responsibility. They became my responsibility while I was sitting in a puddle of their mother's blood promising her that *he* wouldn't hurt them."

He cupped her cheek in one hand, unexpectedly moved by the picture she painted. She shouldn't see such things; she shouldn't know about pain and blood and sick bastards. Heaven help him, he wanted to protect her the same way her parents and her uncle always had. He wanted to make the world right for her. It was possibly the most ridiculous notion he'd ever had.

"You couldn't have known," he said sensibly. "Walking into that apartment didn't make you responsible for those kids!"

"Why do I feel like it did?" she whispered.

He should've made love to her at the lake, this afternoon. As they'd cooled themselves in the water he'd thought about it. He'd actually wondered how Livvie would react if he joined her under the waterfall and took her in his arms.

She wouldn't have pushed him away, he knew that. But it was just as well that he'd come to his senses before things had gone too far. She had enough mistaken notions about him as it was.

"It'll be risky," he said.

"I don't care." Livvie laughed, a little.

She had to know how serious this decision was. "If you go back into Menéndez's palace, you might not make it back out again. You saw Scarface, you made the connection. The general will kill you, if he gets the chance. And death might be the easiest option. Believe me."

"Do you know who I have to go home to?" she asked almost desperately. "Do you know who cares if I make it back or not? No one. My parents have been gone a long time, my personal life is in a shambles, I have no children, no obligations, no…"

"Don't forget about Max."

"I see my uncle once or twice a year," she argued. "Maybe he does love me, in his own way, but I'm more a responsibility than a loved one. If the worst were to hap-

pen and I didn't make it back, he might mourn me for a little while, but his life wouldn't change. No one's life would
change." She touched his face, raking her soft fingers
across his cheek. "The risk is all my own, and I'm willing
to take it. Didn't you ever feel so obligated to an innocent
person that you'd do anything to save them?" There was a
passion in her eyes that had nothing to do with him or any
other man. It was a passion of the heart, of the soul.
"Weren't you ever willing to risk everything to do what was
right? We're talking about two innocent little girls, Cal. I
can't walk away from that. I just can't."

She knew right where to strike to hurt him the most, to
weaken his resolve. "We'll move out in the morning."

Adriana was annoyingly beautiful, and Livvie couldn't
help but wonder why she and Cal were so close. Like she
had to wonder! She didn't enjoy imagining Cal and Adriana together, but when the three of them sat around a small
table in the woman's room and had dinner and wine, she
couldn't help it. Adriana was exotic and lush, from her lips
to her breasts to her hips. Cal was all male, wicked and in-
flexible and demanding. The two of them together seemed
so right. If she wasn't here with them, an unwanted third
wheel, would they be doing something other than having
dinner? Very likely yes, she decided.

Had Adriana come before or after Claudia? Livvie wondered. Had Cal ever loved her, the way he'd loved Claudia, or had theirs been a strictly physical relationship?

The beautiful woman called Cal *Quinnie,* and Livvie
wondered if he would allow anyone else to call him by such
a silly, cutesy name. Probably not.

Over more wine after dinner, Adriana told them that the

scarred man was relatively new—the man she knew only
as Roberto had been with the general less than two years,
though he had risen quickly through the ranks and was now
one of Menendez's most trusted men. Roberto had spent
much of the past two weeks here, Adriana complained.

So she wouldn't see and recognize him at the palace,
Livvie knew. Yes, the general had been careful, where his assassin was concerned. Had he planned all along to do away
with her? Of course he had. He couldn't allow her to live,
since she'd seen Scarface up close. She still couldn't think
of the man as Roberto. Such a normal, ordinary name…

Livvie realized that she'd probably only lived as long
as she had because Menendez had plans for her. Plans that
included diamond necklaces and a candlelit bedroom and
sweetly scented sheets. She shuddered at the very thought.
By showing up when he did, Cal hadn't just saved her
from being attacked…he'd saved her life.

After they'd talked for a while, Adriana glanced at her
bedside clock and sighed. She had to get back to work or
else the bartender would be up here looking for her. After
making sure the hallway was clear, she escorted Cal and
Livvie to a small room at the end of the hall. They each
had a chance to visit the bathroom first. Indoor plumbing!
Rustic and inelegant as it was, the bathroom was a welcome sight.

Beneath them the decadent establishment was already
getting noisy. Through the floor and up the stairwell Livvie heard coarse laughter, the clink of glasses and many
raised voices. As they closed the door she heard footsteps
on the stairs, laughter and soft words, as a woman who
worked here escorted a soldier up the steps.

Cal set the latch on the door and pulled the drapes tightly

over the single window before lighting a lantern that cast yellow light over the small, dingy room. "Not exactly four star accommodations, but at least you won't have to sleep on the ground tonight." He nodded to the double bed.

Livvie unconsciously wrinkled her nose, and Cal laughed at her. "You insist on storming the palace to rescue two little girls who don't belong to you, but you're going to get all girlie on me about sleeping in that bed?"

"There's no telling what's gone on there," she said softly.

"If it makes you feel better, this is where the bartender sometimes sleeps. I can't guarantee that he never…"

Livvie raised a silencing hand. "That's good enough. As long as the door is locked and you're sure Adriana won't tell anyone we're here, I'm fine."

"She won't tell," he promised.

Again, she wondered what they'd be doing if she wasn't here. Her imagination was much too vivid for her own good. Not that she had to rely entirely on imagination. She remembered too well what Cal felt like, how his skin felt against hers, how…what a waste of precious time. She was a victim of mistaken identity, nothing more.

"How can you be so sure?" she asked too sharply. "I swear, even the most levelheaded man will occasionally think with his lower extremities instead of his brain."

Cal raised his eyebrows. He looked slightly shocked and offended. "You think I'm levelheaded?"

Livvie sat on the edge of the bed. It dipped unevenly and squeaked a little. "You? Levelheaded? No, not really. After all you're here, aren't you?"

"So are you. We could be camping close to the Guyana border tonight, and instead we're here talking about a very foolish rescue attempt." He sat beside her, and again the mattress dipped and squeaked. "Major Benning, the man I work for, is a former Marine. When he started his own security firm he took great pains to put together an impressive crew. Some are former military, like Benning and me. Others used to be cops. All of them are the best at what they do, and they're a thousand times more capable of doing this job than you are. Think about it, Livvie. Let's forget about this idiotic plan, and after we get you to Guyana I'll put together a team to come in and get the kids out. It's the only logical solution."

"That would be fine if not for the rebel uprising." He sat right beside her, and she was tempted to slip her arm around his waist. Like it or not, she was scared, and the idea of having someone to hold on to didn't seem so bad, at the moment. But she kept her hands to herself. "I've been thinking about this all day. I know what the general is like, and so do you. How has he treated their daughters over the years, Cal? What are the rebels going to do when they get their hands on Menendez's daughters?"

He didn't have an argument for that—not at first. "Raul won't let anyone harm…"

Livvie stood and glared down at Cal. "Raul?"

He nodded.

"Raul is a…" She shook her head. "And you knew all along."

"Livvie…"

If he didn't look so tired she'd be furious with him. But right now, she just couldn't make herself be angry. Not with Cal, who had literally risked his life to save her butt. "I really am an idiot where men are concerned." She sat again.

"He's a good man."

"Maybe," she said, "but the palace is a big place and he won't be able to watch all the rebels all the time. I don't think Raul is the kind of man who would tolerate violence against children, but he can't be everywhere at once and he can't possibly protect the girls."

Cal grabbed a pillow and tossed it onto the floor.

"What are you doing?" Livvie asked.

"I'm going to get some sleep, and you should do the same thing."

Livvie snagged the pillow and returned it to its place. "Nothing personal, but I want you right here."

Again, his eyebrows lifted slightly.

"Don't get any ideas," she said quickly. "I'll be beneath the covers and you'll be on top."

"Then what's the point?"

She smiled. "I don't trust you not to get the grand idea to sneak out of here without me tonight. I'm a light sleeper. This bed squeaks. If you get out of bed in the night, I'll know it."

"I thought you were going to say I deserved to spend one night on a soft mattress."

"That, too." Her smile faded. "I'll be terrified if you leave me here," she said softly. "The scarred man, he saw my face. If something happens and he sees me here, I'm dead."

"Maybe even if he does see you he won't recognize you. From what you've told me things happened pretty fast. When the adrenaline is pumping, the mind does strange things."

No, she remembered every detail of that man's face, and she suspected he had not forgotten hers. "He was as close to me as you are now, and I hit him in the face with a half-gallon of ice cream."

Cal laughed. "You did?"

"He was about to shoot me."

That cut his laughter short. A muscle in his jaw twitched and his mouth thinned. "Staying here with Adriana is risky, but it won't be as dangerous as what we're about to do."

We. He'd said *we.* "Then I guess we'd better get a good night's sleep." She kicked off her boots and scooted over, then slipped beneath the covers and patted the pillow beside her. "Lie down, Quinnie. I think we're past the bashful phase of our relationship."

He reclined on the bed and closed his eyes, then reached out to douse the lantern on the bedside table. After about five minutes he said, "Princess, we don't have a relationship."

He knew it was a dream, but he couldn't make himself wake up. He'd had this nightmare a thousand times, and every time he thought he could change the outcome. Claudia wouldn't do what she'd done, or else he would make a different choice. But the dream progressed as it always did, and no matter how he tried he couldn't change anything.

And then he was in that room, his arms stretched over his head so tightly he felt like they were about to pop out of the sockets, his back on fire. The general stood before him with modified jumper cables in his hands, jumper cables attached to a large battery that sat on the table behind him. He talked nonstop while he delivered electrical shocks that made Cal's body snap and jerk. The worst part was…just when he thought the torture was over, at least for a while, Menendez delivered another shock. He waited for Cal to relax, and then he moved back in and produced another painful jolt.

Claudia dead, his body throbbing with pain, his mind

clouded…he'd cried for his mother like a baby. While Cal hung there, Menendez had gleefully whipped out a letter. A letter he had saved for just the right moment. He'd shone a flashlight on the page so Cal could see the handwriting, and he'd read the words in a singsong voice.

His mother was dead and had been for months. Claudia had asked her cousin to keep the news from Cal because she hadn't wanted him to go home and leave her behind. She'd loved him so much she hadn't been able to bear the thought of losing him, even for a few weeks.

The general reached for his whip again. "And you killed her," he said. With a wave of his hand he ordered the soldier who stood guard to turn Cal so that his face was pressed against the wall and his back was exposed. "She loved you, and you killed her."

There would be no more electric torture, not for a while. The general delivered his blows with a different method, now, and the blows would continue to fall until Cal passed out. No, they continued even after he was no longer conscious….

Cal woke up in a sweat, and leapt from the bed. He couldn't escape quickly enough. The dream was still with him. Dammit, dammit, *dammit!* It was coming here that brought the old nightmare back. He never should've agreed to return, not after all this time. Not when the past was almost buried so deep it couldn't come back. He ran his fingers through his hair. His heart beat so hard he could feel it, pounding in his chest, threatening to break free. The blood ran cold through his body, and he shivered. One day that dream was going to kill him.

"What are you doing?" a sleepy voice asked. The mattress squeaked as Livvie sat up.

"Nothing," he growled. "Go back to sleep."

"No," she grumbled. "You'll leave me here if I do. And I was sleeping so good. Come back to bed. Please."

He returned to the bed and reclaimed his place, and a sleepy Livvie draped one arm across his chest. "There now," she said sleepily. "You can't move without me knowing it." She took a few deep breaths, and then she said, "You're cold. Why are you cold? Get under the covers."

"I'm fine," he protested.

Livvie rose up on her elbow and looked down at him. Her hand rested on his chest, gentle and soft. "Now I'm awake," she said, her voice only a touch clearer than it had been before. "What's wrong?"

"Nothing."

"Nothing my foot. Your heart is racing, you're sweaty and cold…" She raked her hand higher to touch his cheek. "Oh, no. It's the fever, isn't it? Your wound is getting infected again. Maybe we shouldn't have gone swimming and gotten the bandage wet. Maybe we shouldn't have…"

"I just had a bad dream, that's all." It was embarrassing to admit such a thing, even to Livvie. Especially to Livvie.

"Nah," she said, easing down to lay her head on his chest, since she found no evidence of fever. "You were trying to sneak out on me—admit it."

She didn't sound at all angry. Maybe she was too tired. Maybe she didn't believe what she said, but preferred that explanation to something so ordinary and naked as a nightmare.

He rested his hand in her hair. "Do you want to know the real reason why I won't leave you here?"

"Um-hmm," she murmured.

"I have a sister, did I tell you that?"

"No family, you said."

"I haven't seen her in years. While I was in Camaria last time, my mother died."

Livvie's hand began to stroke. Bad idea. Her fingers were soft as silk, slender and beautiful and arousing. He captured that hand and stilled it, but he held on. "When I got home I found out my sister Kelly had disappeared. Our stepfather was a real son of a bitch. He used to hit me, when I was small enough for him to get away with it, but I never saw him raise a hand to Kelly. But after Mom was gone…" He laid there in the dark, and in the aftermath of an old nightmare he began to relive the one he carried with him every day.

Again, Livvie raised up to look down at him. "What happened?"

"I don't know. Neighbors heard fighting frequently, and one day Kelly was just gone. My stepfather reported her as a runaway, but…but no one heard from her, after that night." He had only voiced his worst supposition aloud once. To Benning. But now, with Livvie's hand in his and the future so uncertain, he asked, "What if he killed her?"

"Can't the police get him to talk?"

"He's dead. The bastard died long before I got home. I've been looking for Kelly ever since." Which was the reason Max had hooked him up with the Benning Agency, a couple of years back. The search for Kelly was an ongoing case. He'd gotten nowhere with the investigation on his own, and Benning had access to techniques and people Cal had never dreamed of.

"So," he said, a touch of unnatural brightness in his voice, "that's why I won't leave you here in the same town with Scarface. That's why I'll put my ass and yours on the line to rescue two little girls I've never met."

He'd save all the little girls…except the one he should've rescued seven years ago.

"I'm sorry," Livvie whispered. "Is that what the nightmare was about? Your sister?"

"Yeah." It was a lie, but a small one.

Livvie kissed him on the forehead before laying down again. He couldn't remember the last time anyone had kissed him like this. Sweet. Comforting. He'd probably been nine years old the last time he'd been touched in such a tender way.

He'd been nine when his mother had remarried.

Livvie was half-asleep, and she snuggled against him with a sigh. If he touched her just so, if he whispered the right words, he could seduce her. He wanted to. He wanted to be inside this woman when he was clearheaded and knew who was laying beneath him. Not only that, she'd be a great way to forget the nightmares of the past, to forget the little girl he hadn't been able to save.

But he didn't make a move, and she quickly reclaimed sleep. Livvie was already beating herself up for getting involved with the wrong men. Picking two losers and being fooled by a slick SOB like Menendez wasn't exactly a tragic record, but he didn't want to complicate matters for her. He realized, even if she didn't, that she wanted a normal life. *Normal* was one thing he could never offer her or any other woman.

If he didn't know anything else, he knew that he was the worst kind of man for a woman like Livvie. Those other two assholes had used her, and so had the general.

He wouldn't do that to her. He wouldn't sleep with her—again—and then drop her on her uncle's doorstep and walk away.

But he held on to her more tightly than he should, and eventually fell into a blessedly dreamless sleep.

Livvie opened her eyes and found Cal staring at her. She was using him as a pillow and he had one arm wrapped around her. It was very nice. Very intimate.

The way he looked at her…at the moment he knew very well who she was, and he wanted her. All she had to do was touch him, kiss him, maybe give him a smile that would tell him that she wanted him to make the first move.

She should have expected this, she supposed. They'd been thrown into close quarters, he'd been injured rescuing her, they'd made love, they'd swum naked in paradise. Surely it was only natural to awaken feeling as if they were true lovers, not just a hallucinogen-based blunder. Maybe it was even natural to believe, at least for the moment, that when they walked out of this jungle they'd stay together. That was surely the silliest thought of all.

His hand rested against her back, and it began to move. Not a lot, just a flutter and a stroke of his fingers. Livvie licked her lips. She raked her hand down his arm and let it stop over his hand. His fingers threaded through hers, almost automatically.

She was lying on a lumpy bed in a cathouse, in a disgusting little town she had no desire to explore beyond these walls. She was about to embark on what might be called the most foolish adventure of her life. But at this moment, with Cal lying beside her and holding her hand, she was content. She didn't want to be anywhere else in the world but here.

There was something so strong and tender in the way he held her hand. Something so deeply natural in the way his body rested against hers. Livvie brushed the tip of her nose against Cal's throat. She could hide here. She could be happy here. This man was hers in a way no other man had ever been, or ever would be.

"Cal…" she whispered.

"Time to go," he said gruffly. He gently put her aside, and then he turned away and left her alone on the bed.

Livvie rolled up into a sitting position. Just as well. She hadn't had a proper bath in days, she needed to brush her teeth, her hair was in tangles…no wonder Cal had run. She cast a quick glance over her shoulder. Why was it that the rigors of the jungle looked so good on him and just made her look grungy?

"How long will it take us to get there?" she asked. Back to business. Please, please forget that I almost made a fool of myself.

"Not long. Two hours, maybe a little longer. But I'd like to scout around the palace before we go in, and we'll have a better chance of getting out of town unnoticed if we leave before noon."

"Before noon? What time is it?" Cal nodded to a bed-side clock. "Eleven-thirty?" Livvie bounded out of bed. "I can't believe I slept so long. You should have awakened me sooner. I don't want to slow you down…."

He smiled at her, and she stopped speaking. He didn't smile nearly often enough—not that he'd had much reason, of late. "You needed the sleep, and we're fine on time. Don't worry."

They were just about to walk back into the lion's den. Menendez had well-armed soldiers and a palace built like a fort. She had Cal, one gun, and a handful of knives. And he was telling her not to worry.

"Think we'll make it?" she asked softly.

He wouldn't lie to her, not now. Maybe not ever. "Fifty-fifty."

She nodded and headed for the door. "I found toothpaste in the bathroom last night. If I'm going into battle I might as well have fresh breath and a white smile." She gave him a wide grin, for effect. *I'm not afraid. This is not a mistake.*

Heaven help me, what have I done?

Chapter 8

They stayed in the jungle, moving through and around lush, dense growth, much as they had during the earlier days of this bizarre journey. The difference today was that, now and then, Livvie caught a glimpse of the road just a few feet away. The dirt road that was just wide enough for a car or a jeep led from the little town where the general's soldiers went for recreation—the town where she and Cal had spent the night—to General Menendez's palace. With every step they took, they were closer to the palace.

With every step she took, Livvie's heart came closer to choking off her breath.

"If we get separated," Cal had told her as they'd walked away from town just before noon, "you follow this road back to town and you go straight to Adriana."

She wasn't fooled. Separated? What he really meant was if he got hurt or killed, she was to hightail it back to town. She needed to do this—she didn't feel that she had any choice. But if Cal got hurt…

"I wish there was more time," she said softly.

He didn't so much as slow down. "Time for what?"

Time to get to know you; time to take a deep breath; time to enjoy this beautiful place… "Time for you to get me out of here and come back in with a proper team to rescue Elsa and Ria."

He glanced over his shoulder.

"Yes, that was your idea," she said. "And it was a very good idea. There's just no time. Do you think I like this?" she asked. "Do you think going back into that awful place for even a minute is on my list of things I want to do before I die?"

"We can turn back anytime."

She hurried to catch up with him. "No, we can't."

They hadn't seen a vehicle or another living person for the past hour, since they'd left town. And they still had at least an hour's walk ahead of them. Cal had assured her they wouldn't have any trouble on their journey to the palace. Menendez wouldn't be looking for her so close to home, not after all this time. He wouldn't think she could be so foolish.

The coming journey away from the palace, with Elsa and Ria in tow, would be an entirely different story.

"So, what's with you and Adriana?" she asked casually.

"She's a friend," Cal answered in a low voice.

She tried not to make that noise, she really did. But there it was. A scoff. A huff. A reaction that told Cal she knew exactly what kind of friend Adriana had been to him. And still was? She tried to cover up her response with a quick "She's very beautiful."

"Yeah."

"Of course, what does that matter to a man who says no woman is worth fighting for?"

Cal just shook his head and kept on walking.

"She seems smart, too. She could probably do other things. Why would she choose to…you know?"

"Be a prostitute?" Cal clarified.

He said it so coolly, so matter-of-fact. "It just seems like she could do something else, if she wanted…."

Cal stopped and turned to face her, his mouth set in a tight frown. "If you must know, Adriana is where she is because when she was seventeen she caught the general's eye. He took her to the palace and kept her there until he got tired of her, and then he sent her to work in his own personal brothel. She was told from the beginning that if she ever caused a scene, if she complained or tried to run or refused him or any of his men, her family would pay the price."

Livvie was horrified. "Menendez threatened to kill her family?"

"No," Cal said softly.

She didn't want to know more. She didn't want to imagine what Menendez had threatened that was worse than death.

After they resumed walking, Livvie quickened her step so she could remain beside Cal. "Before I came here, I had no idea there were men like Menendez in the world," she said.

"Blame the Ozzie and Harriet upbringing."

"And Uncle Max," she added. "He drives me crazy, he's so overprotective."

"Maybe he has reason," Cal glanced down at her, without softness, without mercy. "Maybe on one too many occasions he's seen for himself that there are men like Menendez in the world."

It was a frightening thought, one she didn't want to dwell on at the moment. No wonder her uncle and Cal were so hard. They had seen things she'd been sheltered from. They'd seen ugly, terrible things that they'd diligently protected her from. She wanted to protest that she didn't need to be protected from anything or anyone, but the truth of the matter was she was glad there were men like Max Larkin and Quinn Calhoun in the world. Not that she would ever admit as much to either of them....

"Speaking of Uncle Max," Cal said casually, "you do know he's going to kill us both for going back into the palace when we were so close to getting out of the country."

"Max won't kill me," Livvie said brightly. "He might try to ground me. Twenty-six years old and grounded. That's just sad." She smiled at Cal. "You on the other hand…"

Cal grabbed her hand and pulled her deeper into the jungle. A moment after he reacted she heard the sound of an engine—a car or truck on the road. He led her behind a wide-trunked tree where they'd be completely shielded from view, and placed a finger to his lips to caution her. She didn't think anyone in a passing car would be able to hear over the sound of the car's engine, but Cal was right…better safe than sorry.

As they waited for silence to come once again, Cal didn't press her to the tree with his body, as he had on that first night when soldiers had passed close by. She almost wished he would. He had wanted her then, when he'd known full well who she was. He hadn't confused her with anyone else that night.

But they stood face-to-face with a good foot or so between their bodies. He kept his eyes on her face, as if studying her critically. She was a mess and she knew it.

She'd passed too many days without her good shampoo and scented soap, some days without any soap or shampoo at all. And she was getting mightily tired of these same damn clothes. Makeup wasn't a part of her everyday routine, but a little lip gloss and mascara would go a long way right about now.

She wondered for a moment what Cal would think of her in her good black dress, with the high heels and the pearl studs and some tastefully applied makeup. How would he look at her then?

At least this morning she'd had access to real toothpaste, and Adriana had given her a rubber band to pull her hair back. Still, she had to present a less than enticing picture. Too bad...

When the vehicle on the road had passed and all was silent again, Cal stepped even farther away from her. "Uncle Max has more than one reason to want me dead."

True, her uncle would hit the roof if he knew...but he wouldn't. What had happened between her and Cal was no one's business but their own. "What Max doesn't know won't hurt him," she said casually, as if that afternoon meant nothing to her, as if it had been a hot vacation fling.

Some fling. She'd been swept away and ready to fall over the edge of love everlasting, and the whole time Cal had thought she was someone else.

Ah, romance. Ah, her romantic life! When it came to men, no matter what the decisions offered to her were, she always seemed to make the wrong one. Her love radar was wonky. It had to be! Why else would she look at Cal and wish that he would kiss her the way he had last night? And why on earth did she want him to make love to her again...only this next time she'd make damn sure he knew who she was. She wanted him to look at her…she wanted him to call her name…

"Let's go," he said crisply, turning his back on her.

Cal parked Livvie in a safe, secluded spot and ordered her to stay put while he did a quick recon around the palace. She had everything she needed here; the backpack of supplies with plenty of water and a couple more protein bars. He even gave her one of his knives…not that he thought she'd actually use it. But the way she gripped the handle so tightly—maybe it made her feel better to be armed.

"I don't want to stay here by myself." She kept her voice low, even though there was no one else around to hear. The palace was close, but they were far from the grounds proper.

"I'll just be gone a few minutes," Cal said. He couldn't possibly circle the palace with Livvie beside or behind him and remain unseen and unheard. Surely she knew that. She didn't argue again. He took her face in his hands, tipped her face back, and made her look into his eyes. "Now is not the time to worry. In a couple of hours, when we go inside, that's when you can start worrying."

She nodded quickly.

"Unless you get smart and change your mind…"

"No." She actually gave him a smile. "We're in this together, Cal. You never give up, do you?"

"Me?" He let his hands fall. "You definitely have Larkin blood, princess. You're a lot more like your Uncle Max than you'd like to admit."

There were no more words of complaint. Livvie settled down in a clear spot, sitting on the folded tent with the knife in her hand, and Cal dismissed her as best he could and crept silently to the hidden entrance and beyond.

Menendez had gotten sloppy in the past few years, since the rebel activity had slowed to a trickle. At the palace itself security was slim—two inattentive guards at the front gate and one around back. If not for the automatic rifles those guards carried, Cal might be tempted to simply go through the front door and take what he'd come here for.

Inside those double doors Menendez was probably having regular temper tantrums, thinking Livvie and whoever had assisted her had escaped from the country. He hated disobedience of any kind, and was one of those nuts who really would shoot the messenger who brought him bad news.

There were times when Menendez could appear to be perfectly normal. He charmed businessmen and dignitaries. He entertained visitors to Camaria with flair and charisma. But it was all a show, as anyone who knew him for very long could attest. The general was all about power and control.

The rear of the palace was even more vulnerable than the front. Cal dropped down and watched the back gate for a few minutes. All was quiet. He was tempted to go in now and grab the girls, leaving Livvie where she was and blessedly ignorant until he had the job done. But he didn't know where the kids would be this time of day, or what kind of guard they might have. Just because security looked lax on the outside, that didn't mean it hadn't been ratcheted up on the inside. Best to wait, to stick to the plan.

The palace was a beautiful place, if you were blind to what went on inside those walls. Menendez insisted that the place be well-tended, inside and out. Nothing but the best for the general.

Cal had spent happy days here, in this awful place. Happy, blissfully ignorant days. Claudia had brought him here, and he'd been so incredibly blinded by the beauty and extravagance of the palace that it had taken him too long to see beyond the glitter. Much too long.

She'd found him in a Mexican bar. There had been a fight that night. A drunken, no-holds-barred brawl, to be specific. Cal had been the last man standing. Literally. Claudia had been so impressed she'd offered him a beer and a job.

That hadn't been all she'd offered him.

When he looked back he tried to use his youth as an excuse for the mistakes he'd made. He'd been barely twenty-four when he'd met Claudia. She'd been thirty and gorgeous and exciting. He'd been fresh out of the army and at loose ends—but youth was no excuse. A child should have been able to see through Claudia's schemes.

Her cousin the general needed top-notch security because on occasion the rebels threatened to rise up, that's what she told him. There hadn't been any real fighting for years, and there wouldn't be as long as Menendez maintained his strength. Who would dare to take him on when he had his own personal army? They did face a handful of annoying rabble-rousers now and then, she'd explained, and they needed someone like Cal to train the newer recruits.

He'd done it. He'd taken Camarian boys and turned them into soldiers. Menendez's soldiers. Claudia had shared his bed, Menendez had treated him like a long-lost son, and the money…the money had been great, better than anything he could have gotten back home.

And then it had all fallen apart, on one really bad day….

Cal made his way to Livvie's hiding place. He didn't want to go back into the palace, he didn't want to face the general or his men. He didn't want to smell that sweet co-

logne that made him gag or pass by the door to *that room.*
But he would, because he had no choice. If he didn't get
the girls out of there before the uprising, the rebels were
going to tear them apart.

Livvie was right where he'd left her, with the supplies
close around her, that knife in her hand, and her eyes on
the path he'd taken when he'd left her here. When she saw
him she jumped up, ran to him and threw her arms around
his neck.

For one too-brief moment, he didn't breathe.

"What's wrong?" he asked. Could be so many things.
A snake, a spider, an iguana, a bug she couldn't identify…

"Nothing now," she said softly. She didn't let go. He felt
her hand in his hair, her breathing quick and warm on his
neck. "I just, I just…" she drew back a little but did not let
go. "Don't leave me alone again, please."

Livvie wasn't at all like Claudia. She wasn't like any
other woman he had ever known. It was so easy, so natural, to wrap his arms around her and hold on. Was he being
a fool all over again? Another beautiful woman was leading him into Lazaro Menendez's palace. He had to wonder if the outcome would be any better than last time.

"Now what?" she whispered.

"We wait."

Livvie nodded. Her arms stayed around his neck for a
few seconds longer, then she dropped them slowly and
backed away.

"You're speeding," Livvie said as she peered over the seat.
Cal kept his eyes on the road and ignored her. She pos-
itively hated being ignored!

"Are we going to eat soon? I'm starving." They were

still hours away from D.C. and the coming confrontation with Uncle Max.

A silent Cal reached onto the front passenger seat, grabbed something that crinkled loudly, and tossed it into the back seat. Livvie grabbed the package and grimaced as she realized what it was. "Beef jerky? I don't eat beef jerky."

"Sorry, princess, I'm all out of caviar."

It was the second time he'd called her princess. She didn't like the way he said the word, as if it were an accusation.

She spotted the road sign indicating the restaurants at the next exit. "A hamburger," she said, trying to remain reasonable. "We can go to the drive-through window. You must be hungry, too." He'd driven all night and through the morning, in fact. He stopped for gas, he reluctantly allowed her to go to the bathroom, he bought soft drinks and crackers…and jerky.

After a quiet moment he pulled into the right lane. Right before he drove onto the off ramp he glanced over his shoulder. Livvie's heart did a strange little flip. She had been annoyed and angry and indignant, since he'd grabbed her and tossed her into this back seat. But damn, in the right light he was a nice-looking man. Even though there was a day's stubble around his goatee, now. Even though his eyes were without sympathy for her situation.

They were nice hazelly-green eyes, anyway. And there wasn't an ounce of fat on the man, not an ounce of softness. His face was lean and edgy, his hands were large and strong. His entire body was definitely drool-worthy.

And then he ruined her moment of admiration.

"You're getting a small soda," he said.

Livvie leaned back in her seat. She couldn't figure out

why he was so testy. She'd only tried to escape through a bathroom window the one time.

"Can I sit in the front seat?" she snapped. "I'm getting damned tired of talking to the back of your head."

"Whatever you want, princess," Cal said as he pulled into the drive through line.

Once more before they began this rescue mission, Cal tried to convince Livvie that he could handle the job alone. She wouldn't hear of it. The girls would make a terrible fuss if a complete stranger, especially one who looked like Cal, entered their room through a hidden door, she said. They wouldn't get far once an alarm was raised.

Unfortunately she was right.

He lifted the trap door an inch and listened. From below all was silent, so he opened the door completely and dropped into the tunnel, a knife in one hand. When he was satisfied that all was indeed clear, he gave Livvie a silent signal and she began to climb down the ladder. She closed the door behind her, as quietly as possible.

"Cal," she whispered before he'd taken two steps.

He turned to face her, just to tell her to be quiet, but she surprised him with a kiss. A desperate, passionate, heart-filled kiss. It didn't last nearly long enough, and when she took her mouth away she whispered, "For luck."

Cal nodded and turned his back on her—on the kiss, on the luck, on the impossible ideas that had been bouncing around in his head all day. She was Max Larkin's niece, for God's sake, and he could no longer blame Raul's loco juice for the direction his mind—and another body part—had taken.

First things first. If they got out of here alive, maybe he'd see about risking his life to get laid.

There was no need to coax Livvie along, as he'd done the last time they'd worked their way down this corridor. She stayed close behind him, and even hung onto the waistband of his pants as if they might get separated if she didn't maintain contact. It was unnecessary, but he didn't tell her to let go.

She didn't know her way through these hidden tunnels, but she knew where in the palace the children's rooms were located. Together they had been able to figure out how to reach the girls by way of the secret passageways. By now Elsa and Ria would have eaten and bathed and dressed for bed, but Livvie said they usually read in bed for a while before going to sleep.

The kids should be alone, and if Livvie entered the room first maybe they wouldn't make enough noise to alarm their father or anyone else.

In and out without being noticed. He'd managed it once—but twice? The first time had been tricky enough, and this time he'd have three women with him, not one. It was a foolish mission, an unnecessary risk. He hadn't had a choice in the matter, not really. This was for Kelly, as much as it was for those girls or for Livvie.

Cal told himself that as he passed the door to the room where Lazaro Menendez had tortured him for days. Even now, he wasn't exactly sure how many days. More than a week, less than a month. With no windows, no clocks, no scheduled meals, time had lost all meaning, for those days. Was there anyone in that room now? All was quiet, but that didn't mean some poor slob wasn't in there, just waiting for Lazaro's next visit. They'd be quiet, if they could, hoping not to draw attention to themselves. Hoping Menendez would forget they were there…

They reached a turn in the hallway and found themselves in a narrow, dimly lit corridor that ran behind the rooms in the wing where Menendez's daughters lived. It had not been used recently, by the look of things. A massive spiderweb draped elegantly along one side of the hallway, a piece of nature's art. Dust, dirt and mold covered the concrete floor and the stone walls. Livvie didn't say anything about the conditions, but she crouched behind Cal and held onto his waistband a little bit tighter.

Cal stopped before a narrow door and laid his hand on the doorknob. "If we figured right, this is it."

Livvie let go of him and stepped to his side. She would go in first, as planned, but he would be right behind her.

He opened the door, and they were both relieved to see the little girls' dresses that hung in the closet. Frills and lace, lots of pink and yellow and pale blue. Livvie moved those dresses aside and very cautiously opened the closet door from the inside.

The room was lit with the dim light from a bedside lamp, and Cal looked beyond Livvie's shoulder to see two young, dark-haired girls watching from their beds with wide, surprised eyes. They both held small hardback books. The eldest one wore glasses.

The girl with the glasses, Elsa, spoke first. "You're alive," she whispered.

Cal waited in the shadows of the closet while Livvie walked across the room to the girls. She raised a finger to her lips to caution the girls to speak softly, and then she whispered, "Yes, I'm very much alive."

"Papa said you were dead," Ria said in awe as she lowered her book to the bed. "He said you got all blown up in a helicopter."

Cal gritted his teeth. Fine thing to tell a child! He shouldn't be surprised.

Livvie stood between the twin beds and reached out her arms. She took one of Ria's little hands and one of Elsa's in hers and held on tight. "Girls," she said softly, "I think it would be best if we all left the palace tonight. Would you like to come with me?"

They didn't have to think twice, but leapt from the beds with smiles on their faces. Both girls hugged Livvie with all their might, thin arms wrapping around her for a quick, enthusiastic, group hug. The reaction was only confirmation for Cal that their father would not take care of them, as any proper father should. They wanted out of this place as much as Livvie had, as much as he once had. So they wouldn't be alarmed, Livvie told them that someone was here to help them, and she nodded to the closet. Cal stepped out. The girls were startled by his appearance, but since they had been warned they were not afraid.

Cal turned his back while the girls dressed. No need to rush them out in their nightgowns. He didn't mind waiting here for a few minutes. This room didn't reek of the general's cologne, the way Livvie's room had. But a few minutes was all he could allow.

While the girls dressed and gathered a few of their personal belongings, they talked. Livvie cautioned them to speak in soft voices and they did, but their words were chilling. One of the reasons Elsa was so anxious to leave was that her father had told her it was time for her to marry. She was fourteen years old and could pass for twelve. She was to meet her husband-to-be in just a few days. He was an older man, a political ally, and the marriage would make him family, her papa said.

When Elsa had complained to her father she did not want to get married, he'd told her she had no choice in the matter.

No wonder Nina Menendez had run from the general and taken the girls with him. At least she'd been smart enough not to come back.

For all the good it had done her...

The girls dressed in jeans, T-shirts and tennis shoes, and they each carried a small backpack stuffed with favorite clothes and books and personal things. Cal studied them critically and shook his head as they filed into the closet. The kids were small, skinny, weak. Getting them all out of the country without incident was going to be tough.

But not as tough as leaving them here.

Livvie again cautioned them to be silent, and held their hands as she followed Cal. They retraced their steps, heading for the tunnel exit. As long as the girls weren't missed until morning, they'd be fine. They wouldn't rest tonight, but would head directly for the Guyana border. If they were far enough from the palace and stayed off the roads, no one would find them.

Did he have that much luck left?

They reached the ladder, and Cal climbed quickly. He'd make sure all was clear above before letting the women make the climb. He was halfway up the ladder when the trapdoor opened quickly. A guard pointed his gun down, into the tunnel and directly into Cal's face.

"Run," he ordered as he dropped back down into the tunnel and drew his pistol.

Livvie and the girls turned, but they didn't get far. Four

armed soldiers had crept along the tunnel behind them. They stood there, weapons raised, and blocked the path. Cal had the pistol in his hand and the bullets that remained in it, and three knives. If he was alone he'd give it a try…but in this narrow, confined space, there was no way to take them all on without certain danger to Livvie and the girls.

Behind him, the guard who had been waiting at the top of the ladder dropped into the tunnel. They were trapped.

The soldiers in the corridor parted, and Lazaro Menendez stepped through. Cal placed himself in front of Livvie and the girls, for all the good it was going to do them. The scent he despised, sweet and nauseating, reached him like a wave of sickness.

Menendez was truly surprised to see Cal. His dark eyes went wide, and he actually gasped. Once he recovered, he smiled widely. "You! I thought you were dead."

"A common misconception," Cal said. He didn't drop his gun.

The general nodded to the ladder behind Cal. "After Miss Larkin's unfortunate escape, I added a silent alarm to the tunnel exits. I thought the cautionary measure too little too late, but apparently it was a good decision." His false smile faded. "Drop your gun."

"I'll make you a deal," Cal said. "I'll hand over the gun and I'll stay, if you'll let the women go."

"No deals," Menendez said. "You have nothing to deal with."

Cal aimed his pistol at Menendez. "Your life for theirs?"

The general was not concerned. He looked beyond Cal to the soldiers who had come down by way of the hidden hatch. "If Mr. Calhoun doesn't lower his weapon within five seconds, shoot her." He pointed. Cal glanced back to see that one of the soldiers shifted his weapon so the muzzle almost touched Ria's head.

The little one. The bastard. Of course. He had plans for Livvie, and Elsa was to marry one of his political allies, so that left the eleven-year-old as the expendable daughter.

"One…" the general began.

Cal stared at Menendez and mentally reviewed his options. He could kill the general anyway. The soldiers would be surprised. If all went well maybe Livvie and the older girl would get out. Maybe. He wouldn't be quick enough for Ria, though.

"Two…"

It should be an acceptable sacrifice. A little girl he hadn't met until tonight for the life of this man. This sick…

"Three…"

…murderous, disgusting man who took pleasure in the pain and suffering of others. Who didn't deserve to live….

"Four…"

Cal dipped down and placed his gun on the concrete floor, muttering a curse.

"I had no idea you when you came to work for me that you had a weakness for children. How odd. How unfortunate for you. The knife, too," Menendez said with a wave of his hand. "All of them. If I remember correctly, you will be wearing more than one."

Cal drew one knife from the sheath at his waist and another from his pocket, and he placed the two knives on the floor beside his gun. Before the night was over would he have the chance to go for the blade strapped to his ankle? Maybe. Maybe not. "Let them go," he said as he stood. "You don't need them."

"Perhaps I don't *need* them, but I *have* them. They are mine to do with as I wish, all three of them." This time Menendez's wide grin was genuine. "As are you, Quinn Calhoun."

Chapter 9

"Wait just a minute," Livvie said in her best school-teacher voice. "Where do you think you're taking us? Get your hands off of me!" One soldier handled Elsa in a much-too-rough manner, and Livvie reacted. "There's no reason to drag the child. Release her this instant!"

Cal said nothing. He walked directly before her, only this time she didn't get to hold on to his waistband. Menendez had handcuffed Cal's hands behind his back. The four of them were surrounded by armed guards who moved in a synchronized step. She should be scared, but at the moment she was mostly angry. This was her fault. She'd insisted that Cal bring her back into the palace—she'd willingly put her life and his on the line for Elsa and Ria. And now all four of them were in serious trouble.

They reached a series of doors and Menendez stopped. The entire entourage came to a halt behind him, and Cal finally turned to look down at Livvie. She could read nothing from the expression on his face. Not fear, not anger. Not regret. "I think this is where I get off." He lowered his head slightly and whispered in her ear. "Hang on, princess."

She knew exactly what he meant. The rebels would be arriving in another day—or two? Soon, anyway. Maybe they could escape during the chaos. All they had to do was be strong for a while longer. A day or two had never seemed like such a long time! "You, too."

He shook his head slightly, and his eyes darted to the closed door of one particular room. One of Menendez's guards stood before that door, searching for the right key to unlock it. The rattle and the grating scrape of metal on metal as he tried a key that would not fit was loud in the narrow hallway. He muttered, the general added a word of coarse encouragement, and finally the right key slipped into the lock and turned. The unlocked door swung open.

No light burned in the small room that was revealed, but enough drifted in from the hallway for Livvie to see chains anchored into the wall. A sturdy wooden chair with straps on the arms. A car battery with wires attached. A whip hanging from a peg in the wall.

Cal's back….

"No," she said softly. Her eyes cut to Menendez. "You're not taking him in there."

The general wore a sick, smug smile. She had seen this same smile before, as he looked at her over the dining room table and planned the evening to come. "I owe you a debt of gratitude, Miss Larkin, for bringing Mr. Calhoun back to me so I can finish what I started such a long time ago. I do so hate unfinished business."

Her heart started to beat so fast and hard she could hear

it. Feel it. She'd been willing to come back here because she didn't have anything to lose, but suddenly she realized she did have something to lose. Something precious. Cal. And she had brought him here. She had all but forced him... She took a step toward Menendez.

"Livvie," Cal said calmly.

She stopped.

The general was surrounded by armed men. The girls were watching, wide-eyed and afraid. Rushing forward would only get someone hurt—and it probably wouldn't be her. Not yet, anyway.

"Livvie," Cal called her name again as one of the guards grabbed his arm and steered him toward the room. "I'm glad it was you," he said softly.

Two more soldiers joined Cal and they escorted him into the small room. Menendez promised that he'd join them shortly, and then he turned to Livvie. He had never looked so pompous, so satisfied with himself. "My soldiers will assist you in making yourself at home here once again, Miss Larkin. I will discuss your distressing behavior with you after I am finished here." Before she could respond, his eyes cut to his frightened daughters. "Girls, I'm very disappointed in both of you. A man has every right to expect loyalty from his family, as well as his employees."

Ria started to cry, and Elsa's lower lip trembled.

"We should talk right now," Livvie said, trying to divert the general's attention away from the room where Cal had been taken. She couldn't see him, but she heard the sound of heavy metal clanking. The chains. Cal said a few words in Spanish, words she didn't understand. His statement was followed by the smacking sound of flesh on flesh and the loud squeal of a disturbed piece of furniture scraping across the floor.

The general was also listening to what went on in that room, but his reaction was very different from hers. He smiled. "I will deal with you later." With a wave of his hand, he ordered the soldiers to take his prisoners away. Livvie's heart fluttered. That's surely what they were. Prisoners.

The armed guards took Livvie and the girls away, and the general entered the room where Cal waited. He closed the door firmly behind him, and the sound reverberated down the long, cold hallway.

He should've made her stay in the back seat. At least then he wouldn't have to look at her.

Lucky for him D.C. got closer with every mile that passed. Also lucky for him, Max Larkin's niece had fallen asleep a couple of hours ago.

It wasn't like he was looking for a woman. He was never going to look for a woman again, except for the occasional casual encounter for purely sexual reasons. Women were nothing but trouble, and he had the scars to prove it.

He still had nightmares about shooting Claudia, which was one of the reasons he didn't sleep much anymore. He played that day over and over again, in his nightmares. In his dreams he saw Claudia drag that kid from his group of friends, boys who'd been playing ball in the street. He watched her shoot him in the head, shocked and unable to move. Then he watched in horror as she grabbed hold of another frightened child—another boy who was not as quick as his friends who ran away—and take aim once again.

She'd heard him when he told her to stop; he knew it. She'd lifted her head and looked him in the eye and smiled, while she continued to hold on to the child and the gun, and that's when he'd known the truth. The woman he was in love with didn't really exist. She was a picture painted in his mind out of smoke and mirrors and hope. Claudia was as sick as her cousin Lazaro. She'd just shot one boy and was about to shoot another one, all because there were rumblings that the rebels were organizing in this little village.

Rumblings were all they had. There were no weapons here, no rebels. The general had probably started the rumors himself. This was his way of making sure the people stayed afraid. Of him, of his soldiers.

Cal felt his heart climb into his throat. He couldn't let Claudia shoot another child.

Maybe if he'd aimed for her arm or her shoulder, things would've turned out differently, but he hadn't. He'd shot his lover between the eyes. If he'd made a quick escape then and there, maybe the other soldiers wouldn't have gotten their hands on him and taken him back to Menendez, but he hadn't. He'd stood over her body and mourned for the woman who had never existed.

"Are we there yet?"

Cal jerked his head to the side to find Livvie Larkin staring at him. Her smile was soft, her cheeks flushed with sleep, her hair was mussed. She looked almost as if she'd just…no, he could not allow his mind to go there.

"Five more hours, maybe," he said.

She nodded and closed her eyes again, but didn't go back to sleep.

"So," she asked in a purely conversational voice. "Do you work for Uncle Max's company?"

"I'm a troubleshooter."

"For the government?"

"*Freelance.*"

She nodded and hummed, and tried to comb her hair with long, pale fingers. "Is getting women out of troublesome situations part of your job description?"

"*No, thank God.*"

Instead of being insulted, she laughed. He liked that about her, that she could laugh. "If this isn't an usual assignment for you, then how did you know to plant yourself outside that bathroom window when I tried to sneak out?"

"*It's what I would've done,*" *he admitted.*

Livvie sighed sleepily. Maybe if he was lucky she'd drift off for a couple more hours.

"*So, you and I are a lot alike,*" *she said.*

He'd never met anyone he was less *like.*

"*No way in hell.*"

It wasn't a nightmare this time, it was real. Cal's arms were suspended over his head, just as they'd been last time, his ankles were bound with thick, coarse rope. Somehow the guard who'd tied that rope had missed the knife at Cal's ankle. Not that he could get to it himself. Not now, anyway. Eventually, they might release him for a few minutes so he could eat. Menendez liked his victims to be healthy for as long as possible.

But that wouldn't happen for a very long time, not until they were sure he was incapable of causing them trouble. Then again, if they remembered that that's how he'd escaped last time, killing two soldiers in the process, they might just let him hang here.

His shirt had been cut off almost immediately, but Menendez had started this game slowly. He'd talked for a while, making Cal wait, giving him a good chance to look over the whip, and the knives, and the car battery and attached jumper cables sitting on the small wooden table at the general's side. Menendez played with a small knife while he talked. He spoke with emotion about his beloved cousin Claudia, about his trusted employees Reiner and Alejandro. He even talked about Livvie and how beautiful she was, how much fun he was going to have with her when the time came.

The scent of the general's cologne was as flowery and sickening as it had been six years ago, getting stuck in Cal's nose and his lungs. He could almost gag on it, the scent was so strong. It brought back old memories, that odor. It filled his lungs and caught in his throat, and for no physical reason his back began to hurt. To sting and burn. And Menendez hadn't touched his back, this time. Not yet, anyway.

The first blow came without warning; the general's fist landed solidly on the still-healing wound on Cal's side, the wound Raul had worked so hard to doctor. He hit it again, and again, and then ripped away the bandage to expose the injury and deliver another blow to the raw wound. Cal saw stars, his body lurched, fresh blood began to run…but he didn't make a sound.

"Who sent you here to collect the woman?" the general asked as he almost daintily wiped blood off his fist. "Tell me and I will reward you with a quick death."

It was such a blatant lie, Cal almost laughed. He did manage a smile. "But before that happens you can sell me some swampland in Florida."

Angry—not about the swampland comment, which he probably didn't get, but because Cal had dared to smile—Menendez swung his fist again. Hard, and with precision. Pain radiated from the point of contact outward, seeming to reach through his entire body in waves that wouldn't end. Cal's vision swam and he almost blacked out. Almost.

The longer he stayed awake, the more time Livvie and the girls would have. The guards wouldn't harm them, he knew that. They were keeping the girls and Livvie on ice until Menendez got bored with Cal. So—he couldn't black out, and he couldn't allow the general to get bored.

Only two days, maybe a day and a half, before the rebels' attack. If she played it cool, Livvie would last that long, and maybe she'd even be able to protect the kids. She'd try, that's for sure. She'd put herself between them and harm, he knew that about her.

Cal didn't think he'd last two days. Even if he did, there was no guarantee that the rebels who found him wouldn't put a bullet in his head. Or worse—what if they didn't find him at all? This room was soundproofed, and it was in a secret part of the palace far away from the fine hallways and lavishly decorated rooms. He could yell all he wanted, and no one up there would hear.

He should've run from this place years ago, as soon as he'd been told about the secret hallways and the sound-proof room where the general *interviewed* his enemies. Only a truly sick man would've built this secret section, with its escape hatches and hidden doorways. But he hadn't run. He'd let Claudia explain it all away

"Maybe I didn't come here for her," he said, his voice gruff. "Maybe I came here for you and decided I liked her better."

"I don't believe you," Menendez said softly. In contrast with his soft voice, the blow to Cal's wound was fierce.

Cal screamed this time, and the blackness that had threatened earlier engulfed him. He fought, pushing away the darkness, hanging onto the pain because it kept him lucid, but it was a losing battle. His body had already been pushed to its limits, and it shut down in self-defense.

When Cal opened his eyes a few seconds later, Menendez was opening the door. He'd had enough of Cal, for the moment. It was no fun to torture an unconscious man.

Livvie was next.

"You've lost your touch, you sick son of a bitch," Cal said hoarsely. "Is that all you've got?"

When Menendez turned, Cal smiled.

She and the girls were being held in the same room, at least for the time being. The same room where she and Cal had found Elsa and Ria reading in bed. An armed guard was posted in the secret corridor and another stood in the hallway proper, just outside the door.

All was quiet, for now. An hour ago Elsa and Ria had both managed to fall asleep. Elsa hadn't said a word, but she'd cried herself to sleep. Ria had not cried. She'd held on to her sister and hidden her face from everyone—even Livvie.

The girls slept in the same bed, leaving one twin bed for Livvie. But she couldn't sleep. She couldn't even sit.

What was happening to Cal?

Now she knew why Reiner hadn't simply shot Cal, on that night when the two mercenaries had blown up the helicopter and injured Cal so badly, before dying at his hand. Now she understood why the fair-haired mercenary had ordered the other one not to kill Cal. Menendez wanted him alive—at least for a while. He wanted Cal alive and in that room, so he could finish what he'd started years ago. She shuddered, and tears stung her eyes.

Her mind didn't want to wrap itself around the concept
that any man would actually do such things. That there
were rooms like that one, where men were tortured and
killed. Cal was in that room, and there was no telling what
Menendez was doing to him. Her body trembled, her blood
ran cold. What was happening to Cal wasn't fair, it wasn't
right. With every ounce of her body and soul, she wanted
to stop what was happening. And she had no idea how to
do that.

Cal's last words to her should be cryptic, but they
weren't. She'd known exactly what he'd meant as the
words left his mouth. *I'm glad it was you.* Maybe he had
made love to her thinking she'd been someone else in another time, but now that the drug had worn off and he was
himself again, he was glad to know that she'd been the one
in that bed with him. Not a woman from the past, not a
memory or a ghost, but *her.*

Even though he was here again, even though she'd
dragged him back into this palace and he was in that terrible room…a place she now knew he had been in before… He said he was glad.

Livvie went to the window and looked out on darkness.
She'd been in a similar position before, hadn't she? She'd
asked for a miracle and gotten one, in the form of Quinn
Calhoun.

Now it was her turn to save him…but how?

*Livvie's stomach turned as she glanced through the
windshield to the top floor of the apartment building, where
her uncle was waiting. Uncle Max. She dreaded the coming confrontation.*

"He just doesn't understand," she explained to Cal.

"Max is so rigid and unemotional and boring. He's a stodgy old man, and he wants me to be just like him."

Her escort left the driver's seat, rounded the car, and opened her door for her. Was it her imagination, or did a small smile threaten to soften his harsh face? Cal, smiling? Must be a trick of the light.

"All right, he's not all that old," she said as she left the car. *"But he acts like an old man. He's a dreary stick in the mud and he wants me to be an old woman before my time."*

"He's protecting you because you're family," Cal explained as they walked toward the well-lit main entrance to the apartment building.

"Maybe I don't want to be protected."

He didn't respond to that statement, but the hint of a smile was gone. Instead his jaw twitched and his eyes went hard.

Cal asked the doorman to call up and alert Max Larkin that his niece was on the way. He walked with Livvie to the opposite side of the lobby and pushed the up button, and they waited silently until the doors opened.

"Can I trust you not to try to escape before you get to the top floor?" he asked as she stepped onto the empty elevator.

So, this was it. *"You're not riding up with me?"*

He shook his head. *"You're on your own, princess."*

"You really shouldn't call me that," she said as the doors began to close. *"It's kind of insulting for a grown…"*

The doors closed before she finished her sentence and the elevator began to rise. Before she reached the top floor it occurred to her—she didn't even know Cal's last name.

He'd been in this room for hours, surely, but time had ceased to have meaning. Cal licked his dry lips and took a breath that didn't come easily. With no clock, no window, no routine to mark the passage of time, everything slowed. No, it came to a complete stop. It seemed as if he'd been here for hours.

What if he was wrong? What if he'd only been here for minutes, and it just seemed like hours? It was a horrifying thought, one Cal couldn't afford to dwell on.

There were just three of them in the room now—one armed guard at the door, the general and Cal. A soldier or two probably waited in the hallway, not because there was any chance that Cal might escape, but to make sure the general was not disturbed.

Cal knew the drill. When Menendez got tired of his games, one of the soldiers in the hallway would be given the order to execute the prisoner. That order wouldn't come for a very long time. Days, weeks, months.

A while back, Menendez had gotten tired of hitting Cal's wound. Maybe he was physically tired of delivering the blows; maybe he was simply bored. A knife came next; a small, sharp bladed weapon the general used to make small cuts across Cal's stomach while he talked about the old days. How much he'd trusted Cal, how disappointed he'd been, how glad he was to have him back again.

Cal didn't make a sound. He didn't beg or yell or scream. He couldn't stop his body from flinching and jerking, but he didn't have to give the general the satisfaction of showing how much it hurt.

When the knife failed to have the desired effect, the general reached for his most-favored weapon. That damned whip. Menendez didn't order the soldier at the door to turn Cal's face to the wall. Not yet, anyway. He used the whip on Cal's torso, aiming for the wound but delivering the blows sparingly since he realized Cal was close to passing out once and for all.

He didn't want death; he didn't want Cal to drift off into comforting darkness of any kind. Not yet, anyway.

No, there was no time in this room. There was just pain, and the smell of cologne and blood.

And her. Whenever he thought about passing out or giving up, Cal turned his mind to Livvie. She had no real survival skills, no special weapons training, no way to defend herself. But she had a good heart and she insisted on doing what was right, no matter what the cost. He had forgotten there were people like that in the world.

So he thought about her when he smiled at Menendez, when he shook himself out of the unconsciousness that threatened. He wasn't a saint himself so he didn't simply think about her heart. He thought about her body, and her face, and the way she kissed. He tried to remember making love to her, but the images were fuzzy. Indistinct. He should have bedded her one more time, when he'd had the chance, so he'd have a decent memory to hang onto. Max be damned.

She deserved so much better than the hand she'd been dealt. Her parents, Max, the men in her life, coming here…him. She deserved a man who would help her to recreate that sitcom childhood she remembered so fondly. Picket fences; meat loaf on Tuesdays and spaghetti on Thursdays; alarm clocks and minivans. All the things he wasn't and would never be.

Since he couldn't be that man, he thought about her body, and the way she laughed, and her eyes…

Cal was chained to the wall and his feet were bound together. Since he wasn't Houdini, he wasn't going anywhere. But occasionally he thought about striking out. He thought about summoning all the strength he had left, lifting his legs, and kicking Menendez square in the chest with his feet.

He was saving that for the time when the general got bored.

Before that time came, the door swung open. Annoyed at being interrupted, the general spun on the intruder with his whip raised.

"*General,*" the young soldier said as he took a step back. "*Rebeldes.*"

The whip lowered. Annoyed, the general asked, "Where?"

"*En el palacio. Están por todas partes.*"

Menendez sent the soldier who had been guarding the door and the one in the hallway to fight, and he turned to Cal one last time. "You did this."

"I wish I could take credit, but I can't." He did wonder about the timing. The attack was early. For once, the general's soundproof room had worked against him, not for him.

"No, it is your fault. All of it." Menendez walked toward Cal, that damn whip in his hand. "I am not blind or deaf! In the months after your escape, I heard whispers of the way they worshipped you. You turned my own people against me with your defiance."

Only this time they were smarter than they'd been in the past. They'd hung back for years, building their base, buying weapons, getting stronger so when they struck they wouldn't be swatted down. Even Menendez had relaxed, believing the movement to be dead.

"I'm glad I lived to see this," Cal said.

Menendez raised his whip and rushed forward, but this

time Cal didn't hang there and wait for the blow. He raised up his legs and kicked with all the strength he had left. It was enough to send Menendez back and back until he fell, sprawling half inside the door, half out.

When the general raised up he didn't reach for the whip that had fallen to the floor. He unholstered his pistol.

"You won't live to see anything," Menendez promised as he took aim.

"This way!" Livvie ran, leading the way along the austere, narrow corridor. Raul and two of his men were right behind her. It was strange to see the healer dressed in a dark green uniform and armed to the teeth, but the look suited him. Too well, in fact.

The girls were safe with Dulcinea, who had turned out to be an ally in this quick war. Remembering some of the things the maid had said to her during her stay, her warnings to be careful, Livvie had decided to take a chance. She'd told the guards she needed food and something to drink, and when they'd balked she'd asked for Dulcinea. A quick explanation and her job had been done. Dulcinea had taken one of the general's vehicles to the village where Solana lived. She'd raised the alarm, and in a matter of hours the place had been swarming with rebels who were better armed and more dedicated to their cause than the general's soldiers would ever be.

When the first angry rebel had suggested holding the children hostage in order to bring their father out, Livvie had been there to protect them.

There was no one posted outside the door where Cal was being held, but the door to that room was open and she heard voices. Angry voices. She smiled as she increased her pace. He was alive. She'd know that aggravating, beautiful voice anywhere.

Raul placed a stilling hand on her arm as they neared the open door. Cal wasn't alone in there. The other voice belonged to General Menendez. Did the general know he had nothing left to lose? The rebels had taken control of the palace in less than half an hour.

Livvie paid no attention to Raul's caution. She ran forward until she could see into the room.

The sight almost stopped her heart. Menendez held his gun on a very still, very bloody Cal. She couldn't tell if he'd been shot or not, there was so much blood.

"Hey!" she shouted, and Menendez turned to face her. "Get *away* from him! Game's over. You lose."

"The game isn't over until I say so." He shifted quickly so that his gun was aimed at her.

Behind the general, Cal moved. Not a lot, just a flinch, a lifting of his head. His eyes opened slowly and he looked at her. He mouthed the word *duck,* then lifted his legs slowly.

Before Menendez could fire, Cal kicked the man in the back, sending him flying through the door. Livvie did as he had instructed. She ducked, making herself as small as possible and rolling out of the way. When the general flew inelegantly through the door Raul fired. Two shots.

Menendez went down hard and Livvie ran into the room where Cal dangled from the wall, much too bloody and much too still. He had put everything he had into kicking Menendez into Raul's line of fire…and he hung there as if he were…no, not dead. She wouldn't allow him to be dead.

"Cal," she said frantically. "Wake up. Come on." She reached up and grabbed one of the chains that restrained him. "Where are the keys? I can't get you down unless I can find the keys."

He lifted his head, his eyes drifted open. She could see the pain in those eyes as if it were a tangible thing. "On the general's belt," he said softly.

Relieved, she actually managed a smile. "Raul, did you hear that?"

"I got it," he called from the hallway.

A moment later Raul and two rebels were there to unlock the chains and cut the ropes that bound Cal's ankles together. Raul and one of the nameless rebels handled Cal's weight. Raul tsked and cursed over the wound in his side. Cal couldn't stand on his own, so they had to hold him up as they led him out of the room where he'd been tortured. Cal only glanced at Menendez's body as they stepped into the hall.

"He's dead," Livvie said.

"Good."

"The rebels have taken the palace."

"They're early."

"Thanks to Miss Larkin," Raul said.

"Careful," Livvie said sharply as one of the rebels jostled Cal. "This is Quinn Calhoun, you know." The man took a misstep again, and this time Cal made a soft sound that told her how much that jostling pained him. Unable to stand seeing him suffer, Livvie stopped the parade and moved the clumsy man out of the way so she could take his place. Cal hesitated when she tried to place his arm over her shoulder and her arm around his waist, so she could support him as Raul did on the other side.

"I'll get blood all over you," Cal protested softly.

She held him even closer. "I don't care."

"I do."

Fortunately for her, he was in no position to argue. Livvie moved herself into place and they began to walk down the hall. One small, easy step at a time.

She had never been so angry in all her life. Cal was weak, he was hurt, every step was an effort for him…and it was all her fault.

"We make a good team, don't you think?" she said, trying to make her voice light, trying to chase back the tears.

"The best," Cal said weakly.

"When we leave this place, I say we use the front door." Her voice cracked, but just a little.

"Fine by me."

They took a few more painstaking steps. "Cal," she said softly, not caring that Raul and the others could hear. "I'm glad it was you, too."

Chapter 10

He must be dead. The bed he rested upon was soft, the light was dim, and a small, warm, delicate body curled up next to his as if it belonged there. The way it fit, so snug and right... Maybe it did belong alongside him. There was one small problem—Cal had never expected to find himself in heaven.

His body throbbed and ached from head to toe, but the pain was dull. Eventually it would fade away completely. All he needed was a little time to heal. No, he wasn't dead. Not yet, anyway. It felt so good just to lie here, with that soft flesh resting against his.

"You're awake," Livvie whispered as she rose up to look down at him.

Of course it was her. "Where are we?"

"My room in the guest wing."

Menendez was dead. The rebels had taken over. They were safe here, at least for now. "Where are the girls?"

"They're fine," Livvie answered, her voice low, as if she were afraid the full sound of her voice would hurt him. "When I called Max I asked him to do a little investigating for me. Nina Menendez has a sister who lives in Florida. As soon as traveling is a bit safer, we're going to take the girls to her."

"You talked to Max?"

She nodded and smiled. "At first he was glad to hear my voice, but then once he recovered he had far too many questions." Her smile grew a little. "We got cut off."

Which meant Max Larkin was on his way to Camaria. He would not be happy to find his niece sleeping in Cal's bed. "When did you talk to him?"

"Two days ago. He did call back a couple of hours later with the information about the girls' aunt, but—" she shrugged her shoulders "—we got cut off again."

Cal sat up slowly. His aching torso was thickly bandaged and his shoulders were strained and sore. But he was not as badly hurt as he might've been, if Menendez hadn't thought he had all the time in the world. "Max is probably already in the country."

Livvie laid a gentle but strong hand on his chest. "Doubtful. There's fighting in the capital city. The rebels have already taken the presidential palace and closed down the airport and the main roads, but the war isn't over."

"If you think a war will stop Max…"

"The palace is well-guarded," Livvie argued. "This is where their new leader has set up camp until the battle is over, the country is in complete rebel control, and elections have been arranged." She bit her lower lip, and then added, "It's Raul, did you know that? Raul Velasco. He finally told me his last name. I guess that means he trusts me now. Anyway, he's running everything by phone and computer, and he's also doctoring you because he doesn't trust anyone else to do a proper job of it."

Cal shook his head. No, he hadn't known that Raul was the rebel leader—but he wasn't surprised. The guy was young, but he was sharp and very motivated. "It'll take a while to get the country stabilized." Months, maybe years. "Max is not going to wait that long. Trust me." But he did fall back to lie on the cool sheets.

"We're not leaving here until you're completely healed." Livvie laid her hand over a neat, thick bandage, her hands so gentle he could barely feel her touch. "This time there are antibiotics and proper dressings, as well as chicken soup. We have everything here that a man needs to get better." She lowered her head and very gently kissed his chest, just above the bandage. "Cal, when I saw what he'd done to you…" Her voice broke, and Cal threaded his fingers through her hair and held on.

"Don't cry."

"I can't help it."

He held her and she cried silently, but not for very long. Livvie really did have some of her uncle in her. She was tougher than she appeared to be. In truth, she had never really needed him to rescue her.

"I lied to you," she whispered as she kissed his chest again.

His heart hitched. He didn't want to hear this, he didn't want to know. He'd ended up painting himself such a pretty picture of the princess… He didn't want to know what part of that picture was false. He didn't want to know that she wasn't perfect.

"Everybody lies," he said beneath his breath.

Livvie rose up slowly, so he could see the tears in her

eyes. "No, I don't lie. At least, not on purpose. But when I told you I could come back into the palace and risk my life because I have nothing to lose…I was wrong. I put your life on the line, I dragged you back into this terrible place and…and he might've killed you."

"He didn't."

She licked her lips. "I've never wanted to hurt anyone before, but I wanted Menendez dead when I saw you hanging there. Not in jail, not out of power. Dead. I would have killed him myself if I'd had the chance."

"No." Cal hung onto her hair a little bit more tightly. "Don't say that."

"It's the truth."

She drifted down and kissed him on the mouth; gently, as if she were afraid she'd hurt him. If he had the strength he'd turn the kiss into something proper and arousing. But he didn't. He'd lost so much blood he couldn't manage anything other than this too-sweet kiss.

Livvie took her mouth from his and smiled down at him.

"Don't go anywhere," he said in a sleepy voice.

"Not planning on it." She snuggled beside him and draped her arm over his chest. It was nice, even though he knew it wouldn't last. Couldn't last.

No, it couldn't last, but he hadn't been lying when he'd told Livvie he'd been glad she was the one. Claudia had been a bad time in his life. He'd thought what he felt for her was love, but he'd been wrong. There hadn't been anything beyond the physical with Claudia. He didn't fool himself into thinking there had ever been anything more on her end, either. She'd been sent out to find someone to train Menendez's boys, and she'd found Cal and used what she had to in order to get him here and keep him here.

He didn't want to go back to that time…not now, not ever.

If he was a different man, he might be tempted to think he and Livvie had something worth holding on to long after they left Camaria. But he was who he was, and she was Max Larkin's niece.

"I know what you did, Cal," she whispered. "Raul told me."

"I've done a lot of things."

"You know very well what I'm talking about."

He'd just as soon she'd never found out about that day. "It's not what you think. I did what I had to do, nothing more."

"You shot and killed a woman who was about to ruthlessly kill a child. A woman you cared about. You did what was right even though it cost you dearly." Her hand rested on his chest for a moment and then she made a small, tender fist. "Don't tell me you don't have a heart, Quinn Calhoun."

Cal grabbed Livvie's hand and held on. Dammit, he wasn't noble, he wasn't a damned saint. But at the moment he didn't have the strength to argue, so he fell asleep holding her hand.

Under Raul and Livvie's care, Cal healed once again. Dulcinea took over the supervision of Elsa and Ria until arrangements for travel to Florida could be made, and the job agreed with her and with them. The girls remembered their mother talking often and lovingly about the aunt they had never met. When Menendez had been alive, his estranged wife had been afraid to visit or even telephone her sister, certain she'd be found and her family would be in danger if she dared to contact loved ones. Now that the general was dead, that danger was past.

The girls were anxious to get out of the palace where

their father had made them prisoners. They remembered very little of their lives before their mother had taken them from this place and hadn't realized it was their father who was so dangerous to them. They didn't need diamonds and a fancy palace. They wanted cable TV and fast food and public school where they could make new friends. Things they would not have gotten here.

It had been three days since the rebels had stormed the palace and taken it in a brief battle. Menendez had gotten lazy and overly confident in the past four years or so. He'd taken the rebels inactivity as a sign that there was no more resistance. He thought he'd finally won.

Some of the soldiers he'd considered loyal were not; some were actually rebel spies. The employees the general had been so sure loved him, in reality detested him and were happy to assist the rebels. No wonder the palace had been taken so quickly and easily.

Livvie had been truly surprised to find that Raul wasn't just one of the rebels, but was actually their leader. He had been present that day six years ago, when Cal had shot Claudia. The child Cal had saved was Raul's little brother Tadeo—and Tadeo was also a rebel. He was Raul's right-hand man, in fact, and was more in awe of Cal than anyone else. As he should be. Cal had saved his life, and he was determined to do something with that gift.

He hadn't known it at the time, but Cal had started this new revolution. He'd inspired a handful of young men who were smart enough not to strike until they were strong enough to take the general and the president, who had run the capital city of Santa Rosa in much the same way Menendez ran his palace and enterprises in the north. There had been no hot-headed, desperate attacks.

No small strikes against the general that might alert him, or the president, to their growing strength. The rebels had planned well for the past six years, and they'd sought and found financial support outside the country. They'd waited until the time was right, and at last the waiting was over.

There was only one fly in the ointment. Scarface—Roberto whatever—had not been accounted for. He hadn't been at the palace at the time of attack. It was possible that he was one of the unnamed soldiers who had been killed or jailed in another location, but that supposition wasn't enough to ease Livvie's mind. She half expected to round a corner and see him standing there before her, waiting.

And still, she wasn't in any hurry to leave this palace she had once run from. They were safe here—she and Cal shared a room—and she knew darn well that once they left Camaria everything would change. Maybe Cal would drive her to her uncle's apartment again, and maybe this time he'd even get on the elevator with her and ride to the top floor.

But that would be as far as it went. She'd go back to Indiana in time to be there for the first day of school, and once Cal was properly healed he'd offer himself up for any and all dangerous jobs that were offered to him.

When she entered their room, Livvie found Cal standing before the window, staring out at the night just as she had been when he'd found her here. She walked to him as quietly as possible, sneaking up on him to wrap her arms around his waist and hold on tight. She grabbed him much as he had her…only he didn't fight.

He laid his hands over the arms that encircled his waist, and she rested her head against his back. They just stood there for a few moments, quiet and content and together. Both of them were much too aware that time was running out.

"I think I should get another room," he said softly.

"I don't."

Cal turned in her arms to look down at her. His arms wrapped around her but he didn't hang on tight; he just held her in place, his hands warm and strong on her back. "I'm better now. I don't need a nursemaid to keep an eye on me all night. I never did."

Livvie sighed. "Is that what you think I am? A nurse-maid?"

He didn't answer.

"Do you really think I've been sleeping beside you because you might need a doctor in the middle of the night?"

Again, she was answered with silence.

"Are you really better?"

"Yes."

"You're completely clearheaded and free of pain."

"Yes."

"Good." She took Cal's face in her hands and drew him down for a kiss. He didn't resist, but kissed her deeply. Oh, he had such a nice mouth—such an intense and perfect kiss. She didn't want to let him go, not ever again. This was right and good; her body and her heart told her so. But just when the kiss was about to move beyond perfection to something entirely new, he took his mouth from hers much too abruptly.

"Livvie…"

"Don't tell me we can't," she interrupted. She began to unbutton the shirt he wore, a plain chambray button-up Dulcinea had found for him in the soldiers quarters.

"We can't," he said softly.

"We can."

"We shouldn't," he said with less conviction.

"And you've never done anything you shouldn't before?" she teased.

She could see the silent battle within him, in his eyes and in the tense set of his jaw. "I'm trying to do the right thing, here. For the first time in my life, I'm trying to do the right thing." He swallowed hard. "You're not making it easy for me."

"You always do the right thing," she argued. "You can kid yourself, and you can kid everyone else, but I see the truth. I see all of you, Quinn Calhoun. Yeah, you're a bad-ass. I'm shaking in my boots. But guess what I found out?" She kissed him—quickly, this time. "You're a badass with a really big heart."

"Livvie…"

"Fine," she interrupted with a smile. "We won't talk about your heart, and I won't tell you what a wonderful man I think you are. We'll keep it simple. Just let me play with you for a little while, and if you still don't want to…"

"I didn't say I didn't want to," he began, and then he paused. "Play?"

She pushed his shirt off his shoulders and it fell to the floor. Smaller cuts on his torso were uncovered, but the bandage over the knife wound in his side was a stark reminder of what had happened to him. No, Cal was not completely healed. That would take a long time, she imagined. But he was here, and he was hers…and she wanted him to make love to her once, just once, when he looked at her and knew exactly who she was.

Cal had done a lot of things in his life that he knew were wrong, and this was one of them. Livvie Larkin wasn't the kind of woman who had casual sex, and she didn't use her body to get what she wanted from a man.

She put her heart and her soul into everything she did, including seducing him.

She undressed him. The shirt was easy, and when that had been tossed aside, she worked the zipper of his trousers as she pushed him gently, very gently and patiently, toward the bed. Her hands were tender but insistent, soft but relentless. He was already hard. No surprise, since lately all she had to do was look at him and he was ready.

He tried to reason this intense infatuation away. His body remembered having Livvie, his brain didn't. His brain was just playing catch-up, that's all this obsession was. It had nothing to do with the fact that she was beautiful, and sexy, and funny, and sweet, and took care of him, and wanted to save the world...

She pushed his pants over his hips and then gave him a gentle shove that sent him onto the bed. Livvie actually laughed as she pulled off his trousers and tossed them aside. Hell, if she wanted to play, he'd let her play. He might try to do the right thing, but no matter what the people in these parts thought of him, he was no saint.

Besides, it wasn't like he could hide the fact that he wanted her.

The room wasn't completely dark; light from the adjoining bathroom spilled onto the floor and almost reached the bed. But it wasn't enough to suit Livvie. She turned on the bedside lamp before she began to undress herself. No more jungle camo for her. She'd recovered her own clothes upon returning to the palace, including this little slip of a sundress that she so easily pulled over her head and threw aside. Underneath she wore a silky pair of panties. No bra.

She slithered out of the panties and joined him on the bed, crawling toward him like a cat.

Cal ran his finger from her chin to her belly button. Slowly. "You're so beautiful."

Her smile faded. "Raul hasn't been giving you any loco juice, has he?"

Cal shook his head. "No."

"I just want to make sure you're not hallucinating."

"Not tonight." He cupped one of her breasts and brushed his thumb over the taut nipple. She closed her eyes and took a deep breath, and then she damn near purred. "You are beautiful. Always, but especially now."

He drew Livvie to him and kissed her—the way a man kisses his lover. His tongue danced with hers, without awkwardness, without restraint. He caressed her while they kissed, and this time when she purred he took it into his own mouth, as if he could catch and taste it.

They kissed, mouth to mouth and flesh to flesh. Livvie was almost too tender at first, being very careful around the bandages he wore, but soon she forgot all about them. And so did he.

She took her lips from his with a low moan and laid her damp mouth on his throat, where she sucked and kissed and licked as if she were starving. Cal closed his eyes. If he were given to purring…this would be the time. Livvie's hands, soothing and sweet, swayed over his skin. She examined his arms and his chest, those curious fingers fluttering over every muscle, every curve and edge. Her hand skimmed down to his navel and lower, until her fingers wrapped around his erection and she stroked him.

Apparently she didn't want to play for very long. Very quickly, her passion soared beyond graceful seduction and into out-of-control heat. Her hands moved faster; her mouth sucked harder.

When he tossed her onto her back and the mattress bounced beneath her, she laughed. He loved the sound of that laugh because it was so real. It reached inside and grabbed him, somehow, almost as tangibly as the kisses and the caresses.

He'd been with women before and after Claudia, but this kind of pure laughter was new. The genuineness of Livvie was new.

She stopped laughing when he took a nipple into his mouth and suckled it deep. She arched, she sighed, she definitely purred. Cal dismissed every reason he had for keeping away from Livvie Larkin. For now, for this one night, her body belonged to him. He could make it purr, and dance, and he could make it scream. His tongue teased her, his hands stroked. He parted her thighs and touched her, and the purr turned into a moan.

He guided himself to her and her eyes opened. There was passion in her dreamy blue eyes. There was such fire there, in the uncontrolled desire that made her more beautiful than she had ever been. More beautiful than any woman had ever been. Her arms snaked around his neck and she held on tight.

"Look at me," she whispered.

He kept his eyes locked to Livvie's while he entered her. Slowly, gently, until she was wrapped around him tight and hot and he couldn't think about anything else but this. Her body and his, the way she moved, the way she purred. Her eyes drifted closed and she moved against him, taking him deeper, asking for more. Her legs wrapped around his, her arms held on as if she'd spin out of control if her hold on him didn't keep her grounded. Their bodies were tightly intertwined and swirling on the edge of perfect pleasure. Every small move sparked another purr, a gasp of delight, an answering move, as if they danced on this bed to their own music. Nothing else mattered. Not the past, not the future. Nothing.

He drove deep and Livvie shattered beneath and around him. She didn't purr anymore, but moaned while she held on to him and trembled. He came while she shuddered, while she whispered his name and ground against him one last time and speared her fingers through his hair.

And then he lowered himself to rest on her soft body, while she sighed and held on and kissed his neck as if they were starting all over again.

"You closed your eyes," she whispered.

"So did you." He raised himself up and brushed a length of hair away from her face. "I'm looking at you now."

"Cal, that was…"

He didn't know what she was going to say, but he suspected it would be something important. So he kissed her. He kissed her so well she couldn't possibly remember what she'd been planning to say. Tongues danced, sweat mingled, they shared a moan or two. Somewhere along the line, pretty quickly in fact, he got so lost he forgot why he'd kissed her to begin with.

He could happily remain in this bed forever. He could live here, die here, even love here…

No, this was entirely physical, like every other relationship he'd ever had. There was nothing here but need and pleasure and the perfectly natural magnetism between a man and a woman. He took his mouth from Livvie's and kissed her sweet neck, letting his lips linger and taste and arouse.

"This isn't fair," she whispered. "I want you again."

"What's not fair about that?"

"It's too soon."

He lifted his head and smiled down at her. "No it's not."

"But…" He moved inside her and she took a deep breath, then let loose with a soft, "Oh…"

All the lights were off now, but they didn't sleep. The air was too charged for sleep, her body was too uneasy for sleep.

Cal was propped up on his elbow, lying beside her. She didn't need the lights on now. She could make out the vague outline of his body, here in the dark. Most importantly, she didn't doubt that he knew very well who she was.

"I never had a teacher like you when I was in school," he said.

She laughed lightly. "Somehow I doubt you were the ideal student."

He answered with a noncommittal hum and reached out to cover her breast with one very large, very talented hand.

Livvie closed her eyes and relaxed. It was as if Cal touched her and her body went boneless. "I wish I had known you then," she whispered. "I wish I had met you when you were a child."

"Your overprotective parents would *not* have allowed you to play with me," he teased.

Livvie knew very well that she and Cal came from different worlds, that outside this bed they had nothing in common, that if she hadn't gotten herself into hot water again she never would've known what it was like to kiss Cal, to hold him, to make love in such an earthy and wild way. But she didn't want to think about such annoying realities. Not tonight.

"I would have made you take me to the prom," she said dreamily.

Cal growled.

"What kind of response is that?" She laughed lightly. "Oh, wait, I know. You don't dance."

"Never." His hand left her breast and traveled downward. Fingers brushed very lightly around her navel.

"And you don't sing."

"No."

"Well, you must at least like to *listen* to music."

His hand rested over her belly, in a proprietary manner. Just the touch of his hard hand there, just the brushing of his skin against hers, was arousing.

"Some," he said. "However, I am not especially fond of old disco tunes sung off-key."

"I'm offended," she said, halfheartedly since there was more than a touch of jesting in his voice.

Cal's hand trailed lower still and gently parted her thighs. He touched her intimately, tenderly, and the insistent throb in her body grew. He knew just where…and just how…

"You're forgiven," she whispered.

Livvie woke aching all over but also warm to the pit of her soul. She'd never known a night like this. If only it would last forever. It was still dark out, but morning all the same. In an hour or two she'd have to get up and pretend that nothing had changed.

She had changed. Everything had changed! Had Cal? For all she knew, he passed nights just like this one all the time. Maybe sex with her meant nothing to him but recreation. Fun, release, a pleasant way to pass the time. He certainly hadn't told her that he loved her, the way he had when he'd been hallucinating and thought she was another woman in another time.

Maybe he hadn't mentioned love, but she knew without a doubt that there was something extraordinary going on here. Something magical and precious. Something other than his ability to make her body do incredible things she had never known possible.

Four times.

What kind of lover would Cal be when he wasn't wounded? Last night he had been tender and demanding, raw and sweet, thoughtful and wicked. Surely no woman had ever been so thoroughly loved. Would Cal be so attentive and passionate after something so ordinary as a movie or a dinner date? She wanted the chance to find out, but she knew without a doubt that once they left Camaria everything would be different.

She didn't want to waste a minute of the time they had here by worrying about the future—or lack thereof. Beneath the lightweight coverlet, her hand rested possessively on Cal's bare hip. Her lips brushed against his shoulder, and she trailed the tip of her tongue there, tasting his skin. He had awakened her just this way, once in the night, and before she'd come completely awake he'd been inside her.

Livvie raised up slightly and brushed a strand of hair away from his face. "Cal?" she whispered. "Are you awake?"

Cal barely stirred, but from a dark corner on the other side of the room a low, tense, all-too-familiar voice answered her question. "I certainly hope so. I'm getting damn tired of waiting."

Livvie sat up, clutching the sheet to cover herself. As she did so, a tall figure rose from the chair in that dark corner.

"Max?"

Chapter 11

Max Larkin dressed like a banker, in expensive suits and silk ties and button-up shirts he did not wash himself. His black hair was always conservatively cut and annoyingly neat, and he was never unshaven—not even in the jungle. But looks could be deceiving. Cal wasn't afraid of any man, but if he was going to be wary of anyone...

On discovering that her uncle had arrived, Livvie wrapped herself in a sheet and ran to the bathroom, slowing down only long enough to grab a handful of clothes from the dresser drawer. While he waited for his niece to dress, Max paced, muttered under his breath, and cast warning glances at the bed. Cal pulled on his trousers and stood.

"How'd you get here?" Cal asked. "The borders are closed and the airport in Santa Rosa is shut down. There's a war going on, in case you haven't noticed."

"Money got me in," Max said succinctly. The pacing

stopped and he glared at Cal with surprisingly calm eyes. Not a good sign, Cal decided. "The new government is in need of cash, and I'm here representing a faction who is willing to offer them financial support."

"You bought your way in."

"You're damn right I did." Beneath that conservative suit, Livvie's uncle was solid. He was in good shape and he was quick.

He was also armed.

"Listen…" Cal began.

"Save it," Max said tersely. "There's nothing you can say to make this better. If you tell me you love her I'll know you're lying and I'll be forced to shoot you. If you tell me you don't love her and this episode was just a casual diversion, I'll be forced to shoot you."

Max was right; there was nothing he could say to make this right. Livvie deserved better…he'd known that all along. Max wanted better for her, as he should. Cal knew that if he ever found Kelly and was able to protect her, the way he should have years ago, he wouldn't want her anywhere near a man like him.

But that didn't mean he was sorry about last night. He would never be sorry.

"How about I just tell you Livvie's not a kid anymore and she doesn't need you to follow her around cleaning up after her mistakes."

"We agree on one thing." Max took a single, small step toward Cal, and there was an unspoken threat in that move. "This is a mistake."

"I didn't say that." Even though it was the truth. "Max…"

Max lifted a silencing hand, and Cal obeyed it. He had a feeling he was wasting his time trying to reason with the man.

"There's only one thing that needs to be said." Max crossed his arms over his chest and glared at Cal. "You stay away from my niece. You come anywhere near her and you'll regret it."

Most men who were on the receiving end of that glare just nodded and skulked away. Not Cal. "You'll shoot me, right?"

"If I have to."

He'd been an idiot to forget who she was and why he was here. He'd been a fool to think that he could have just one night…and what a night it had been. Before Livvie, he'd never laughed in bed before. It had never felt so good just to lie beside a woman. Was any woman worth this?

"I've been shot before," he said.

Max took one more step forward, so his face was no longer in shadow. He was pissed, and rightly so. "You've never been shot where I'm going to shoot you. Trust me, you won't want to survive." It was possible there was a subtle softening of his hard face as he studied the bandages and bruises on Cal's torso. Possible. Not likely. "What happened to you? You look like hell."

"Long story," Cal said. He wasn't about to complain to Max about anything. Not now, not ever. None of it mattered anymore, anyway.

Livvie burst out of the bathroom, slightly red-faced. Her hair was loose and her feet were bare, but she was dressed. The pants and blouse she'd grabbed from the drawer didn't match—not even close. Even Cal, who was definitely not into fashion do's and don'ts saw that much. The button-up shirt was a bright flower print; the capri pants had pale blue stripes. If Livvie even noticed the infraction, she didn't let it show.

She looked from Cal to Max and back to Cal, and then she took a deep breath, visibly unwinding. Had she expected to step out of that bathroom and find a body on the floor? And if that was the way of it, whose body had she expected to find?

"Mr. Calhoun is going to be escorted to another location this morning," Max said, no emotion in his voice or on his face.

"What do you mean?" Livvie asked. She took a step toward Cal. "Where are we going?"

"*We're* not going anywhere," Max said, biting off the words.

"I don't understand…" Livvie began.

"Calhoun's job is done. I'll escort you home myself. We leave tonight." Max looked Cal in the eye. "Tell Benning I'll pay the full fee, but I'm not entirely satisfied. You were supposed to deliver the package, not open it."

"Wait," Livvie said as Cal stormed from the room. "Cal, don't…" He didn't pay her any mind at all. The door slammed behind him, and Livvie turned to her uncle. Hands on hips, she gave him her best I'm-very-annoyed scowl. "What have you done?"

The scowl worked very well on eight-year-olds, but Max was not impressed.

"What have *I* done?" he shouted. "You…you…" Was it a trick of the light or did he blush? "I can't believe…" Max was never at a loss for words. He didn't stammer, he didn't take a moment to search for the right word. But at the moment, he was definitely struggling. "Please tell me you were careful," he finally said in a lowered voice.

This was a conversation she'd be very happy avoiding

for the rest of her life. But of course Max was not going to let her get away with that. "Not that it's any of your business," she said calmly, "but I have hormone implants."

Max made a low animal sound that was halfway between a grunt and a groan. "What about a condom?" He pointed to the doorway Cal had just stormed through. "You don't know where he's been!"

The night had ended too abruptly, her heart was still pounding with surprise and worry… And she was damned tired of explaining herself to Max. "What you really mean to say is I don't know where his…"

"Don't say it," Max interrupted hoarsely. "Just…don't." He shook his head. "Of all the men in the world…Quinn freakin' Calhoun."

He seemed so genuinely distressed she couldn't stay angry with him. Max was an overprotective uncle who seemed to think she was still a girl who needed to be sheltered from the pain of living in the real world. He'd stepped in and taken on a responsibility that wasn't his own, and he'd done the best he could. She shouldn't be angry. He was only thinking of her, she knew that. Besides, he didn't understand.

"Cal saved my life."

His normally passive face turned red and a muscle in his jaw twitched. "So send him a fruit basket!"

Livvie almost smiled. "It's not like that. I didn't sleep with him in lieu of sending a thank-you note, or because I had nothing better to do, or even because I like the guy more than I've liked anyone in a very long time." Again, that grunt, though it was softer this time. "It's more than that. Much more." She crossed the room to give Max a hug. How could she make him understand when she was so uncertain herself?

She put her arms around her uncle and rested her head on his shoulder. For a long moment he was unresponsive, stiff and cool. Anyone who didn't know and understand him might move away, feeling rejected. But Livvie didn't move away. After only a moment, Max sighed and wrapped his arms around her and held her close. "Oh, no. This is worse than I imagined. Please don't tell me you think you're in love with him."

Love. She had such a poor track record. Was her love radar still wonky? It certainly didn't feel that way. Not now, when she could still feel and smell and taste Cal, when the very thought of him made her heart lighten and her mouth twist into a reluctant smile. "What if I am?"

Max squeezed her tight. "Honey, Quinn Calhoun is not the kind of man a woman like you falls in love with. He's done things and seen things you don't ever need to hear about. His world is dangerous and unreliable, and so is he. Something you thought was…special was just another conquest to him. The son of a…"

"You're wrong," she interrupted.

Max took a deep breath and exhaled slowly. "I'm not."

"You don't know Cal the way I do." No one did, she knew that without a doubt.

But Max had never been one to give up easily. "Even if he does—" for a moment she thought he was going to choke on his own words "—have feelings for you, nothing can ever come of it. He lives in a world I've tried very hard to keep you far away from. Not only that, he's obsessed with finding his sister, and the likelihood is he never will. He's not going to stop looking for her, not until he finds his answers even though he knows there might not be any answers to be found. He's never going to settle down, Livvie. Never."

"I know about Kelly," Livvie said. "I also know that Cal will never have a nine-to-five job, or be home every night and on weekends, or coach Little League or…"

Max stepped back quickly and placed his hands on her shoulders. "Little League? You're thinking about Little League!"

Yes, she was thinking well beyond the moment, well beyond great sex. She thought of Cal and she saw more. She saw a glimpse of forever. More nights like this one, more laughter. Love, forever, babies…Little League.

She smiled. "You're right, you know. You always are. I do love Cal. Not because he saved my life, not because he came back here to rescue two little girls he didn't know, not because he makes me feel…"

"You're not thinking straight," Max said with a decided bite in his voice. "Be realistic, Livvie. You were vulnerable and afraid and alone, and Calhoun seduced you."

Livvie remained calm. "Actually, I seduced him."

Max groaned and closed his eyes. "I don't want to hear this."

Livvie leaned in and gave her uncle a kiss on the cheek. "You brought the subject up, not me." She rested her hand on his chest. Trust Max to come to the jungle in his best suit. "It doesn't matter why I love Cal, but I do. I love him with all my heart, and I'm going after him right now. If he leaves the palace, I'm leaving with him."

"I'm warning you, Olivia Larkin…"

"Don't," she said sharply, for the first time close to losing her temper. "No more threats. No more well-meant warnings. I'm not fifteen anymore, Max. I'm not twenty-two and fresh out of college. I'm a fully grown woman, like it or not, and I'm not going to allow you to chase away the only man I've ever really loved. Besides you, of course," she added when a pained grimace crossed his usually inexpressive face.

"But Quinn freakin' Calhoun…"

"Trust me," she said as she headed for the door. "Please trust me, just this once."

The hallway was quiet, and free of the tension that had filled her bedroom this morning. All was cool and serene, without outward signs of the war she knew raged beyond these walls. Livvie headed unerringly for the office that had once been General Menendez's and was now Raul's. He usually got an early start in the morning. Someone would be there, she imagined.

But she was wrong. The office was deserted.

The guard outside the palace was heavy, but inside things were very much as they had been during her stay here under Menendez's tenure. She passed the occasional armed guard, but for the most part it functioned like any other large household. This early in the morning there were only a few servants and a handful of armed guards about. Livvie didn't see anyone she knew well enough to ask about Cal.

Raul would know where he was.

She finally found Raul having breakfast. He nodded politely to her when she joined him in the dining room, then he looked over her hastily assembled outfit and grinned widely. For the first time, Livvie glanced down and realized how silly she must look. Her mismatched ensemble was the least of her problems this morning.

Raul didn't comment on her appearance, but asked her how she'd slept.

Instead of answering the question she asked, "Where's Cal?"

His smile faded. "Gone, I'm afraid."

Livvie's heart lurched. "Already? He can't be. That's impossible. Where did he go?"

Raul shook his head gently. "I'm sorry. I can't tell you."

She had been entirely too nice to Max. While he'd been pretending to listen to her, while he'd held and comforted her, he'd known very well that someone had been dragging Cal away. She'd known all along that their time together might be limited, she knew that once they left here everything would change. But she had not been prepared for their parting to be so abrupt. She needed to say goodbye. She needed to give him her address and phone number.

"I need to see Cal. Surely you can understand."

Raul was unemotional and unresponsive, giving his attention to the eggs and fruit on his plate.

His unhelpful attitude didn't help matters any. "I don't care what my uncle told you or if he paid you or threatened you…"

From close behind her, Max said, "I did none of those things."

Livvie didn't turn to look at her uncle. She stared at Raul. "Then why won't you tell me where Cal's gone?" she snapped.

Raul looked apologetic as he set his fork aside and said, "I'm sorry, Livvie. He asked me specifically not to tell you."

Driving down the road in one of Menendez's jeeps—Raul's jeep now, Cal supposed—was much easier than walking through the surrounding jungle with a woman in tow. A woman who chattered and screamed and sang badly. A woman who clung to him because he made her feel safe, for a while. Cal pushed every thought of Livvie out of his mind. That part of his life was behind him now. No, it wasn't even important enough to be called a part of his life. It had just been a few crazy days, that's all.

All that mattered was that he was armed, he was well-rested, and he was on his way out of Camaria.

He should feel much better than he did at the moment. He'd survived Menendez's abuse and was healing quickly. He'd gotten laid and gotten paid. There were no bonds on Cal, no obligations beyond finding Kelly and taking on the jobs Major Benning gave him. He'd been momentarily insane, where Livvie was concerned. Max was right to be pissed. Sleeping with Livvie had been a mistake—he'd known it all along.

But no matter how hard he tried to readjust his memories…it hadn't felt like a mistake. Not then, not now.

He parked the jeep in front of Adriana's place. Rebel soldiers were sporadically posted along the street, but if any fighting had taken place here it was long over. The soldiers looked him over, but they recognized the jeep and the rebel uniform Raul had given him. A few of them even recognized him and nodded in respect as he left the vehicle.

Cal pushed through the front door of the bar and cathouse where Adriana had been forced to work all these years. Maybe she was still here, maybe not. She didn't have to be, not anymore. Menendez and the threat to her family was gone for good.

But it had been home to her for a long time, and he hoped she had stuck around, at least for a while. He wanted to say goodbye. He wanted to thank her.

The last time, after she'd found him half-dead and nursed him back to health, he'd just left. He'd gotten up one morning, dressed, and walked away without a word.

After several days in that room he'd been in sorry shape, and Adriana had saved him. She'd put her life on the line for him. If Menendez had found him here back then…if he'd had any idea that Adriana had helped him…

There was always someone awake in this busy building, but it was a quiet place in the morning. Two rebels sat at a table in the corner and ate a hearty breakfast. An old woman who had been here since the place was built, in one capacity or another, cleaned behind the bar. He remembered her, from years past, and apparently she remembered him. Orlanda smiled gently when she recognized his face, but it was not the broad grin he remembered.

As if it had been yesterday that he'd last walked through that front door, and not six years ago, she asked, "What can I get for you this morning, Mr. Calhoun? A woman? Whiskey?"

Cal glanced at the rebels' table, and the aroma of eggs reached him. Believe it or not, he was hungry. "Breakfast," he said.

Orlanda nodded and scurried to the back room.

Cal climbed the stairs slowly, trying not to make much noise. Adriana would still be asleep at this time of day, and she might not be alone. None of that mattered. As soon as he said goodbye to her and ate his breakfast, he was on his way to the border and a two-week vacation before reporting back to work. He was going to leave Livvie and every crazy thought she'd ever sparked in him behind. He was going to kill that spark, as surely and as finally as he'd killed Claudia.

The door to Adriana's room hung halfway open. He peeked in and was surprised to see the bed made and the room deserted. She hadn't moved to another room; some of her things sat on the dresser. A brush, a hair clip, her favorite bracelet.

Maybe she'd returned to her family and had departed quickly, leaving these small things behind. He hoped so. He hoped when she got home she'd find a good man who would love her and give her fat babies. That was all she'd ever wanted.

But he wished he'd had the chance to thank her. He'd never been very good at that…thanking the people who helped him. He was much better at walking away.

By the time he reached the main room once again, Orlanda had placed a plate of eggs and ham on the bar. There was a large cup of strong coffee, too. Cal thanked her and dug in. He must be getting better, because a simple meal had never tasted so good. When he was almost finished he said, "If you see Adriana, tell her…"

The pained expression on the old woman's face stopped him. Orlanda shook her head and her eyes went wide with horror.

Cal knew that look, dammit. He set his fork aside and stifled a curse. "What happened?"

The old woman leaned in, drifting toward and over the bar. "Adriana was killed," she whispered.

Cal stood, appetite gone. "By the rebels?" It hadn't been Raul's intention to target the innocent, he knew that. But as Livvie had said…he couldn't control every man under his command, no matter how he tried.

Orlanda shook her head quickly. "No. It was Menendez's man, the one with the scar." She ran a finger over her own cheek, tracing a line from the corner of her eye to her chin. "He was very angry about the revolution, and he accused Adriana of being in league with the rebels. She denied the accusation many times, but he did not believe her. He wanted her to tell him where the American woman had gone, but she wouldn't tell." Her eyes filled with tears. "She wouldn't tell."

Livvie was almost finished packing. She'd had a long bath, and she'd changed into an outfit suitable for travel: long tan pants, a matching blouse and low-cut boots.

She supposed she should cry, but so far she hadn't. Not a single tear. Maybe she'd feel better if she cried, or if she threw something, but she couldn't do either. She felt numb, from the top of her head to the tips of her toes. Completely, totally numb.

She loved Cal, and not only had he left her without a word, he'd told Raul—a man he knew would honor any request from the hero who had saved his brother and sparked a revolution—not to tell her where to find him. Maybe he'd run because he was scared of Max, though to be honest she couldn't imagine Cal being afraid of anyone.

No, he was just finished with her. Since Max was here to take custody of her, Cal's job was done, and she was just an annoyance.

There it was, that first tear.

The tear just made her angry. She was such an idiot where men were concerned! It wasn't like Cal had ever told her he loved her. He hadn't even fudged a little and said he cared for her or was fond of her.

But he had said he wanted her. It had seemed like enough at the time, but now…

The door to her room flew open, and the man she'd been thinking about burst in uninvited.

Cal wasn't alone, she noticed as he advanced toward her.

There were three armed rebels behind him, and he was well-armed himself. He carried more than his little pistol and a couple of sharp knives; he held an automatic rifle as if he knew exactly what to do with it. Cal crisply directed one of the rebels to the passageway off the secret door in the closet and left two posted at the door.

Livvie quickly wiped that single tear away, hoping beyond hope that Cal hadn't seen it. "I thought you'd left."

"Change of plans, princess. I just found out that Scarface is alive and looking for you."

She shivered, and the ugly visage she remembered too well flashed through her mind. "How do you know?"

Cal's face softened slightly, and then a split second later went hard again. "He murdered Adriana, and he was asking about you."

"Oh." Her knees went a little weak. She and Adriana had not been friends, they'd had nothing at all in common, but to imagine what had happened to her sent sick chills down Livvie's spine. Cal saw and understood, and offered a hard, steady arm for her to hold on to.

She grabbed onto that arm and leaned into Cal just as Max bullied his way past the guards. "What the hell is this? I told you, Calhoun…"

Cal turned to face Max, but he didn't release her. Not entirely. His hold on her was distant somehow. Professional. "My job isn't finished until Livvie is home and safe."

"Your job is…" Max began hotly.

Cal didn't let him get far. "The man your niece saw leaving Nina Menendez's apartment after she was murdered is searching for her. Two days ago he didn't know where she was, but I'm betting he's found out by now. Argue all you want, Mr. Larkin, but I don't work for you this time. I work for the Benning Agency, and unless Major Benning personally calls me off, I'm not backing down from this."

Max didn't have an argument. For once. "We're not waiting until tonight to get her out of the country."

"I agree. We'll make separate plans for the Menendez girls," Cal added.

Livvie touched his arm. "I don't want to send Elsa and Ria off with someone they don't know. They've been through so much already."

Cal looked rough, but oddly beautiful. He was dressed like the rebels, in dark green and gunmetal. He needed a shave and a haircut, he needed a real doctor…he needed her. "It will be safer for the girls if they're not with you," he said crisply. "I'm sorry. Dulcinea will travel with them to Florida."

Livvie nodded.

Cal returned his attention to Max. "Raul has offered vehicles and a few of his soldiers as escort to the border."

"Unacceptable," Max barked. "We'd be much too vulnerable on the road. I can have a helicopter here in less than two hours."

"Then do it."

"And I can get her home without your help," Max added.

The two men stared at one another for a moment, until Cal said, "I'm not going to allow you to put Livvie's life in danger because you're pissed. You need me, Larkin."

Max's response was obscene…but it was also affirmative.

Chapter 12

The trip by helicopter was too noisy for conversation, so Livvie spent most of the time watching the jungle below fly past. Caught in that lush growth that could not be tamed, the traveling had been slow and dangerous. Beautiful and more than a little frightening. Exciting and scary and uncertain. Watching it go by so fast was almost unreal. In the jungle each step had been a struggle. So why did she wish to be there once again? Her life had been so much simpler, just a few days ago.

At one point Livvie spotted a lake below. Was it the same lake she and Cal had stopped at? She couldn't be sure. But as she watched that small body of water disappear from view she remembered…her time with Cal was already turning into memories. Precious moments in the past that she could never reclaim.

Max and Cal didn't speak to or even acknowledge one

another, and neither of them spoke to her, either. Livvie told herself that it was because of the noise in the helicopter, but she didn't really believe that. Thanks to her two men who had once been friends—the two men she loved— were no longer even talking to one another. And she had a feeling that if she wasn't here as a buffer, things would be even worse.

To look at them, you'd think Max and Cal had nothing in common. Cal was rough and Max was smooth. Cal was heat and Max was cold. Cal was as down to earth as any man she'd ever met, and Max was too rich and aloof for his own good. But they did have a few traits in common. They were each tough, in their own way, and they were capable men. Yes, she was almost positive that they had once been friends…and she'd destroyed that friendship.

Another thing she suspected they had in common— neither of them could afford to lose a friend.

They reached Guyana without incident, and by early evening Livvie was settled into her hotel room. The hotel was not as extravagant as the palace, but it was very nice. She felt safe here in a way she hadn't for a long time— thanks to the two men who remained with her.

Max and Cal were not visibly relieved to have reached this place without incident. Maybe they'd wanted Scarface to attack. She didn't. She wanted to be as far away from the murdering man as possible, and she wanted both these men with her.

The three of them would be staying in one very nice and roomy suite, courtesy of Max's demanding manner and his platinum credit card.

Livvie sat in a fat padded chair against one wall. She hadn't unpacked yet, and probably wouldn't. They were only here for one night. Max had promised to make arrangements to get them out of here first thing tomorrow. She wanted to go home, she needed to get back on her own turf. But so many things here were unsettled. Undone.

Would she ever have even a minute alone with Cal? There was so much she wanted to say to him, so many questions she wanted to ask. But for the conversation she had in mind they needed to be alone. It didn't look as if Max was going to allow that to happen.

Maybe that was just as well. What would she say if she did get a minute alone with Cal? I love you? That would send him running for the hills for sure. I'm sorry? No one should have to put up with Max just because they'd behaved as any two unattached, healthy, consenting adults might, but she didn't want Cal to think for even one minute that she was sorry. No matter what happened tomorrow, she wasn't sorry.

What she really wanted to do was ask Cal one simple question. Am I going to see you again?

"Now what?" she asked instead, directing her question to both her uncle and her lover.

Cal looked at Max, not at her. "While it would be incredibly stupid of Scarface to follow Livvie to the States, he does know where she lives. Arrangements for security need to be made."

"She can stay with me for a while," Max countered.

"School starts in a couple of…" Livvie began

"She could be found much too easily at your apartment," Cal argued, shaking his head and laying one hand over the knife at his belt as if he might need it here and now. "It'll be the first place he goes when she doesn't show up at home."

"I'll put a guard on her, if I have to," Max snapped.

"Santana and Mangino," Cal suggested. Normally he'd think of Harlow for this assignment, but when he'd left the States Benning's only female agent had been on a long-term bodyguard job.

Max shook his head. "Since we have no idea how long this detail will last, a low profile will work best. Mangino will stick out like a sore thumb in my building."

"Yeah, but he's the best."

Max hesitated, then nodded in agreement.

"But I'm…" Livvie began.

"Do we have a name for this guy?" Max asked. His voice and manner remained sharp, but he no longer seemed to be directing all of his anger at Cal. For the moment, they were allies again. "Something besides Scarface," he clarified.

"Roberto," Cal said. "No last name yet but I have people on it."

Max nodded in obvious approval. "Once we have that name we'll turn the tables and go after him with everything we've got."

"I want in on that job," Cal said in a lowered voice.

"Hold it!" Livvie stood and walked toward the men, placing herself between them. They were taller than her, bigger and tougher, but she would not allow them to run roughshod over her and make plans that concerned her without even asking what she wanted or thought.

She studied Cal, trying to see something of the man she loved on his stony face. He looked very much like the man who'd dragged her out of a Texas bar, four years ago. Like the man who'd dragged her out of Menendez's palace and called her princess as if it were an insult. There was no hint of love or tenderness in his eyes or on that fiercely harsh face.

So why was she so certain the love was there?

"First of all, why can't you be my bodyguard?"

Max offered a sharp "No way." But just as painful was Cal's silent and completely unemotional shake of the head.

"But I trust you," Livvie argued. This was the man she had fallen in love with, and she was not ready to let him or that love go, not without a fight. "I don't know Santana or Mangino, and I don't care how good they are, I don't want a complete stranger following me around. After everything that's happened, how can I possibly trust a stranger?"

"Santana and Mangino are not strangers," Cal said. "Not to me and not to Max. We wouldn't ask them to take on this job if we didn't know damn well that you can trust them with your life. You won't have to put up with them for long. Once we have a name we'll get this guy who's looking for you and you'll be out of danger. I promise."

She started to argue, but he stopped her.

"I promise," Cal said again, in a softer voice. "You know I don't make many promises, Livvie."

"I just…why can't someone else go after him?" Her hands curled into tight fists of frustration. "You did your job and got me out, and no one expects you to do anything else. Look at you!" She waved a trembling hand. "You're hurt. You've been shot and stabbed and given experimental homemade medicine and—" her breath caught in her throat "—and tortured. When I think about…" No, she couldn't allow herself to imagine everything Cal had been through, not if she wanted to finish this conversation without breaking down. "You're better, I know that, but you're not well. I won't have you running around Camaria looking for Scarface when you should be in bed. Resting," she added sheepishly.

"I'm fine," Cal said. "And if you think I can rest while that SOB is out there hunting for you, then you don't know me at all."

"I understand that, I do." She took a single step toward him. "But why do you have to go after him? Let someone else track him down. Ask Raul to send his soldiers after Scarface. He has an army, Cal, an entire army!"

"I can't do that. Scarface is mine."

She didn't have any doubt that Cal was capable of taking care of himself. Scarface should be the one afraid, not her. But she didn't want Cal to face that awful man. Not now, not a week from now, not ever. She wanted Cal with her, always. Heaven help her, she wanted to protect him from the darkness in the world the way her parents and Max had always protected her. Had anyone ever sheltered Cal before? She didn't think so.

"You told me women aren't worth fighting for, right?" she argued.

"Maybe I changed my mind," he said between clenched teeth.

"You're fired," she said calmly. "You can't go back to Camaria and chase after that awful man if you're not working for me anymore. There are other jobs, right? Something…safer?"

Cal shook his head. "Safer? Are you kidding? And honey, I don't work for you. I never did. So you can't fire me."

They both started talking at the same time…she insisting that he not return to Camaria, Cal arguing that he had no choice. Gradually, they moved toward one another. She took a step…then he took one. They drifted together until they were standing almost nose to chest…and the argument didn't cease just because she was close enough to reach out and touch him. If anything, it became more heated.

Eventually, Max started cursing. His voice wasn't loud, but his comments were surprisingly vile and they took Livvie's attention away from her argument with Cal. Cal must've heard, too, because he went silent as well. They both turned to face her uncle, who stood by the parlor sofa with his arms crossed over his chest and an absolutely deadly scowl on his face.

"What's wrong?" she asked.

"Everything, apparently," Max said. "I can't believe this. It's a nightmare."

"Scarface?"

"I can handle Scarface a lot better than I can handle..." His hand flitted from her to Cal and back again. Several times. Then he headed for the door. "I'm going down to the bar to get good and drunk. I won't be back until late. Very late. You two do whatever it is you have to either get this out of your systems or work out all the kinks." He stopped in the open doorway and turned to glare at Cal. "You were right. She's not a kid anymore."

Livvie laid a hand on Cal's arm. Had he defended her this morning, before she'd had her own confrontation with Max?

"She's definitely too old for me to be threatening her...her...boyfriends," he finally finished. He turned around with a nasty sounding grunt. Right before the door slammed behind him he muttered, "Little League!"

The room was so quiet. Too quiet. Cal looked down at her. She couldn't tell if he was glad they were alone or not. "Is that what I am? A boyfriend?"

"I don't know. Are you?"

He was more than that, she knew it in her heart. She just

wasn't sure he knew it yet. She rested her hand over his chest, glad to touch him even in such a simple way. If she pressed her fingers just so, yes…there was his heartbeat, sound and steady.

"I was never anyone's boyfriend." He gave her a crooked smile. "I was the boy no one wanted their daughters to go out with. The troublemaker. The juvenile delinquent. Never the *boyfriend*."

"Maybe you can try it on for size and see how it fits," she suggested. "There has to be a first time for everything."

His smile disappeared. "I'm not sure that's a good idea."

"Why not?"

"I'm still not boyfriend material."

No, he wasn't. For one thing, he wasn't a *boy*. He was a man. "How about friend," she suggested. "Partner. Guardian angel."

That last one got her a disbelieving lift of the eyebrows.

"Lover," she added.

He took her in his arms. "That one I can handle."

Last night she'd seduced him. Now it was his turn. He didn't know why Max had changed his mind and left them alone, and he didn't care. The argument wasn't settled, but there wasn't much time left, not for them. Tonight would be the last of it, he imagined. No, he wouldn't be her bodyguard, and he sure as hell couldn't be her boyfriend.

But he could be her lover. Tonight.

Cal led Livvie to the nearest bedroom and kicked the door shut behind them. He lifted her off her feet, and she wound her arms around him and held on tight. With her arms and legs wrapped around him, her mouth moving gently on his neck, he carried her to the four-poster bed that dominated the small room. In the air-conditioned hotel, the netting around the bed was for decoration only. It was atmosphere…local color.

"I don't want you to go back," she whispered.

"We're not going to talk about that now," he said as he laid her on the bed.

"But…"

He sat beside Livvie and began to unbutton her blouse. Not without restraint, but idly. Easily. Her breath came slow and deep, the blue of her eyes changed slightly, went darker and dreamier. His fingers brushed the flesh beneath that plain shirt as he undressed her. She was so warm and silky, so responsive to the simplest touch.

"We're not going to agree about this, and right now…I don't want to argue with you." He spread the blouse open and flicked open the little nothing of a bra she wore. The silky garment had a front clasp, and it easily came undone in his hands.

"I don't want to argue with you, either," she said softly. A hand reached up to touch his beard-roughened cheek. "I don't. I just…"

"Tomorrow, Livvie," Cal said as he lowered her zipper and bent his head to lay his lips on her skin. He started with the soft skin between her breasts, but he wasn't going to stop there.

"Tomorrow," she whispered.

Livvie cuddled up against Cal's body in the dark. The air was turned up high, making the room chilly, and she was naked. So she snuggled closer, stealing a bit of warmth from Cal and trying to go to sleep.

She should be sleeping. Max had come in hours ago,

slamming the door behind him, then slamming the door to the room on the opposite side of the parlor. He'd muttered something as he'd crossed the room, but since the door to this room was closed she had no idea what he'd said. Something vile, she imagined.

It was his earlier words that kept her awake. *You two get this thing out of your systems.* Was that all this was? A *thing.* Energy. Sex. The tumult of an intense situation misdirected into a false feeling of love.

No, that wasn't it. Not on her part, anyway. But would Cal eventually get tired of her? Would he work her out of his system?

He rose up on his elbow and looked down at her. There was very little light tonight. Dark shadows filled the room beyond the mosquito netting that encircled the bed, but she made out Cal's form fairly well. She couldn't see his face clearly enough to suit her, though. What would she read in his eyes if she could see them now?

"You should be sleeping," he whispered.

"I don't want to sleep." She reached up and her fingers found the small scar high on his forehead. Her fingers traced the slightly raised skin as if she could wipe the evidence of violence away. "How did you get this one?"

"Beer bottle," he said softly.

She shuddered slightly and rose up to kiss the mark. Once. Twice. "Please tell me you didn't get this scar in a bar fight over some tacky big-breasted woman," she teased.

For a long moment, he didn't answer. Finally he said, "Stepfather with a hangover. I was making too much noise, apparently."

Livvie kissed the scar again, more tenderly this time. She borrowed a few of Uncle Max's most vile words to express her feelings on the matter. "How old were you?" she asked when her tirade was finished.

"It doesn't…" he began.

"How old?"

Again, he was quiet for a few moments. But he did wrap his arms around her and hold her a little closer. "Ten."

She held on to him. "Your first scar."

"Yeah."

Did he know how much it hurt her to know what had happened to him? Did he have any idea how much anger was rising within her? She wanted to make the stepfather pay for hurting Cal, she wanted to go back in time and somehow make his life better. Safer.

But she couldn't go back in time. All she could do was love him here and now.

He released her and very gently forced her onto her back. "You really do need to get some sleep," he said. "We have a plane to catch in the morning."

"Yeah." Livvie knew she couldn't fix the past, and she didn't know if they had a future together. She reached out and touched Cal. His beard-roughened face, first—then his chest, there above his heart, his tight stomach and lower.

"Of course, we can always sleep on the plane," he said as he lowered his head to take a nipple into his mouth.

Livvie closed her eyes and sighed. One touch, and her body throbbed for him.

Cal played her like he was a musician and she was his instrument. In the dark, in an overly cool room, he used his warm hands and his mouth and his tongue to make her body sing…and he did make music. He told her she purred like a cat when he touched her just so, and maybe she did.

She was caught on a fine line…reveling in the sensations that rippled through her body and needing more so badly she wanted to cry. And Cal seemed to know just how to keep her on that edge.

"Cal," she whispered, threading her fingers through his hair and pulling his mouth to hers. He rested atop her, heavy and warm, and her soft curves met his hard planes until they fit together perfectly. He speared his tongue into her mouth and she wrapped her legs around his hips, drawing him closer. Drawing him into her.

"Love me," she murmured. "Love me." The room was no longer chilly, but had turned hot. A sheen of sweat covered her skin and Cal's. "I love you," she whispered as he pushed inside her.

He made love to her hard and fast, breathless and primal. Their bodies were locked together, and they moved in time. Quick and hot and exquisite, he did love her. He drove deep and she shattered with a soft cry that was ripped from her, and while she shuddered around him he came. Cal didn't purr. He growled. He trembled.

It was impossible that her soft body and his hard one should fit together so perfectly, so rightly, but they did. She ran her hand slowly down his side, amazed by the beauty that brushed against her palm. Scars and all—Cal was beautiful.

He didn't rush to leave her, but stayed joined with her, his lips on her shoulder, his body heavy and hot against hers. As Livvie's breath came back to her, her heartbeat gradually returned to normal.

"I love you," she said again, not at all afraid of what he might think or say. It was the truth. She laughed lightly at the freedom saying those words brought her. She'd denied the truth for too long, she'd been so afraid to tell him how she felt. "I love you. That's why I can't let you go after Scarface, that's why I don't want anyone else as a bodyguard. I want you close, Cal. I want you here, always."

He kissed her very gently on the forehead, laying his lips there and letting them linger...which was odd since he was still cradled inside her. One gesture was completely intimate, the other almost sweet.

"We'll talk in the morning," he said. "You need to sleep."

She felt sleep coming, drifting in on easy waves at last. "Okay."

And she did sleep. She slept deeply and had wonderful dreams.

When she woke, Cal was gone.

There were a lot of things in the world worse than being shot, stabbed and whipped. Hearing a woman say those three little words was one of them.

Cal starred at Raul, not at all intimidated by the healer's new position in the government. "All right, you keep saying you owe me something. I don't agree, but since you insist I'm going to ask for a favor."

Raul lifted one expressive eyebrow. "Another one?"

"The last one," Cal said. "I want the scarred man who worked for Menendez. You do have a name for me by now, don't you?"

"Roberto Vega."

"Vega," Cal repeated. "The man assassinated Menendez's estranged wife and has been looking for Olivia Larkin because she can identify him. He killed Adrianna. I want him. Now." The sooner this last little detail was taken care of, the sooner he'd be able to get Livvie out of his life, once and for all.

It had been two days since he'd walked out of the Guyana hotel, leaving before sunrise and without a word. Walking out without saying goodbye was a crappy way to end things, he knew that, but he also knew a quick and simple ending of the affair was for the best. Max had been right all along. He and Livvie, they weren't going to work. She might not be out of his system, she might not ever be out of his system. But when it came to kinks…there were too many to count.

Claudia had told him how much she loved him. Every day, every night, with a smile, with a moan…and he had believed her. He had begun to think what he felt must be love, too. But he was older now. Wiser. And he wasn't falling for that old line again.

He refused to admit to himself that Claudia had never meant the words, and Livvie did. At least, she thought she did. Whatever she was feeling, she'd get over it soon enough.

"Here." Raul slid a slim packet of information across the table. "Vega has taken up with a group of former soldiers who claim to be loyal to the late president. In fact, they are no better than bandits, and they've been terrorizing small villages. Inside you will find a list of the places they have been seen in the past week. I cannot guarantee that Vega will be in any of these places, but it's a start."

Cal snatched up the envelope. "Thanks. Men?"

Raul sighed. "I can give you three."

"Three?" Cal placed his hands on the table and shouted. "That's your idea of gratitude?" He could call in a couple of the guys from the agency, but this was dangerous business and besides…it wasn't their fight. It was his.

"They are three of my best." The intimidating man sitting at Lazaro Menendez's desk looked very little like the kid who'd so cautiously tended Cal. Like everyone else, Raul Velasco had more than one face for the world. "I offer you these very talented and dangerous men along with a bit of advice."

"Advice," Cal deadpanned. "Just what I need."

Raul was not deterred. "Get over it."

"Get over what?" Cal asked without emotion.

An elegant hand gestured impatiently. "Whatever it is that makes you look back instead of forward. Her, I suspect, though I hate to think that a good man might waste years of his life pining over a woman who was not and never would have been worthy of him."

"Healer, rebel and philosopher," Cal said dryly.

"Do with the advice as you wish," Raul said, not at all offended. "But great men look forward."

"I'm not…"

"That is a matter of opinion," Raul interrupted before Cal could finish.

The healer and rebel didn't look so much like a kid these days. His new responsibilities were already weighing heavily on him. Cal knew he and greatness would forever be strangers, but this kid…Raul had a grand future ahead of him. He was going to do great things with his newly attained power.

"You're going to make a good president," Cal said.

"That remains to be seen," Raul said in a lowered voice. "The elections will decide."

He would definitely be president soon—of that Cal had no doubt. The people of Camaria would love Raul the way Menendez had always wished to be loved. He would instill courage and loyalty in those around him, without fear.

Without a secret room filled with the stuff nightmares were made of.

"A good president," Cal continued, "but a lousy philosopher."

Raul smiled. "I believe I am a very fine philosopher. You will invite me to the wedding?"

Wedding. The very mention of the word caused a lump to form in Cal's throat. A lump of fear. "There's not going to be any wedding."

"If I am truly mistaken and there will be no marriage forthcoming, then please know you are always welcome here. I could use a man like you beside or behind me when I go to Santa Rosa. I would never worry about my back if you were there."

"I'll think about it." He needed to be stateside to look for Kelly…but the trail was cold, and there were half a dozen agents with the Benning Agency who could handle the case. Camaria had changed dramatically in the past few days, but it was still a good place to hide.

Cal took the information Raul had obtained, the three soldiers he supplied and a fully loaded automatic rifle, and he headed back into the jungle. Truth be told, he hurt all over. He could use a week in his own bed. Alone—or not. He'd learned to like being alone, but Livvie had tried to change that.

He couldn't afford to need her.

What he was about to do was a much more dangerous task than picking up a package, and look how wrong that job had gone. Vega and the men he'd taken up with would be looking for trouble—they'd be waiting, and they'd be armed.

But Cal wasn't going to rest until Vega was dead and Livvie was safe.

It was the least he could do for her.

Chapter 13

"Ma'am, are you sure you don't want something to eat?"

Livvie spun on Dante Mangino and answered with a much too sharp "No." How on earth could he think about eating at a time like this?

Max had been right when he'd said Mangino would stick out like a sore thumb in his upscale, conservative apartment building. The six-foot-three, long-haired, profusely-tattooed man *definitely* did not fit in.

Lucky Santana did, though. He fit in very well. The second man who'd been assigned to this duty dressed almost as nicely as Uncle Max, and had that smooth, polished look that Cal and Mangino would never pull off. Not that they would ever try. Or want to.

Staying at Max's apartment with a constant guard made Livvie feel like she was fifteen again. She couldn't sleep. She was constantly on edge and she had no appetite. She'd tried to pass the time putting together her lesson plan for the first few weeks of school, but her mind wouldn't be still long enough for her to get far.

"Sorry," she said in a softer voice. "I didn't mean to snap at you. I'm just…not hungry."

Since Santana, who had been working the night shift, was sleeping in the spare bedroom next to her own, Mangino sat down alone to the meal Max had had delivered. He poured himself a glass of soda. When they were on duty, which was apparently all the time, Benning's agents did not drink.

They did, however, smoke, curse, and—in Mangino's case—tell off-color jokes. He was particularly fond of limericks. Under ordinary circumstances Livvie might've enjoyed spending time with the men Max had hired, but these were not ordinary circumstances.

She missed Cal. Worse, she had no idea if he was still in Camaria, if he'd found Scarface, if he was all right…

Mangino's cell phone rang and he answered. Whatever the caller said to the big man made him smile, and then he turned his face up and winked at Livvie. There had been a time when a man of Mangino's type winking at her might give her cause to smile, at the very least.

But everything had changed, in her world. She had a feeling nothing would ever be normal again.

"What is it?" she asked. "Is that Cal?"

He shook his head, so she didn't snatch the phone from him. Mangino moved the phone an inch or so from his ear. "Vega's dead," he said softly.

Livvie nodded, relieved. Max had told her Scarface's name, on the long trip back to D.C. It was about the only thing he'd told her. Her uncle had refused to so much as mention Cal's name, and when she'd tried to explain to him how she felt he shut down completely. The last leg of the journey had been silent and decidedly uncomfortable.

"What about Cal?" she asked.

Mangino ignored her and returned to his phone call… listening intently to whoever it was who'd called, nodding and giving noncommittal answers.

"Cal?" Livvie whispered.

Mangino waved her off. He didn't even look her in the eye, he simply *waved* her *off!*

Livvie reached down and grabbed his hand, took hold of his little finger, and twisted it back.

"Hang on a minute," Mangino said. He put the phone down beside his plate and looked Livvie squarely in the eye. "Ow," he said softly.

Livvie did not release her hold on his little finger. "Is Cal back? Is he hurt?" She had a hundred more questions, but none she'd dare to send through a second party.

Mangino lifted the phone to his ear. "Calhoun," he said simply.

He nodded as he received his answer, then told whoever he was talking to that he and Santana would be back late in the evening. He disconnected the call and turned his undivided attention to Livvie.

"Well?" she snapped.

"My finger?"

She let go and he shook the digit out. "Cal's fine," he said. "He's home and it sounds like he's going to take a couple of weeks off."

Livvie dropped into the nearest chair, boneless with relief. Her heart beat too hard…she'd been so worried about him! "He's okay. That's good." She was glad he'd be taking some time off. He needed his rest, he needed to get healed. For the first time in days, tears stung her eyes. And her stomach growled. She looked at the spread on the dining room table.

"He said you were the best, you know," she said as she grabbed a plate from a stack at the center of the table.

"Cal said that?" Mangino asked with a smile. It was an absolutely brilliant smile, the kind that surely broke women's hearts. Not hers, though. Her heart was already broken.

She nodded.

"Don't tell Santana," Mangino said. "He might get his feelings hurt."

"I doubt that." Livvie put a sandwich and some fruit on her plate, then reached for the potato skins. She had to wipe away a single tear, though, a move Mangino neatly ignored.

Cal rounded the bend, driving too fast as always. Without warning, the familiar building appeared as if by magic. *Last Chance. Gas. Ice. Beer.* The ramshackle building rose up in the middle of nowhere, a weathered wooden shack on the side of this two-lane Alabama road. The gas station really was the last chance for gas in either direction for at least ten miles. Last chance for beer if you were headed east, since the next county over was dry.

He pulled his Mustang sharply into the gas station lot, claiming a parking space on the side. Just a couple of days ago he'd told Benning he was taking some time off, but vacations had never agreed with him. Cal had a tendency to get into trouble when he had too much free time on his hands.

Wallace, who looked ninety years old but claimed to be

a young seventy-two, stepped into the doorway, his tall, thin body appearing deceptively frail. The old man was tough as leather. Cal had no doubt Wallace could give him a good fight, if he cared to.

"Mr. Calhoun," Wallace said, his voice soft and low. "I didn't expect to see you today."

"Is Benning in?"

"Major Benning and Mr. Murphy are in building two."

The war room.

Behind the gas station and down a hill, beyond a stand of thick pine trees, Major Flynn Benning had built his center of operations. Four long metal buildings, nondescript on the outside, state-of-the-art on the inside, were the headquarters for the Benning Agency. Cal nodded to Wallace and then took the path that wound through the trees, ignoring the well-hidden security cameras he knew recorded his arrival.

By the time he reached building two, Major Benning and Murphy would be waiting. Wallace had probably called ahead, an unnecessary courtesy since the alarm system had surely sounded the moment Cal stepped onto the path.

He opened the metal door and stepped inside building two. Maps and diagrams were spread across the long table that dominated the room, and two fair-haired men studied those maps carefully. Benning and Murphy lifted their heads as Cal approached.

The two men were very dissimilar, physically and in character. The Major was big and crude, and still wore his dark blond hair in a style fit for the military. Short and precise. Murphy had a computer nerd thing going for him. He was tall and lean, with pale blond hair worn in a much more fashionable style. When he took off those ridiculous glasses he was prettier than a lot of women Cal knew. There had been a time when Cal believed Murphy to be a pansy who had no business working for Benning. But as it turned out, he was a god with a computer and he'd saved their asses more than once.

One man was rough and the other was a nerd, but they were both good men and Cal considered himself lucky to have them on his side.

"What are you doing here?" Benning asked. The words were gruff, but he smiled.

"I got bored."

The smile faded. "You can't possibly be physically ready to return to work. I saw the doctor's report, Calhoun. I'm surprised you're able to walk in here under your own steam."

"It's not that bad. Besides, anything he can do I can do." Cal pointed to Murphy.

"Hey! Don't be pointing at me," Murphy protested. "From what I hear you're lucky you made it out of South America with your head." The computer geek grinned. "The big one *and* the little one."

Cal glared at Murphy and the nerd's grin died quickly.

"Sorry, man. I didn't know it was a touchy subject."

It wasn't like they hadn't talked about women before. But not this one. Livvie was different.

The mistakes made had been his, not hers.

"You must have something I can do around here." Cal looked around the war room. It was as much home as his house up the road.

"Go home," Benning ordered. "Sleep, take your medicine, eat, watch TV, read…just get better."

"But…"

"Go home and take it easy for a few days. That's an order."

Cal turned away. Nobody argued with the major. He'd tried in the past, and it was always a waste of time. But he couldn't possibly take it easy! How could he, when he couldn't get Livvie out of his head? Everywhere he looked, everything he saw or heard or tasted, somehow she was in it. He'd never minded living his life alone…he usually liked being alone. But in the past few days he'd just felt lost.

"Calhoun," Benning barked.

At the door Cal glanced over his shoulder.

"Good job."

Cal laughed without humor and shook his head. "Major screwup from beginning to end."

"You got the package out alive. That's all that matters."

That wasn't all that mattered, dammit. Not anymore. "Olivia Larkin is a woman, not a package," Cal said as he let the door close behind him.

School started, and something Livvie had never expected happened. Terry the rat came to her on his hands and knees—figuratively speaking, of course—and begged her to take him back. He *begged!* He called, he sent flowers, he wrote sickeningly emotional love letters. She hadn't been able to muster any semblance of emotion at all for the man who had once been her fiancé. She didn't love Terry, and she didn't hate him…she had nothing to offer the man and she wanted nothing from him.

It had been ten days since Flynn Benning had called Dante Mangino and told him Roberto Vega was dead and Cal was fine. The next day Max had allowed her to return home, and since then Livvie kept expecting the phone to ring. She'd answer and hear Cal's voice on the other end, and somehow everything would be fine.

But that scenario was just a fantasy. Cal didn't call. Just as well. He was obsessed with finding his sister, and he obviously hadn't gotten over Claudia, and besides, all they really had was an unusual adventure to remember when they grew old and gray. And sex. Great sex, yes, but still—just sex.

She told herself that, anyway. She'd even made a list. A very sensible, detailed list of pros and cons where Cal was concerned. The list of cons was long. He didn't have a normal job. If he didn't change something about his life, he wouldn't live to see old and gray! She'd never held him or kissed him when he hadn't been seriously banged up in one way or another. Did he stay that way all the time? With the job he had it was entirely possible.

He had scars, inside and out. He had baggage. Lots and lots of baggage. If Quinn Calhoun by some miracle became the man in her life, there would be no office parties, no quiet evenings at home. No arguing over what wallpaper to choose for the den.

No Little League.

The pro side of the list was short but powerful. She loved him.

She'd thought about stopping on her way home from school for ice cream and cookies, but drove right past the grocery store. That could turn out to be a bad habit, she supposed. She went straight home instead, parked her car and planned her evening while she walked into the building. A microwave dinner, a little television, maybe a review of her plan for tomorrow's class, even though she knew the plan by heart since last night she'd gotten antsy and reviewed the entire week.

She didn't want another quiet, safe evening at home by herself. What she really wanted was to sit in the jungle with Cal and talk about his sister and her parents and everything they'd done wrong—and everything they'd done right. They had done a few things right, hadn't they? She wanted to laugh in bed and kiss Cal's scars and become the one person in the world who protected him.

Cal truly believed that he didn't have any family; Livvie believed that she was his family…and she'd never found the right time to tell him so.

She knew the minute she saw the denim-encased leg that it was him. From her vantage point on the stairs, that was all she could see for a moment. One leg. Blue jeans. Someone was leaning up against the half-wall beside her front door, one leg jutting out just enough…just enough. Heart beating too fast, she climbed quickly to the top of the stairs, walked down the hallway, turned a corner, and saw his face.

"Hi," she said.

Cal looked her in the eye, and she felt that gaze as if it ripped inside her and grabbed her heart. He'd shaved, and looked years younger without the beard. Not soft, never soft…just younger. The lines of his face were sharp without the beard to soften them. He hadn't cut his hair, and even here it looked as if he'd combed with his fingers. Instead of jungle green or black he wore a gray button-up shirt and those blue jeans and a pair of boots that had not been dragged through the jungle. Not yet, anyway.

He was beautiful.

"I think we should get married."

Of all the things he might've said… Everything caught in Livvie's throat. Her heart, her stomach, her words. In the excitement of the moment, all she could manage to say was, "Huh?"

"Married," he said again. "If we just shack up, your uncle will eventually kill me, no matter what he says about you being an adult. We'll catch him on a bad day and that'll be all she wrote. Do I have to ask him for your hand or anything like that?" He sounded vaguely horrified by the idea. "I was thinking maybe we could elope and tell him the news after the fact."

Livvie let the surprise fade, and she was left with a smile and the realization that Cal had just asked her to marry him. "You're moving kinda fast, don't you think?"

"No, I don't." He pushed away from the wall and wrapped both arms around her. He rested his head alongside hers and held on tight and said in a low, husky voice, "I've been thinking about things lately. A lot of things. Things like…Little League."

"Oh…"

"Mostly I've been thinking about you." His arms tightened around her. "I am so amazingly and completely in love with you, Livvie. I've never felt like this before. Maybe this is happening too fast, and maybe I was a jerk when we were in Guyana. We'll go slow, if that's what you want. If you want to risk my life by shacking up instead of getting married, then that's what we'll do. But I'm not going to let you go. I'm never going to let you go."

A wide smile spread across her face. "I like the married idea. I like it very much. And the Little League. One day, that is." She kissed him quick and deep, then pulled back and slapped him lightly on the chest as she laughed. "I love you, too, but you already know that. Quinn Calhoun, what took you so long! I thought you'd never get here."

His smile faded, a little. "I had to make a side trip. Kelly called an old friend from high school."

Hope and joy washed through her, because she knew how much this meant to Cal. "You found her!"

He shook his head. "No. She called from a pay phone in Atlanta, and no one around there remembers seeing her. I looked all over, I talked to a hundred people…and I found absolutely nothing." His smile crept back. "But she's alive. I'm going to find her."

"I know you will."

He traced her cheek with one finger. "When I found out Kelly was alive, all I could think about was telling you. I kept wishing you were with me, so I could hold you close and share the good news. Even when I was in Atlanta trying to find someone, anyone, who remembered her, I wanted you there. I kept thinking…this jerk that won't talk to me, Livvie could charm him into telling everything he knows. While I was there I searched all day every day and half of every night, but for the other half of those nights I wanted you beside me. I needed you there."

Livvie took Cal's face in her hands and kissed him. Not easy, this time, not gentle. She kissed him the way a woman kisses a man she can't live without. She began to laugh while she kissed him, a light and easy laugh of pure joy, until he lifted her off her feet and spun her around until she was dizzy and he was laughing with her.

"Why did you wait in the hall?" Livvie asked as she unlocked the door to her apartment. They both knew very well no lock would keep him out.

"I didn't want to jump out of your kitchen and scare you," he said as he closed the door behind them. "Besides, something like that might've cost me a broken little finger," he added softly.

"You've been talking to Dante, I see," Livvie said as she tossed her purse onto the couch. "In case he didn't tell you the whole story—he deserved it. And I didn't break his finger. I just twisted it a little because he wouldn't tell me how you were."

"It's a good thing he likes you, honey. Twisting Mangino's little finger is kinda like going after a bear with a pea-shooter."

Livvie wrapped her arms around Cal's neck. "He wouldn't tell me if you were okay or not. That justifies any action. I couldn't stand it when I thought you might be hurt again, Cal. I just couldn't stand it."

Cal kissed her again, and there was no laughter this time. It had been a long time, too long, and she didn't want to ever let him go.

He took his mouth from hers, gradually, as if he couldn't bear to end the kiss. Then he kissed her again, quickly and passionately. "Before I forget…" he reached into the pocket of his shirt and came up with a dainty gold chain. The chain was wrapped around his finger, and it swung slightly, dangling before her. The light from an open window caught and sparkled on the stone that hung there.

"This diamond isn't very big or fancy," Cal said, "but I bought it with fairly earned money and I mean every word I'm saying to you, now and always."

"My honest man," she whispered.

"Yeah."

Once again she took his face in her hands. Her fingers brushed over smooth, beautiful cheeks. Her breath caught in her throat again, with happiness, this time. With pure, deep happiness.

"I'm glad it's you, Quinn Calhoun," she whispered before he kissed her again. "I'm glad it's you."

* * * * *

Watch out for Linda Winstead Jones's next story,
TRULY, MADLY, DANGEROUSLY
coming in February 2005

SPOTLIGHT

**Every month we'll spotlight
original stories from Harlequin
and Silhouette Books' Shining Stars!**

Fantastic authors, including:
- Debra Webb
- Julie Elizabeth Leto
- Merline Lovelace
- Rhonda Nelson

**Plus, value-added Bonus Features
are coming soon to a book near you!**

- Author Interviews
- Bonus Reads
- The Writing Life
- Character Profiles

SIGNATURE SELECT SPOTLIGHT
On sale January 2005

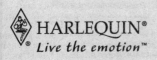

HARLEQUIN®
Live the emotion™

Silhouette®
Where love comes alive™

INTIMATE MOMENTS®

#1339 DANGEROUS DISGUISE—Marie Ferrarella
Cavanaugh Justice
Mixing business with pleasure wasn't in detective Jared Cavanaugh's vocabulary—until he saw Maren Minnesota walk into the restaurant where he'd been assigned to work undercover to catch the mob. But when their smoldering attraction for each other threatened his disguise, would he have to risk everything to protect the woman he loved?

#1340 UNDERCOVER MISTRESS—Kathleen Creighton
Starrs of the West
After a hit-and-run accident forced Celia Cross from Hollywood's spotlight, her only refuge was the beach. Then homeland security agent Roy Starr washed ashore, bleeding from an assassin's bullet. Little did she know her mystery man had gotten too close to an international arms dealer. With the killer determined to finish the job and Roy's feelings for his rescuer growing stronger, would this be their beginning—or their end?

#1341 CLOSE TO THE EDGE—Kylie Brant
Private investigator Lucky Boucher knew his attraction to fellow investigator Jacinda Wheeler was a mistake. He was a bayou boy; she was high society. But when a case they were working on turned deadly, keeping his mind off her and on their investigation proved to be an impossible task, because for the first time since he'd met her, their worlds were about to collide.

#1342 CODE NAME: FIANCÉE—Susan Vaughan
Antiterrorist security agent Vanessa Wade felt as false as the rock on her finger. Assigned to impersonate the glamorous fiancée of international businessman Nick Markos, she found herself struggling to remain detached from her "husband-to-be." He was the brother of a traitor—and the man whose kisses made her spin out of control. Could she dare to hope their fake engagement would become a real one?

#1343 RUNNING ON EMPTY—Michelle Celmer
Detective Mitch Thompson was willing to risk his life to uncover the mystery surrounding Jane Doe, the beautiful amnesiac he'd rescued from an unknown assailant. But the more time they spent together trying to unravel the secrets hidden in her memory, the more evident it became that they were falling in love…and that Jane's attacker was determined to stop at nothing to destroy their happiness—not even murder.

#1344 NECESSARY SECRETS—Barbara Phinney
Sylvie Mitchell was living a lie. Pregnant and alone, she'd retreated to her ranch to have the baby in hiding. Then her unborn child's uncle, Jon Cahill, appeared, demanding answers, and she had to lie to the one man she truly loved. She'd lived with the guilt of his brother's death and the government cover-up that had forced her into hiding. When the truth surfaced, would she lose the only man who could keep her—and her baby—safe?

SIMCNM1204